The Travel Agent
by
MICHAEL ROTHERY

Weatherdeck Books

The Travel Agent
Copyright © 2020 Michael Rothery
All rights reserved
United Kingdom Licence Notes
The right of Michael Rothery to be identified as the Author of this work has been asserted by him in accordance with the Copyrights, Designs and Patents Act 1988
Apart from any use permitted under UK copyright law no part of this publication may be reproduced, stored in a retrieval system, or transmitted, in any form or by any means, without the prior permission of the publisher.
Disclaimer
This is a work of fiction. Names, characters, places, events and incidents are either the products of the author's imagination or used in a fictitious manner. Except for crucial elements, events, people and organisations in the public domain that form the story's geopolitical background, any resemblance to actual persons, living or dead, or actual events is purely coincidental.

Revised Edition: 1st February 2021

ISBN: 9798697933213
Imprint: Weatherdeck Books

CONTENTS

Gibraltar - Key Locations	vii
January 2017 - Western Russia	1
Episode One - The Mark	5
Episode Two - The Traffickers	61
Episode Three - Rosie's Doubts	91
Episode Four - Michael's Mission	115
Episode Five - The Interview	153
Episode Six - The Training Course	189
Episode Seven - Galene's Mission	239
Episode Eight - Surveillance & Capture	287
Episode Nine - The Discovery	359
Episode Ten - The Rogue Agent	405
About the Author	III
Rosie Winterbourne Book 3	V

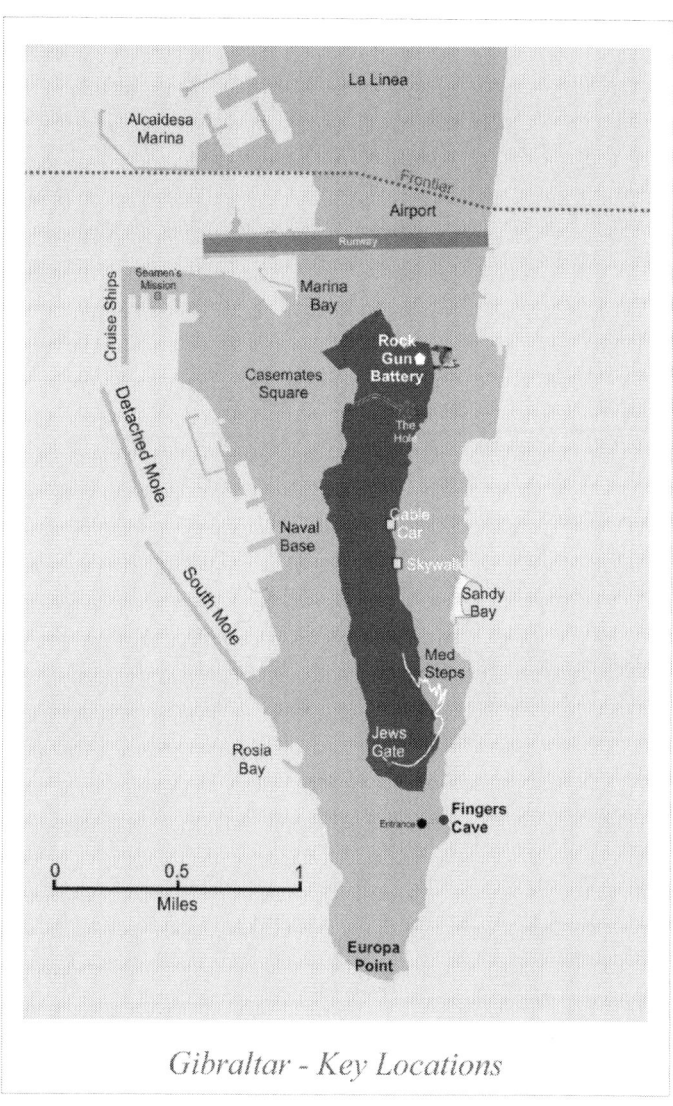

Gibraltar - Key Locations

PROLOGUE

January 2017
Western Russia

A servant emerges from the lodge, alerted by the rattling growl of a snowmobile. The young man's exhaled breath crystalises with a sound like tiny wind chimes. Shivering in the sub-zero air, he rubs his hands briskly together and smiles at the two men climbing the steps to the wooden terrace.

'Welcome back, Sir,' he says, relieving the hunters of their rifles. 'Any luck?'

'Thank you, Anton, yes, a good day's shooting. Some sables in the trailer, have Ludo deal with them before the wolves get the scent.'

'Yes, Sir,' says the houseboy, taking the rifles inside.

'Wolves, Vladimir?' exclaims the guest, startled. 'You didn't mention wolves.'

His host snorts derisively. 'Don't be such a *mysh*, Sergey,' he chides. 'Of course, there are wolves. There are always wolves in the Urals. But you can walk these forests for days and never see one. Ha, you should worry more about those cute little things we shot

The Travel Agent

today? Sables are known to carry rabies. Now come, let us get down to why I invited you here.'

Sergey gives a wry smile as he follows his host into the dacha, knowing an invitation from this man amounts to a command. Entering the hallway, the two men tug off their boots and socks and shrug out of their heavy furs.

'Come, let us go to the Karpinski Room and you can drink some of that overpriced vodka you like.'

'You have *Russo-Baltique*?' Sergey asks incredulously, following his host barefoot along the cedar-floored corridor.

'Of course. It is still your preferred tipple, yes?'

'But these days, it is so exp…'

Sergey has stopped in the doorway, astonished. Vladimir is known for his extravagant tastes, but such opulence seems out of place in this remote hideaway. A log fire blazes in a walk-in fireplace; above the mantlepiece an elk stares down glassy-eyed at a luxurious black bearskin – jaws agape - on the floor. Fine artwork adorns the surrounding walls: Sergey recognises a Kandinski, a Serov, a Chagall, no doubt originals. A dozen plush leather armchairs are spaced in a semi-circle around the room, each with its own glass coffee table. Sergey imagines the Decisions of State that must have been taken in this luxurious mountain retreat.

The dacha's owner stands commandingly before an enormous window and gazes out at a stunning view. A snow-covered pine forest slopes gently away until beyond its horizon stands the towering massif of Mount Karpinski.

'I love the winters here,' he murmurs.

Prologue

Vladimir is short but powerfully built: a youthful complexion and finely-toned physique belie his sixty-five years. Abruptly, he turns, heel squeaking on the polished wood.

'You look like an imbecile, Sergey. Come, sit and enjoy the view.'

While his guest chooses his armchair, Vladimir crosses the room and opens a cold-cabinet behind an ornate cocktail bar. Selecting a crystal tumbler, he pours ice-cold vodka for Sergey and cracks open a beer for himself.

'I trust you enjoyed the day, Sergey?'

'Very much. Thank you for inviting me. I didn't know about this place.'

'You are now among the privileged few, my friend.'

Vladimir hands him his vodka and grins, then walks back to stand by the window.

Sergey sniffs his drink and nods approvingly. 'I am grateful for your generosity, Vladimir, but I think you didn't invite me to the mountains merely to shoot sables and drink fine vodka.'

Vladimir sighs without turning, 'No, you are right. We have a serious matter to discuss.'

Sergey tenses at the tone, 'Is this about Salisbury?'

Vladimir half turns, gives the ghost of a grin, then returns to viewing his mountain domain.

'Salisbury?' he says to the window. 'Why would I be concerned with a quaint little English town?' He turns and walks back into the room.

'Salisbury is your problem, Sergey, not mine.'

The guest sips his vodka in silence; the man's self-assured obfuscation is as maddening as ever.

The Travel Agent

'No, Sergey,' continues Vladimir, taking an armchair by the fire and crossing his athletic feet on the bear's head. 'I want to talk about oil: specifically, *Tomsk Oblast* oil and *Transneft*.'

'The pipeline to China, my President?'

'Mm. Chinese demand last year was down forty percentage points. Why was that?'

Sergey shrugs. 'They are importing Libyan light crude. It's cheaper, and they prefer it to the heavy stuff from the Siberian fields. I don't see what we can do about it, Comrade Pr–'

'Oh, please, Sergey, don't go all Soviet on me.'

Sergey frowns and takes refuge in sipping his vodka.

Vladimir sighs again; a trace of annoyance briefly crosses his face.

'I think you might be losing your touch, my friend. Back in the KGB days, you would have found a solution before I asked.'

'A... solution?'

'Yes, Sergey,' Vladimir taps his well-developed chest. 'My solution. A little more ambitious, and certainly more useful than going after ageing defectors. I want SVR to devote their considerable skills and resources to the wealth of the Motherland.'

EPISODE ONE

The Mark

The Travel Agent

1: The Mark

1/1

Contact

The woman drinking coffee alone at the station café seemed quite ordinary: a little gamine, perhaps, and evidently carefree in her attire choice. But otherwise, quite the everyday traveller. A trio of teenage girls chatted noisily nearby about boyfriends and clothes while dexterously thumbing their phones. The arresting but somewhat passé figure at the next table drew their occasional glances.

Rosie Winterbourne had never been a girl to submit to Millennial trends: she had always travelled her own road. Now at thirty-two, her only priorities were decency and comfort. For this hot summer's afternoon, comfortable was a pair of well-worn flip-flops below grey cotton pedal-pushers and a loose-hanging cheesecloth shirt. Jewellery was a no-no, the legacy of a naval career she had maintained into civilian life. The only exception was a diamond stud she wore in her left earlobe – given by her mother on Rosie's twenty-first. In short, the way she looked suited Rosie

The Travel Agent

just fine: five-feet-nine with the figure of a sprinter and an unblemished, rather elfin countenance.

'Boyish' was how her friend Doc once described her. Another vestige of life at sea in a predominantly man's world? Not entirely. A lifelong passion for bodily fitness, independence, and the pursuit of challenging goals had also played their part. Those qualities, if you could call them that, were what Rosie put her boyishness down to. It was all about attitude washing over into the physical. And then there was *Pasha*.

A passion for Pasha.

She allowed herself a grin at Dad's cheesy pun.

At precisely ten-past-five by the station clock, Rosie finished her second Americano, picked up her holdall and crossed via the underpass to Platform Three. As the train arrived, she walked alongside Coach 'D' until it stopped. The door hissed open and, when a trickle of arrivals had disembarked, Rosie climbed aboard. She shunted her heavy holdall along the aisle until she reached her reserved seat, D:27A, a forward-facing window seat. Seat D:26A - opposite and facing hers - was empty. She stooped to read the reservation ticket:

THIS SEAT RESERVED
SALISBURY TO GUILDFORD

Her mark alright. But he was leaving it awfully late. She heaved her bag into the overhead luggage rack then flopped down and stared glumly out of the window.

Rosie would have been out having fun with friends right now, had it not been for the text on the Blackphone this morning. Her instructions were to

1: The Mark

drive here to Salisbury, park at the station and get on the train. This train - the 1716 Intercity to London Waterloo. This reserved seat.

Rosie was usually okay with a short-notice gig. In fact, she enjoyed the spontaneity and having to think on her feet. But today had been her final day at University, and the unscheduled triage had meant missing the students' farewell night out. And now she was going home, and Dad would have to pick her up at Guildford. And besides, she had checked out of her digs today, so was hampered with an exceptionally heavy holdall.

All these small annoyances combined to leave Rosie feeling rather pissed off when she should be rejoicing at having completed a long and challenging three years of study. It was the continuation of the history degree course she had started fourteen years ago and dropped out after a year. Going back to Bristol, she had changed direction. After all that had happened, the Humanities seemed just too frivolous – too esoteric. 'Middle Eastern Languages and Culture' suited the reinvented Rosie much better, and as it proved, took more significant advantage of her prodigious gift for recall. More to the point, it better matched her new career strategy.

Departure time approached, and Rosie grew concerned. Change of plan, perhaps? A whistle sounded, and seconds later, the platform furniture began to glide backwards. Damn! She took out the Blackphone and began to text her displeasure to Harry. But just then the connecting door slid open, and an oversized holdall manoeuvred its way through, followed by a gangly young man looking hot and

The Travel Agent

flushed. He swung his cumbersome bag into the rack by the door and made his way towards Rosie, looking up at the row numbers as he came. Rosie knew straight away he was a yachtsman from his blue Musto crew cap, and therefore, she assumed, probably McCaffey.

Reaching his seat, the mark seemed to fixate for a moment on Rosie's holdall in the rack, then threw her a nervous smile. He folded himself onto the seat like a grasshopper, all elbows and knees. He had taken the middle seat rather than his reserved one, which Rosie assumed was to give them both more legroom. She smiled him her thanks then deleted the message she had been typing on the Blackphone and sent simply:

'Contact'

When she looked up again, McCaffey was smoothing out a rolled-up newspaper. He took a ballpoint from his inside pocket and clicked it, then glanced up. Their eyes met.

'Hello,' Rosie offered, beaming politely.

'Hi,' McCaffey mumbled back, then dropped his eyes to his crossword, tapping the pen on his lips. Oddly, his ear-tips were blushing. Something about him kept her looking, an attractive shyness that trumped his somewhat severe countenance.

After a moment she asked, 'So, what are you stuck on?'

He looked up, 'Sorry? Oh, right,' he consulted the puzzle and read: 'Er, eighteen down: "those who criticise devices to attract attention of residents." Eight letters, third one's "O".' He had a slight Irish accent

1: The Mark

but overlaid with a discernible affectation. Public school, perhaps?

Rosie's brow furrowed, even as the answer came to her. It was just the sort of clue she could decipher in an instant. But best not to be a smart arse.

'Er, it's cryptic,' McCaffey added as if to let her off the hook.

'No shit, Sherlock?' She threw him a conciliatory grin and leaned over to glance at his paper.

'Ah, the Telegraph,' she exclaimed. 'Thought so.'

Rosie saw the young man had completed not quite half the puzzle. She moved across into the window seat next to him.

'How far are you going?' she asked him.

McCaffey shifted uncomfortably at her sudden closeness. 'Guildford. You?'

'Huh, same,' she said brightly. 'What do you reckon, time to crack it between us?'

He smiled then. His nose was like a blade, straddled by deep-sunken brown eyes - striking but not pretty. Rosie estimated her mark was a few years younger than she, mid-twenties maybe.

Half an hour later the only clue remaining to be solved was that tricky eighteen down. McCaffey sighed and laid the paper aside and turned to Rosie.

'You live in Guildford?' he asked.

'No, Cobbingden - a small village a few miles south. My Dad's picking me up.'

McCaffey glanced up at the rack. 'I noticed the Bristol Uni sticker on your bag. You teach there?'

Rosie snorted. 'No, I'm a student. '

'Oh, sorry, I didn't mean…'

The Travel Agent

Rosie's laugh cut across his apology, 'It's okay, easy mistake. I'm what they call a "mature student".' She signed finger-quotes.

'Oh, cool. Was that a change of career? Or did you just find yourself at a loose end?'

Okay, so not too tactful – that could be useful.

She said, 'Huh, a bit of both, I suppose. I started Uni when I was eighteen but dropped out after a year to do something more interesting.'

'Yeah, I get that. Nobody knows what they want at that age. So, what did you do instead?'

'Joined the navy.'

'Ouch! How long were you incarcerated?'

A touch of the anti-establishment. Interesting. A bit of a hippy?

She laughed. 'It wasn't a gaol sentence. Nearly seven years.'

'And your degree course now is what, unfinished business?'

'*Was* unfinished business,' she corrected. 'I just sat my finals.'

He nodded slowly. 'Good luck with your results.' He sounded wistful.

'Thanks,' Rosie said.

'Name's Michael, by the way.'

'Pleased to meet you, Michael Bytheway,' she said teasingly. His chestnut eyes could have been quite beautiful had they not been so profoundly inset. 'I'm Rosie, Rosie Winterbourne.'

His handshake was firm. His bony hand felt hard and calloused - like Rosie's had been before three years in academia had softened them.

1: The Mark

'So, Rosie, what's next in your life? You didn't say what your degree was in.'

'It started as History, but I switched to Languages. Next in my life? I have absolutely no idea. I'll be looking for something part-time while I decide what I want to do.'

Michael gave a derisive snort, 'Huh, bit of a waste of a degree, don't you think? I mean, not having a goal in mind before choosing your subject. What are you going to do, help foreign customers with their burger orders?'

Well, that was provocative.

And this one was turning out a nosy bastard, too.

'Probably something more challenging,' she replied with forced diffidence. 'I only went back really because I don't like loose ends. The study of languages is intense enough to fill my endless craving to learn about the World, okay?'

McCaffey nodded, seeming to enjoy her robust response.

'Endless craving?' he prompted.

Rosie just shook her head. She had allowed the conversation to run away from her – amateurish. The young man was strangely amorphous: his speech, gregarious and laced with blarney, while his body language spoke of timidity, shyness. And now Rosie had missed her chance to turn the talk onto him because he moved on.

'You say your Dad's picking you up, do you still live with your parents?' Then he winced. 'Oh, that was crass, sorry.'

Rosie smiled, tickled that his ear tips were glowing again. Over the past fifteen years, her home had been a

The Travel Agent

warship, a psychiatric ward, a sailboat, and a shared bedsit in Bristol. And she had narrowly avoided including a prison cell in the list.

'It's okay,' she said. 'Sort of – it's just my Dad now. Mum's not with us anymore.'

'Oh, I'm so sorry.'

Rosie nodded grimly - annoyed that her mark was not only keeping the focus on her but invoking in her an emotional response. After a moment's struggle she said brightly, 'So what does Michael Bytheway do to earn a crust?'

'Right now, Michael Colm *McCaffey* is between jobs.'

'Mm, Michael Colm McCaffey - nice alliterative ring. Let me guess, Irish Dad, probably Dublin? English Mum?'

'Very good. You from Irish stock?'

'Uh-huh, an Irish Granny who lived with us when I was growing up.' It had been the other way around, but Rosie retained a childhood aversion to admitting how dependent they'd been on Granny Bee. 'So, another guess, private education? Learned to play polo, a bit of fencing?'

McCaffey huffed. 'Private, yes: RHS Holbrook - marching about in sailor suits and messing in boats on the river. Horses terrify me. And the only fencing I ever did involved chicken wire. Besides, I'm a pacifist; else I'd have joined the navy as my Dad wanted me to do.'

Rosie grinned ruefully. 'Well, even the master sleuth gets it wrong sometimes.'

A naval connection, eh? A common interest for another time? She glanced up at her bag, at what had

1: The Mark

caught his eye earlier: Bristol University's quadrantal red crest.

'Is that where *you* went to Uni,' she asked, 'Bristol?'

'He shook his head. 'Wanted to but missed my grades. Ended up going to Sailing School at Cowes—'

Now we were getting there, but the slippery sod moved on again.

'— and after that, I did five years with the VSO in Rwanda.'

Her eyes widened in mock astonishment. 'Michael, you're turning out to be quite the adventurer, sailing school, and now Voluntary Service Overseas. Whatever did you do for money?'

He grinned, somewhat sheepishly, ears turning ruby. 'I have to confess to my family being quite well off. Dad inherited a big construction company over in Dublin and moved the business to Watford when I was eight.'

'Ah! Lucky you.'

He shook his head. 'To be honest, my Dad's a fucking brute, or at least he was when I was growing up. He bullied me into attending Holbrook and then beat me up when I said I wasn't happy there. And when I flunked my A-levels, he didn't speak to me for a year. In the end, he gave up on me and just let me go my own way with an allowance. I was glad to get away.'

For once, Rosie did not know how to respond - she found herself lost for words by her mark's unexpected frankness.

'But to be fair,' McCaffey continued, 'he did cough up for the residential sailing courses and commercial endorsements, and that's not cheap.'

The Travel Agent

'No, I don't suppose it is. Gosh…' Rosie forced a playful grin to lighten the mood, 'So, you said you're between jobs, is that a euphemism for unemployed?'

'Self-employed. I'm *literally* between jobs; just finished one and starting another soon, not sure when.'

She gave him her naively-curious face, 'Doing what?'

'Yacht deliveries, I'm a "professional sailor",' he mimicked her rabbit-ears of earlier.

No surprise. Delivery Skipper, just like the last two Harry had asked her to triage. There came a sudden unexpected flashback to Erik the Viking - making love on a Cape Verde mountain top …

Stop it!

'What?' she demanded, noticing him smirking.

'You went off on one just then, a kind of a wistful look. You got a thing about yachtsmen?'

Rosie laughed. 'In your dreams. So, now you just go sailing, like, when the fancy takes you, is that it?'

He shook his head. 'It isn't a hobby. I do it because I need my own money.'

'And these boats you deliver, what kind are they?'

'Ooh, all sorts. Mainly sailboats - my last contract was a forty-five-foot ketch.'

She flashed him her interested-but-puzzled face.

'A sailboat with two masts, three sails,' he explained. He looked up and down the length of the carriage. 'About two thirds as long as this coach?'

Rosie looked incredulous. 'And they *pay* you for that?'

He nodded. 'Not as glamorous as it sounds. Take the trip I've just finished - I flew out to Malta to pick her up, and I had to sail her to Southampton where the

1: The Mark

owner wanted her delivered. That trip took six weeks, with rough weather most of the way. I was delirious from lack of sleep and physically exhausted. Good money, but not for the faint-hearted.'

She gave him her little-girl-impressed face. 'What, and you did that all by yourself?'

A slight hesitation and a glance to the right before he said, 'Of course, all alone.' *Those pink ears again - something a bit off maybe. Dig deeper.*

'So, where did you stop on the way, anywhere exciting?'

'No time for stops; it was a straight-through run.' He looked at his watch then out of the window as if looking for an escape. Then, as the train began to slow, he said, 'Talking of stops, this is ours, I think.'

Rosie looked out as a small station flashed past. 'That was Wanborough - five minutes yet. I'll just nip to the loo. Oh, and Knockers.'

'I beg your pardon?'

'Eighteen down. It's "Knockers".'

She had been saving that answer for a mood-lifter. Because she wasn't quite sure about this one – she would need to see Michael Colm McCaffey again.

The Travel Agent

1: The Mark

1/2

Cleaners

Here is a shabby suburban street coming alive at the end of schooltime, mothers and grandmothers with pushchairs, toddlers squabbling alongside. The convenience shop on the corner is doing brisk business.

Two-hundred yards down the street, a car is parked: two men inside. Watching.

Five-thirty pm, and here the men come, returning home from work, or from the mosque. A bus draws up opposite the shop, disgorging a new batch of home-comers.

The car's driver suddenly sits up and looks keenly at one of the new arrivals.

'T*here!* Is that Wasim?'

A man is emerging from behind the bus, clean-shaven, white *taqiyah* plastered on his skull like paint. The passenger pans the car's inbuilt camera to bring the man into view on the monitor.

The Travel Agent

'Yup, looks like our number two,' tapping one of the mugshots taped to the dash. 'Are you getting this, ma'am?'

'Give me a close-up,' a disembodied voice, a woman's voice, raspy and commanding.

The camera zooms in; the man is scanning for traffic before crossing the street, for an instant facing the camera and the shot freezes. The mark crosses toward the corner-shop, to a plain door at the side, looks furtively about, unlocks the door.

'He's just gone in. Anything yet, ma'am?'

'Patience, DFR takes longer without their beards. Ah, here we go ... a positive match! Jibril Wasim, born Bradford 1985, Radicalised and flew to Turkey in January 2014. Wasn't heard of again until the following year when he showed up on a YouTube beheading of a journalist, we think that was in Hajin, Syria. Since then he's been sighted by drone several times in action against the Kurds and SDF. Turned up in Libya in March this year after Syrian troops overran the Daesh enclave in al-Bab. No record of him re–'

'Hang on, ma'am, I believe our number one just showed up.'

A car has pulled up outside the shop, a man climbs out, sharply dressed in suit and tie, again wearing the white *taqiyah*. The camera zooms in, catches his face as he looks around before entering through the same door.

'Yes, that's Ammar Awad al-Hajjar - born John Awad, Birmingham, 1981, joined Daesh in 2015, again, no record of him re-entering. Whoever's tipping us off seems to be on top of things'

1: The Mark

'Unlike Border Force,' mutters one of the watchers.

'I didn't hear that,' grates the woman. *'Any sign of number three?'*

'Not yet, oh wait ... is that Cham, walking up on the right?'

The newcomer is bareheaded, also clean-shaven, conventional western dress. He saunters casually up to the shop, lights a cigarette in the doorway, then stands looking lazily about. His gaze pauses for a moment on the surveillance car, then moves on.

'Think he made us?' mutters the driver.

'He'd better not have done,' snaps the woman. *'It's him alright: Eisa Guirguis al-Kassab al-Sarraf.'*

'Phew! What a mouthful,' mutters one of the agents.

'Born Ali Cham 1979 in London. Positive sightings in Syria and Iraq, implicated in several atrocities against women and children – a real bad boy. Rumoured to have fled to Libya last month.'

'I think we're okay, ma'am, looks like he's going in.'

'Right, as soon as he's inside, scram. We have approval, Cleaners in two minutes.'

The Travel Agent

1: The Mark

1/3

Invitation

'How'd your finals go?' Peter Winterbourne asked after he had hugged his daughter.

'Ooh, not too shabby. I'll know at the end of next month. Fingers crossed, eh?'

They took a handle each of Rosie's holdall and walked the platform to the exit.

'Glad it's over?'

'Mm. Guess I'll miss it, but time to move on, I reckon.'

Dad knew better than to ask why he had needed to pick her up or where she had left the Jeep. He knew about her part-time work with Mercury One - and the fact that she had not explained was good enough for him.

Reaching the Renault, they dropped her holdall onto the back seat, and Rosie got in the front. She avoided looking at her Dad as he started the car but sensed his nervousness. He looked around with unnecessary caution (the carpark was empty), slipped into gear and looked again before creeping hesitantly away. Since he had got his licence back, he drove like a little old lady on her Sunday drive to church. The Accident would probably haunt him forever.

As they pulled out of the carpark, Peter said, 'Talking of moving on, a letter came for you yesterday.'

'Oh yeah?' Rosie was studying the card McCaffey had given her, and therefore missed the significance of her father's words. She would need to ask Harry if he wanted her to take up the young skipper's invitation for drinks tomorrow night. It would depend on how much a 'person of interest' he was.

'The Foreign & Commonwealth Office.'

Rosie tensed. 'The FCO, what about it?'

'They sent you a letter in the post.'

'What? Why didn't you say?'

Peter laughed, 'I just did, it came yesterday.'

Rosie could barely contain herself for the rest of the drive home and barely listened to Dad's recounting the past two weeks of village gossip. She was out of the car almost before it stopped in the drive. Fumbling for her keys, she shimmied to the door, unlocked it and stepped inside. There it was on the hall table: a white envelope with the royal coat of arms and government seal. She stared at it for a moment, then picked up the letter. Trembling slightly, she tore it open and scanned the single page. Hardly able to believe it, she reread it, her face lighting up until she was grinning like a coal-scuttle.

'Dad!' she yelled out of the door, 'they've invited me to attend an interview: three weeks on Tuesday in Whitehall.'

1: The Mark

Peter smiled to himself as he carried his daughter's holdall up to the house.

After unpacking, Rosie cooked a Chicken Alfredo Tagliatelle. They ate while watching some mindless TV programme. Or rather: her father watched half asleep, while Rosie, wearing earbuds, played back the conversation with McCaffey from her phone.

After half-an-hour, the Blackphone buzzed in her pocket. Rosie stood and glanced out of the window.

'My Jeep's back,' she told her Dad, pulling out her earbuds. 'I need a word - won't be long.'

Marcus had parked the Jeep in the drive behind her Dad's Renault; she could feel the heat coming off the engine from a yard away and heard it ticking as it cooled. Shaking her head in despair, she retrieved her keys from under the wheel-arch and walked down to the green Range Rover that was parked across the bottom of the drive, engine still running. Rosie opened the rear door and climbed in, pulling it closed behind her. Both men in front twisted to face her.

'Marcus,' she snapped, 'my jeep's twelve years old and built for trundling, could you please not drive her like a Ferrari?'

The young black man in the front passenger seat smirked. 'Want I should bring her home cross country, Rosie, off-road, like?'

Marcus' persona was pure London-street, but behind it lay the sharp intellect of an accomplished undercover investigator, which indeed had been his previous posting. Now deemed too old for the role, he had switched his expertise to human-trafficking and modern-slavery.

The Travel Agent

'Well?' asked Harry from the driver's seat. 'This McCaffey fella of interest or no?'

Harry McAllister was a fifty-year-old ex-Royal Marine from the Highlands. Five years ago, the Secret Intelligence Service had charged Harry with recruiting and training a small cadre of part-time Triage Officers. Specialists in small private boats or light aircraft: their job was to identify British nationals involved in small-scale people-trafficking. This unit was known as Mercury One, and Rosie had been among its first recruits.

'Mm, maybe,' Rosie said. 'What put you onto him?'

'The boat sailed west from Malta then made a detour to Libya. I've sent the Marine Traffic footage to yer Inbox, take a look for yersel. So what got *your* hackles up, hen?'

'Just a gut feeling. He didn't want to talk about the trip, and he hedged when I asked him about being single-handed. And he claimed not to have stopped anywhere on a six-week passage, which frankly is madness. Yeah, there's something off about him, but I can't be sure it's anything of interest to us. He might be just running drugs.'

'No man, he won't be running no drugs from Libya,' said Marcus. 'Maybe refugees?'

Rosie said nothing. Marcus was the expert on all matters North African.

'Are ye set for a follow-up?' asked Harry.

She nodded. 'I've got McCaffey's number. I can call him.'

'Okay, Rosie, take a look at his track, see if ye can figure oot what's going on. Let me know your thoughts tonight.'

1: The Mark

'Okay? Anything else?'

'Er, aye, actually,' Harry said, 'Ye'll remember the wee Australian from last year, aye?'

'The hashish smuggler, Wesley Corcoran? What about him?'

'He called you this afternoon on the burner ye had at the time.' Harry handed her an old-fashioned Nokia. 'Ye'd better call him back, hen. See what the wee chappy wants.'

'And if it's another drug run?'

'Just find oot where he's delivering from, and we'll hand it over to Europol. But we traced the origin of the call to a location just ootside Escalles. That's a few miles west o' the former refugee camp at Sangatte. We think it might be human traffic this time.'

Rosie frowned. 'So why not just hand it over to Europol and Border Force anyway? I don't understand why I need to triage him again. We already know his game.'

'His sailboat's still impounded,' Marcus said, 'we dunno how he's going to work it.'

Harry said, 'Ye'll need to find oot what the wee fella's plannin' – if he's up tae his auld tricks. Find what boat he's using, where aboot he's leaving, and where he's landing. Then we can arrange a nice welcome home party fer the wee man.'

Rosie switched on the phone and watched the tiny screen light up. One missed call: 'Oz'. She pressed the callback button and put the phone to her ear while Harry slipped on a pair of headphones. It answered after four rings.

'That you, Rosie?'

'Hi, Wesley, what's up?'

The Travel Agent

'You ever sailed a Lagoon 45?'

'I've sailed a catamaran, not one that big, but the principal's the same. Why?'

'I need a hand to bring one across the Channel. Quiet overnight job on Monday. There's a grand in it for you.'

She glanced at Harry, who rolled his finger for more information.

'Maybe I can help. Where are we sailing from, and where to?'

'I just need you to come over to Calais on the 2.30 ferry from Dover. I'll pick you up from there, and we'll drive to the boat.'

Rosie grimaced at Harry. If she pushed again, the Australian might get suspicious. Harry gave her a thumbs-up but looked worried.

'Okay, Wesley, I'll be on the ferry. Is it just the two of us?'

'... I'll see you Monday, Rosie.'

The phone clicked off.

'Not quite the result we wanted,' said Harry, 'but can't be helped. You okay with this?'

Rosie grinned. 'Wesley's safe enough - bit of a softy really. Sounds like he might be smuggling refugees this time though, and a lot of them, going by the size of the boat. Border Force is going to owe us, big time.'

Marcus looked anxious. 'Just make sure you keep your Blackphone switched on so we can track you, Rosie. You ain't no superspy yet.'

Rosie grinned. 'Talking of which, guys, I might not be on your team much longer. I've got an interview at FCO in three weeks. It looks like I'm going full-on.'

1: The Mark

Marcus grinned and gave her a high five. 'Nice one, Rosie! Knew you'd be up there wid da stars pretty soon.'

Harry did not look so happy. 'I wouldn'e get too excited. A spook's life's no all it's cracked up to be.'

'Well, thanks for the pat on the back, Harry,' said Rosie, disappointed with her handler's negative response. 'What's up, think I'm not up to it?'

He blew out a sigh. 'I always knew ye'd be moving on, hen - yer talents are wasted in triage. I'm just sayin': it's going to get seriously tough for ye from here on in. But I wish ye luck, all the same.'

'Mm, I'll be sad to leave you both - I've learned a lot from you in the past four years.'

'Hey!' Marcus chimed in, 'you ain't gone yet, Rosie. We still got to crack this McCaffey dude.'

The Travel Agent

1: The Mark

1/4

Suspicions

Rosie found Dad snoring gently in front of yet another televised Brexit debate. She turned it off, took away the dinner things, loaded them into the dishwasher, and then went upstairs to her room.

She logged on to her laptop and accessed her account on the Mercury One VPN with the fingerprint reader. Finding the media file Harry had sent her, *KentishDawnAIS.mp4,* she double-clicked it. The screen went blank for a moment as the file loaded. A marine chart of the central Mediterranean appeared, centred on Malta with the Libyan coast to the south, Tunisia to the west, and Sicily to the north. She clicked the 'full-screen' icon. The title at the top of the screen read:

Marine Traffic: s/y Kentish Dawn MMSI 235113215
Track 29/05 - 14/07

Countless tiny symbols filled the chart like a spilled bag of hundreds-and-thousands - shapes and colours representing vessels ranging from the largest container ships to the smallest of leisure-craft. Rosie hit Play, and the symbols began to creep along their tracks, the DateTime in top-left counting off two hours for every screen refresh. The picture zoomed-in to a flashing pink pleasure-boat symbol off Malta's north coast, a label next to it with the legend KD, *Kentish Dawn* - McCaffey's delivery contract. Okay, his story so far checked out; this boat looked like she had just left Malta's Grand Harbour.

Rosie speeded up the video so that the symbols raced along dizzily. She watched *Kentish Dawn* pass to the north of Gozo, on her way up to the Sicilian Strait. Suddenly the boat sheared off to port, settling on a southerly track towards the Libyan coast. The picture zoomed in as the yacht got closer to shore, then, at about five miles north of Zuwara, she disappeared from the screen. Rosie paused the video and checked the DateTime: 2330 1 June. She wrote down the last position and made a note to check the weather there for that time, and then she clicked Play. The sailboat did not reappear for another fifty hours, and when she did, it was some 240 miles to the north. Having passed through the Sicilian Strait, she now headed west toward the Strait of Gibraltar. Rosie fast-forwarded again and watched as *Kentish Dawn* raced out into the Atlantic and up the Iberian coast.

Rosie shook her head in bewilderment.

'Why on earth didn't you call in somewhere?' she muttered. 'Gib or Lisbon, or even Vigo.'

McCaffey must have been knackered, and living off dried food. It made no sense.

'No, mister, you weren't single-handed, were you?'

1: The Mark

Even if he had a crew, what was his hurry? Had the owner given him a deadline?

She drummed her fingers impatiently as the yacht continued her passage across the Bay of Biscay, scraped past Ushant Light, and towards the tumble of ships pouring in and out of the Channel. When McCaffey's vessel entered the Western Approaches, Rosie slowed down the video once more. The target vessel now approached the south Devon coast where a cluster of fishing boats hugged the coastline. But as Kentish Dawn came within ten miles of Salcombe, another contact was highlighted, moving fast away from the coast towards the yacht. AIS gave the new vessel's name as M/V *Sarirnaqal*, a motor launch. Then, as if by coordinated signal, both AIS contacts disappeared.

Rosie hit pause and noted the time: 0234 14 July. The dead of night. She made a note to check the moon and cloud cover for that time—also, the wind and sea-state. Rolling on, *Kentish Dawn* did not appear again until six hours later - transiting up the Dart Estuary. *Sarirnaqal* never reappeared.

Rosie scribbled some rough calculations in her notebook. She spent half an hour on the items she had noted for research.

After a few more moments of pondering her conclusions, she muttered, 'You've been bullshitting me, Mister McCaffey, and I don't like that.'

Rosie returned to her Mercury One account and typed up her preliminary analysis to Harry.

> No logical reason for the detour to Libya except to rendezvous for a transfer of

The Travel Agent

some kind - someone ashore must have been expecting them. Weather that night was clear and calm with a south-easterly breeze and no moon. AIS was switched off during rendezvous.

I calculate that, in order to get to where she reappeared 50 hours later, KD can't have spent more than an hour in the vicinity of Zuwara.

There was a rendezvous with a vessel reporting herself as *Sarirnaqal* off Salcombe, presumably to transfer whatever he had picked up in Libya. The conditions were ideal for a clandestine transfer at sea.

Agree it all looks suspicious - not the expected behaviour of a legitimate yacht delivery. Whatever *Sarirnaqal* is, she's not in the UK Ship Register even though she has a UK MMSI Number – a pirate AIS transponder. (FYI that's the marine equivalent to a false number plate). Odd name, nothing on Google – could be made up from joint-owners' initials.

Conclusions
IMO Marcus is right about refugees, but the mark doesn't strike me as the kind likely to involve himself in anything more sinister than humanitarian aid (he told me he once worked with VSO in Rwanda). Also note: on a six-week non-stop passage he'd be hard-pushed to provision

1: The Mark

for more than two or three passengers. NB this is advisory: I might be wrong.

I should have a better idea about him after tomorrow night.
R.

The Travel Agent

1: The Mark

1/5

Housekeeper

The console on Rachel Sanderson's desk buzzed insistently for the seventh time in as many minutes. It had been a frantic afternoon. A flashing message told her who was calling: Cleaner Three. She picked up.

'Please, give me only *good* news.'

'All done, Ma'am. Nothing to see here.'

'Splendid. Stand down and await further orders.' She hung up.

After a rare quiet moment, Sanderson sighed and keyed in a number known only to herself. When the other end picked up, she said, 'The Leeds case is closed.'

The call clicked off without a word.

Sanderson leaned back in her chair and massaged her eyelids. She wanted a cigarette, but still had things to do before she could sneak off to her smoke-hole in the underground carpark. Ironic that she could sanction murder but could not escape the no-smoking rule.

The Travel Agent

She buzzed her intercom.

'Yes, Housekeeper?'

'Have Gauntlet and Hammer checked in yet?'

'Ten minutes ago.'

'Send them up.'

Rachel Sanderson was forty-nine, a full Colonel in the Army, though she had not worn a uniform in ten years. Nobody at Firegate knew Sanderson's name or rank; she was known merely as the Housekeeper.

A knock came at the door.

'Come.'

'Good evening, Ma'am. We got your message. What's up?'

Gauntlet suited his codename, 195cm and wiry with cold grey eyes. He was a multi-talented agent: an accomplished sniper, all-round weapons specialist, and a deadly coiled spring in unarmed combat. He was also volatile, impulsive, and prone to amorous distraction. Hammer, by contrast, was shorter of build: 168cm and stocky. Watchful as a barn owl and manifestly geeky, Hammer's skills lay in field-surveillance and covert comms. Although aware of Gauntlet's irritation of his partner's pedantic methods, Sanderson considered Hammer the strategist and steadying influence that made the pair her most valued team.

'Close the door and sit down. We've got a problem.'

The two men sat and waited, quietly curious.

'Earlier this afternoon, C3's team - acting on my orders following yet another anonymous tipoff to the Foreign Office - caught three men preparing explosives above a shop in Leeds. Turns out once again they were Daesh returnees, British nationals, radicalised here in the UK before travelling to Syria.'

1: The Mark

Gauntlet shrugged and said carelessly, 'It's what we do, Ma'am.'

Sanderson glared at the agent for a second, then said icily, 'It's what we do with homegrown terrorists that police can't prosecute due to covertly acquired evidence. Our current brief is *not* about insurgents trained in overseas terrorist enclaves. My point is, Gauntlet, GCHQ reported all three having escaped to Libya with Rasheed al Basara's fighters. And now they turn up in the UK undetected. These three make sixteen so far this year, and our people tracked none of them coming home.'

Gauntlet sighed. 'Not in our gift to do Border Force's job for them. When they cock-up, we clean up. We should round them all up and waste them, no questions, no trial.'

'Out of order, Gauntlet,' Sanderson snapped angrily. 'I'll try to ignore that indiscretion, but watch it.'

'Obviously, it's a well-organised effort,' said Hammer quickly, keen to disrupt the oncoming exchange of views. 'The caliphate must have found themselves a travel agent.'

'Which raises the stakes significantly,' Sanderson said. 'And perhaps allows us the opportunity to revise Firegate's terms of reference. Homegrown amateurs are bad enough. Can you imagine a coordinated attack on our cities by Daesh-trained fighters?'

'Any idea where the tipoffs are coming from?' Gauntlet asked. 'If we discover the guy blowing the whistle, we might get to find the train driver.'

'We need to be careful not to scare him or her off,' Sanderson cautioned. 'We don't want to turn off the tap before we're ready to pull the plug.'

The Travel Agent

'Why turn off the tap at all?' offered Hammer.

'Because there's a political angle,' said The Housekeeper. 'It makes us look incompetent, and frankly, makes our surveillance effort redundant. I want you two to start digging, find this travel agent, find out how these people are getting in and close it down. Usual drill - use all necessary means but don't make a mess. I will not be a happy bunny if you call for Cleaners.'

They nodded in unison; it was a familiar spiel.

'And by the way, you might come across a low echelon team from SIS looking at private aerodromes and yacht marinas for human traffickers. They go by the name Mercury One. One of their operatives is investigating a yachtie who could be smuggling refugees from Libya. If our travel agent's using similar routes, there's a risk of mutual interference. Mercury One are not aware of Firegate - make sure it stays that way.'

When the pair had left, Sanderson retrieved her cigarettes and lighter from her desk drawer and hurried out for a much-needed nicotine fix.

Returning to her office five minutes later, she opened a file folder on her desk - a dossier of Mercury One's part-time agents. She flipped over the pages until she came to the file of a T.O. Rosie Winterbourne. According to The Housekeeper's secret liaison at SIS, Herbert's team was about to interview Winterbourne for a full-time post - a woman with no covert-ops background or training. Sanderson was curious to know why. After reading through the six-page document, she buzzed her intercom.

'Yes, The Housekeeper?'

1: The Mark

'Get me Erin Easterwood on a secure line.'

The Travel Agent

1: The Mark

1/6

Catching-up

Rosie woke to the sound of the lawnmower through her open window. A warm breeze billowed the curtains, flicking bright sunlight around the bedroom. It was Saturday morning. Dad was cutting the grass, and life was back to normal. She stretched luxuriously, loving the comforting feel of her own duvet, the sheer perfection of her orthopaedic mattress. For ten minutes, Rosie just languished in bed, soaking up the joy of home. Then, with a pleasurable sigh, she threw back the duvet and rose.

After her shower, Rosie prepared tea and toast and took it back to her room to check her emails. First up was one from Doc Halliday - her best friend from the navy, now a Chief Writer and shore-based in Plymouth - asking how she had got on in her Finals. Rosie told Doc she would be home for a while now and it would be good to catch up if she wanted to come to stay for a weekend.

The Travel Agent

Scrolling down, she found one from Anna and glanced anxiously out of her window to make sure Dad was still out in the garden. He did not know Rosie had remained in touch with Mum's erstwhile partner, and she didn't want to rake up old wounds. Since his re-awakening from Locked-in Syndrome four years ago, there had been an emotional brittleness about Dad that made Rosie cautious talking about the past.

It had all happened before Rosie was born. Peter Winterbourne had known about Anna; she had first invited him to sail with her and her partner, Margaret. On subsequent occasions, Peter filled in as crew whenever the two women required the third pair of hands. The former Royal Navy sailor had soon become besotted with Margaret, *Pasha's* owner. Despite Margaret's relationship with Anna, the three had developed a friendship that should have endured. But it all fell apart when Margaret, following a brief affair, fell pregnant with Rosie. Peter, already a devoted admirer of the elegant lady sailor, had stepped up to the mark to placate Margaret's imperious Irish mother, later known to Rosie as Granny Bee.

Margaret's marriage to Peter had mollified Granny Bee's Catholic sensitivities by providing the coming child with a legitimate father.

Meanwhile, poor Anna, emotionally destroyed by her lover's betrayal, fled to Florida. A Finnish migrant with a degree in software engineering, Anna was a communications analyst for the US Federal Government.

The whole scandal, including Rosie's falsified paternity, had been kept from her for twenty-seven years. It was not until more than a year after Mum's

1: The Mark

death that Anna lifted the veil of secrecy. It was these astonishing revelations in the aftermath of her mother's death that had been the root of Rosie's delusional psychosis.

Anna's email was brief and to the point: she was moving to Virginia to be closer to her place of work, and how was Peter? A PS offered the use of Anna's Miami house if Rosie or her father visited South Florida.

Rosie rattled off an equally succinct reply then deleted both emails.

She called McCaffey's number - he picked up after three rings.

'Hello, who's this?'

'Hi, Michael, it's Rosie. From the train, yesterday?'

'Ah, I wondered if you'd ring.'

'That invitation for drinks. Is it still open?'

'Well look, Rosie, I've got someone I have to see tonight – business, you know?'

'Oh, okay. It's just you said…'

'We can do early doors and grab a bite if you like? My meeting's at nine-thirty here in town.'

Rosie was disappointed. Early doors with a meeting later would not afford the chance to get him loosened up and talking. He probably would not even be drinking. However:

'Okay, sounds good. Does that mean you'll be driving?'

An exhalation came down the phone, which could have been laughter or a snort of derision. *Driving! Me? Rosie, there's a thing you need to know about me: I've never owned a car – never needed one.'*

'Oh, right. So, where shall we meet, and when?'

The Travel Agent

By the time Rosie made it to the back garden to help her Dad, he was emptying the mower's grass-cuttings. The wheelbarrow was heaped with freshly-pulled weeds.

'Oh, I was going to weed the flowerbeds.'

'Too late, my girl, all done.' He straightened stiffly and arched his back, grimacing. 'Whew, your Dad's getting too old for this. I take it from yesterday's shenanigans, you've got a new mission with the secret squirrels?'

'*Dad!*' she hissed, 'Not outside.' Despite her annoyance, she could not help a grin at his injured-dog act. She knew he did it to wind her up. Shaking her head, Rosie took up the barrow and began rolling it down to the compost.

'Oh, Rosemary?'

She stopped, and half turned. 'What?'

He nodded at the wheelbarrow. 'You won't grass me up, will you?'

Rosie rolled her eyes, but she wheeled on down the garden smiling, not at the cheesy joke, but the fact he'd made it. Perhaps, after three-and-a-half years, Dad was getting his mojo back.

1: The Mark

1/7

Fishing

It was a glorious summer's late afternoon; Saturday - Guildford's streets were teeming with late shoppers and early diners and fun-seekers. The age it took Rosie to dodge her way through the spilling crowds to find a legal parking space resulted in her arriving some ten minutes late.

McCaffey had found them a table outside where an impatient waitress jiggled her notebook while Rosie was getting herself seated.

'Sorry,' she huffed, 'Parking in this town's a nightmare.'

'Oh! The joys of driving,' McCaffey grinned smugly.

'Are you both ready to order?' asked the waitress, standing like she needed a pee. 'Or should I come back?'

McCaffey, who was indeed ready, asked for a Fino Pitta and a pale ale. At the same time, Rosie, after a hurried scan of the menu, ordered peri-peri wings with

The Travel Agent

a green salad and a glass of pressed apple juice. The waitress scribbled it all down, flashed them a lightning smile and straight-legged it back inside.

'This place is like a production line.' Rosie commented.

McCaffey said, 'Peak time and sunshine, who can blame them - this is England, and it'll be raining pitchforks tomorrow. Besides, maybe now you know how their battery chickens feel.' He grinned at Rosie's startled look. 'Only joking. I'm sure the peri-peri wings come from happy free-ranging little cluckers.'

Their drinks arrived, clunked down unceremoniously. Rosie watched the waitress race off to take her next order, then raised her eyebrows at McCaffey, who nodded and raised his bottle.

'To production lines,' he said.

'To battery hens,' she rejoined.

Bottle clinked to glass, and they drank.

'You say you were looking for some part-time work,' he said with a half-smirk. 'Plenty of waitress jobs going, I should think.'

Rosie spluttered, 'I did my share of that in Bristol. And by the way, when you're a waitress relying on tips you don't rush around ignoring your customers - you have to stay and be nice.'

McCaffey grinned. 'Means they probably pay them too well – worth a thought–' He noticed the sardonic set in her expression and shook his head. 'Nah, I can see that's not gonna float.'

'Good, Michael, so move on. Tell me ab–'

'You know, Rosie, you're the first navy person I ever met, so tell me about your life and travels.'

1: The Mark

'Maybe later. And talking of firsts, you're the first man I've ever met that doesn't drive. How have you survived so long without a licence?'

'Oh, I've got a driving licence, alright. Back in Rwanda, I used to bump around dirt trails in a Landrover. Here, I couldn't justify a car's expense when I spend most of my time overseas. Nah, the train suits me fine.'

'So, tell me about this yachting business of yours. And keep it simple, remember I'm a girl of the land?'

'Huh? Navy, you said.'

'Ah, you might not know this, but they replaced the sails with gas-turbines a year or two back. I want to know all the secrets of taking a … what did you call it, a sloop? Yeah, a sloop, all the way from the Mediterranean to here, and why you didn't stop anywhere.'

McCaffey's demeanour changed immediately. He looked down, picking at the label on his bottle.

'And,' she persisted, pretending not to notice his discomfort, 'what really puzzles me: why should someone trust a stranger with her or his expensive yacht.'

He seemed to relax at the generality of the second question.

'Ah, well that's easy enough—online agencies. Skippers sign up and prove their credentials. The agent targets potential customers through online marketing: yachting websites and the like. After you've delivered the boat, the client posts a review, with star-ratings for value-for-money and performance. The clients can compare the meercat for the cheapest, or the most trustworthy skippers. Simples, Sergei.'

The Travel Agent

Rosie grinned slyly. 'And you, Michael, your reviews are five-star I presume?'

His ear tips reddened. 'I do okay. I get to pick and choose the jobs I want.'

'And what kind of jobs do you turn down?'

'Er, I don't cross oceans for a start. Look, what's this, twenty questions?'

Rosie leaned back, hands up in surrender. 'Sorry, sorry. I'm just fascinated, that's all - I've never met a boat captain before.'

He grinned then. 'The navy runs ships by committee, or what?'

'Fair point. But you know what I mean. In complete charge of a boat, out there, all alone. It sounds so, so …'

'So what? So fucking dangerous?'

'I was going to say, romantic.'

McCaffey smiled grimly, 'Trust me, Rosie, there's nothing romantic about getting battered and bruised in a gale and wishing you were sleeping under an oak tree.'

Tell me about it.

'So why don't you take somebody on to share the workload?'

He shrugged, 'Pure economics. I'd have to pay a crew out of my fee - wouldn't be worth my while doing it.'

McCaffey's began picking at the label on his bottle again. A subtle change, a defensive tension whenever Rosie broached the detail of his trips. Now his ear tips were on fire. Antagonising him further risked losing her his confidence. And how would that go down in her coming interview?

1: The Mark

'Yeah, I get it,' she said. She allowed a mischievous grin to spread on her face. 'So, tell me, Michael Colm McCaffey, what was your Irish Dad's connection with the navy?'

The Travel Agent

1: The Mark

1/8

Pasha

It was almost nine by the time Rosie got home, and Dad was watching *Strictly Come Dancing*.

Gently, she squeezed his shoulder, 'You okay, Dad?'

'I made a lasagne and garlic bread,' he said distantly, without taking his eyes off the dancing pair. A beefy sports celeb in a tuxedo was dancing American Smooth with a painted wraith to some crooner from the fifties.

'Just needs a blast of microwaves, and there's a salad in the fridge.'

She bent and kissed his forehead, 'Thanks, I'll have it later. Cuppa tea?'

He did not answer, just stared at the screen, seemingly lost in the world of yesterday and the glamour of the ballroom. Dad did that a lot these days, and that was worrying. As she stood there, waiting for her question to register, she wondered how she could change something in his life. Find him an external interest before he descended into cognitive extinction.

The Travel Agent

Suddenly, Dad looked up, a noticeable jerking out from his sombre demesne.

'Sorry, sweetheart, miles away. How was your evening?'

His eyes were glassy, and Rosie smiled at him fondly, 'You were thinking about Mum.'

'Mm,' he nodded. 'Yes, a cuppa would be nice.'

Rosie swallowed. They had loved their dancing, M & D: The Ballroom Club in town, a Tuesday night ritual from a bygone era that Rosie had ribbed them about incessantly. That was now a touching reminder of her parents' devotion to each other; a cherished memory.

'I'll put the kettle on,' Rosie said with a catch in her voice. She paused by his chair a moment longer, her father's distant, watery eyes seeing memories beyond the dancing. With a silent sniff, she turned and headed for the kitchen.

When Rosie came back into the sitting room, Dad was still staring but at a blank screen.

'I thought you were watching *Strictly*,' she said, putting his tea down on his side-table.

'Huh? Oh! No, darling, *Strictly* doesn't start again till September. That was the 2011 final.'

Rosie put her tea down and folded her arms tenderly about her father's big grey head, 'Oh, Dad. That was the last one you watched with Mum.'

Oddly moved by the gesture, Peter reached around his daughter's awkward embrace and ruffled her short, mousy hair. 'Don't start blubbing, lady, or you'll have me at it.'

Rosie straightened up and sniffed, then slumped onto the settee. 'I remember it because I was home on

1: The Mark

Christmas leave after our Caribbean Guardship deployment. That Harry whatsisname out of McFly won it.'

'Judd. I don't suppose you're going to tell me about your assignation?'

'*Assignation?* What am I, sixteen?'

'I mean, your chat with the secret squirrels out there.'

'You know better than to ask.' Rosie said, then leaned forwards, a sudden sparkle in her eyes, 'What I can tell you is I'm driving down to Mullhaven tomorrow. They're lifting her in. Fancy giving me a hand?'

Peter looked startled for a moment. 'Phew, think I'm getting a bit old for running around on a boat, Rosemary, don't you?'

'Rubbish. There are blokes in their eighties still sailing. It's *mostly* old codgers down there, anyway.'

'Yes, but I've not stepped aboard a boat for ten years or more–'

'Phooey, Dad, this is our old *Pasha* we're talking about. It'll be just like going home. Anyway, we're not taking her out. When we've lifted her in, we'll tie her up at the pontoon and then wash her down. I've got all the clean cushion covers to put on. And I have to go aloft, so I'll need your help. We can get a coffee afterwards in the *Chandlery* and pop by to see Mum on the way home. Back here by teatime - promise. Come on, Dad, what do you say?'

Rosie jumped aboard the moment *Pasha's* deck came level with the dockside. She turned around to help Dad, but to her surprise, he had already stepped over the midships guardrail, cool as you like. Rosie smiled fondly at the sight of her father walking confidently along the narrow deck with the bow rope in hand. It took her back to her teens when they used to sail together almost every weekend. It was hard to believe that for the past six years it had been she, Rosie, who had worn the Captain's hat. *Pasha's* former skipper - now tramping the deck with such panache - gave her a queasy sense of nostalgia for her teens.

When *Pasha's* hull had settled into the water, and the crane slings slackened, Rosie stepped down the companionway ladder and into her cabin in the port quarter-berth. She had earlier lifted out her mattress to allow access to the stern-gland, and now she slid face-down along the boards and shone her Maglite into the shaft space. Rosie reached her hand along the shiny propellor shaft to the stiff rubber collar where it breached the hull. Working blindly, she squeezed the grease-packed sleeve to release any trapped air. That was the best she could do for now - she would recheck the gland for leaks once the propellor had been turning.

Next, she opened the cooling-water seacock in the engine bay and called up to Dad to start her up. After a moment, the engine shook violently on its resilient mountings, turned over twice, then burst into life with a throaty rumble, quickly settling down as Dad adjusted the revs. Rosie shone her Maglite into the bay, checking for oil or water leaks. She checked that the alternator belt was spinning smoothly. The impellor-plate felt cold to touch, signifying that cooling water flowed freely. Satisfied, she replaced the

1: The Mark

engine cover and went around opening the other seacocks.

Back up in the cockpit, she found Dad leaning over the starboard guardrail. He straightened up and gave Rosie the okay sign - the exhaust was punching out cooling water.

'Like old times, Rosemary,' he beamed, looking once more the gritty sailor of Rosie's youth, belying his seventy-three years. 'Shall we take her out for a spin?'

Rosie laughed, swept up in his enthusiasm, but then said, 'You might not have noticed in your excitement, Dad, but we've got no sails at the moment. They're still up in the sail loft.'

Her father pursed his lips and nodded; his disappointment palpable.

'We can go out next weekend if you like?'

'Splendid idea! You're on. Now, let's get the old girl alongside and cleaned up.'

With the boat secured at her allocated berth on the floating pontoon, and the teak deck and coachroof restored to a healthy glow with the pressure hose, it was time for Rosie to go aloft.

She stepped up onto the coach roof, unbuttoned the main-halliard from the mast and hooked it onto her harness. She checked her toolbelt and her bag of goodies were secure around her waist then turned back to Dad on the halliard winch.

'You sure you're okay to do this, Dad?'

'Getaway with you, child. You're a featherweight.'

She grinned at him. 'I was five stone last time you pulled me up the mast - I'm nearly double that now.'

The Travel Agent

He glared at her tight-lipped.

She smiled back. 'Okay, take it nice and slow, then. Ready? Take up the slack.'

She watched critically as he pulled the rope in tight, took four turns on the winch, jammed it into the self-tailer, and slotted in the winch handle. No hesitation. Rosie gave a nod of satisfaction. An old sailor never forgot his craft. As Dad began turning the handle, Rosie was lifted clear of the deck. She took some of the weight as she rose, climbing first onto the boom, then hitching up the mast using her hands, knees and bare feet. Climbing onto the first set of spreaders, then the second, she used the wire shrouds to help her rest the way to the top.

'Okay,' she called down. 'Secure at that.'

From her toolbelt, Rosie selected a medium Philips. She unscrewed the broken wind transducer - all three cups and the vane had snapped off in an Atlantic storm.

That same storm, three years ago, had almost been the death of Rosie: knocked on the head, she had lain unconscious in the saloon for three days while *Pasha* sailed on unmanned. She reached up and ran her fingers along the faint ridge above her hairline and shivered at the memory. It was an Azorean fisherman who discovered the un-skippered boat and called the coastguard. Rosie was airlifted to hospital with a brain aneurism.

She returned to her work, eased out the two electrical wires an extra inch or two through the watertight membrane. Then she disconnected them from the damaged unit, which she exchanged for the new one in her goody bag. Reconnecting the wires, Rosie screwed

1: The Mark

the new instrument into place. Working slowly and methodically, she repeated the process with the masthead tricolour lamp, replacing the whole unit rather than just the bulb - cheaper than risking failure through corrosion. The bigger masthead lamp-holder was a chunky, robust item and required only a new LED lamp. Finally, she checked the AIS whip-aerial was secure and corrosion-free and gave everything a spray of WD40.

When she was finished, she sat there a moment, swinging gently in her harness, and scanned the seascape from her lofty perch. The fifteen-metre elevation gave her a view over the breakwater of the blue-grey expanse of the English Channel. Several transiting ships, seemingly motionless from this distance, plied the shipping routes east and westbound. She thought about the sea, going out there again. Dad would be aboard this time, and that was going to be a fun sail, and a nostalgic one.

But someday soon she would have to bite the bullet and get out there again - alone. That, or admit she had lost her bottle.

'You asleep up there, Girl, or what?'

Rosie snapped out of her reverie. 'All done, Dad, lower away.'

Later, drinking coffee in the Chandler's Arms, Rosie said. 'You enjoyed yourself today, didn't you?'

'Yes, Rosemary, surprisingly I did. And I've been thinking; we should do Weymouth next weekend, like back in the day.'

'Why not? And I've got another idea.'

'What's that?'

The Travel Agent

'Let's drop in at the Arundel Garden Centre, buy some white lilies, and go tell Mum you've got your mojo back - she'll be thrilled to bits.'

EPISODE TWO

The Traffickers

The Travel Agent

2: The Traffickers

2/1

Wesley

Monday morning at the Dover Ferry Terminal, Rosie got a call from McCaffey.

'Hope I didn't get this wrong, but I got the distinct feeling you'd like to meet up again soon. Only you never said.'

Rosie laughed, hiding her annoyance at having heard from him so soon. She preferred to set her *own* agenda.

'Yeah, why not,' she said. 'I've got a few things to do this week, but I'm free Thursday. Would that suit?'

'That'd be great. Now, you said last week you were into Game of Thrones and you'd only seen up to Season Four, is that right?'

Rosie began to get a bad feeling. 'Er, yes, I did say that. Why?'

'Okay, now you sound a bit unsure. Let me come straight to the point. Then you can tell me to take a hike if you want. I've got Season Five, and I want to cook you a Paella at my flat. You can watch a couple of episodes and then drive home, or we can binge-

The Travel Agent

watch the whole thing, drink some wine, and you can crash on my settee. My intentions are entirely honourable, but you'll need to trust me on that.'

Rosie did not answer for a while - allowed the silence to hang awkwardly between them. It was McCaffey who broke it.

'Well, at least you haven't hung up on me… I take it your still there?'

Rosie chuckled. 'Yeah, I'm still here.' After another short pause, she gave a sigh. 'Okay, Michael, you're on. Where do you live, and what time do you want me?'

She had just ended the call when the announcement came for foot passengers for the two-thirty DFDS Seaways to begin boarding.

Two hours later, Rosie disembarked the ship via the zigzag passenger walkway at Calais. She spotted Wesley beyond the chain-link fence as she walked toward the security building. He had grown a beard - a scruffy ginger fuzz - and his hair was longer and greasier. But she recognised his hunched way of standing - he was almost thirty by now but hadn't lost that sulking teenager demeanour. He sauntered over to meet her as she emerged from French security.

'You came then?' he said, not looking pleased to see her.

Rosie spread her hands and looked down at herself. 'Oh look, so I did!'

'Sharp as ever, I see,' he complained. 'Transport's this way.'

'Jesus, Wesley, who's knocked *your* pile of bricks over?' she asked as she fell in beside him.

2: The Traffickers

'S'okay,' he said. 'Been a difficult morning - had one or two problems but it's all sorted now.' He flashed her a yellow grin. 'Thanks for coming, by the way.'

'So, where's this cat,' Rosie asked, 'and what happened to your little Sigma?'

'Oh, you didn't hear, then? After that run from Morocco last year, the filth raided us in London when I moved the gear on. I got off with three months in Winson Green. But *Pepper* got impounded.'

'Oh, so sorry to hear that. Will you get her back?'

'Phew, no way, mate. The Exise'll probably sell her off to pay for the new Brexit border checks.'

Rosie tried not to smile - Wesley would not see the irony in his complaint. She knew all about the incident, of course - that had been last year. On the suspicion he was human-trafficking, Rosie had helped Wesley sail the Sigma to Morocco and back. She had parted with Wesley and his boat when they docked in Chichester – leaving the guileless Australian unaware of her duplicity. Following Rosie's tipoff, Border Force undercover officers had tailed Wesley and his heavy suitcase up to London. Here they caught him in the act of trading with a known drugs baron high on their wanted list. Wesley's luggage had contained fifty kilos of high-quality Moroccan hashish. Still, he had got off with a light sentence for his cooperation.

The transport was a grey Renault panel van. As they neared it, Rosie was dismayed to see a man already in the driver's seat – she had expected it to be just the two of them. The window was down, and the man was smoking a cigarette. He was dark-skinned and sported a colossal moustache under a severely hooked nose.

The Travel Agent

Wesley opened the passenger door and got in and shuffled over, leaving room for Rosie to slide in beside him.

'This is Guran,' Wesley said by way of introduction but gave no further explanation.

'Hi, Guran,' she said, reaching for a seatbelt but not finding one.

Guran grunted, scowled askance at her, then started the van.

'Guran doesn't speak English,' Wesley explained.

'Oh, okay. Er… *Bonjour, Guran. Comment ça va?*'

'He doesn't speak French either.'

'So, what does he sp– '

'Best not ask. Just leave it alone, eh?'

Rosie sighed and wound down her window. The van stunk of stale sweat and cigarette smoke. There was also a bad smell about this operation - Rosie had a sinking feeling that Wesley was not the one in control here.

'Where is it we're going?' she asked, as the van sped south toward the A16.

'It's a forty-kilometre drive,' Wesley replied. 'The cat's moored close to a west-facing beach in shallow water. High tide's around nine tonight – they reckon we'll be okay to float her off.'

'They?'

Wesley shook his head but offered no reply.

'And the cargo?' Rosie said, glancing across him at the driver.

Wesley turned and gave her an almost pleading look. 'That's erm… that's none of our business, Rosie, so don't ask. We just drive the bus and look straight ahead.'

2: The Traffickers

'Mm. Okay, so where are we heading on the other side? Can I at least know where I'm sailing her to?'

'A sandbar near the Winstanley Nature Reserve, between Hastings and Dungeness. We ground her there, collect our cash, and piss off. Job done.'

Rosie got the feeling that Wesley harboured similar misgivings to her own. Absently, she felt for the comfort of the waterproof Blackphone in the pocket of her foul-weather jacket.

For the rest of the journey, nobody spoke. Rosie looked out at the gently sloping mix of agricultural lands rushing by, each usage bringing its own distinct bucolic odour. Herds of dun cows grazed contentedly under the warm sun and hectares of bright yellow rape rolled into the distance. A field of wheat rippled in the breeze like a flaxen sea. A more pungent stink wafted into the cab as they passed a mud-churned enclosure of scattered swine-pens.

Wesley's reticence to reveal the nature of the job was worrying. One thing seemed inevitable: this was not a simple weed shipment. Nor your everyday fare-paying refugees from Sangatte. The guy at the wheel looked like a gangster with a more lucrative cargo on his mind.

'How many people are involved in this job, Wes?'

'Us three, and two more on the boat.'

'Five crew? So why do you need me?'

Wesley cast a nervous glance at the driver then said quietly, 'These guys aren't sailors, Rosie, we can't use 'em. It's just us manning the cat.'

'So ...'

'Please, no more questions now, it'll all come clear later, okay?'

The Travel Agent

Rosie felt her stomach beginning to flutter, and she wondered whether she had got into something beyond her paygrade. Her job was to probe the peripheries of human trafficking – boat-owners compromising themselves to earn a bit of cash on the side. She wasn't trained for deep cover operations among the actual traffickers. And if Guran was anything to go by, these people were dangerous. She cursed Harry for letting her volunteer for this. She was only a part-time amateur, for Christ's sake.

After an hour, the taciturn driver left the autoroute, headed west, and then turned south on the D940. A succession of rustic hamlets now relieved the relentless farmlands. Rosie began to catch glimpses of the sea between rolling hills as the road gradually merged toward the coast to her right.

A small township's buildings showed up ahead, and a signpost that read: *Bienvenue aux Roches*. Then, just short of the town and without slowing down, Guran swerved the van into a right turn. He followed a sandy track headed in a straight line down to where - sheltered from the sea by dunes - a small, isolated building stood. As they got closer, Rosie discerned in her two-o-clock - almost lost amongst the tall beachgrasses - the mast of a sailboat.

Guran pulled up in front of the building - a garage-sized wooden shack with padlocked double doors at the gable-end facing them.

Rosie swung open her door and jumped down with her backpack, Wesley followed close behind.

'Come on, Rosie,' said the Australian, hurrying up a wooden walkway where a fingerpost read *'La Plage'*. A series of wooden steps led up and over the dune.

2: The Traffickers

'Is Guran coming with us?' Rosie called ahead to Wesley.

'Later,' came the terse reply without looking back.

On the other side, the beach was narrow - shallow waves rasped rhythmically on the shingle a few metres short of the dried seaweed that marked the highwater line. The catamaran stood with her stern in no more than a metre of water, aground but bobbing briefly on each incoming wave.

Rosie checked her watch: almost eight, French time. An hour to high water.

'Jesus, Wesley! I only hope she's got a good anchor capstan because we're going to have to warp her off.'

Wesley shook his head, 'That's a non-starter - literally. She's got no engines and no batteries. She's not even anchored, look.' He kicked a rope that Rosie had not noticed, tied to a post of the wooden walkway, leading out into the water and turned up on a winch drum at the catamaran's stern.

'Fuck off, Wesley – you expect me to just float her off, with no engines and no sodding wind?'

Wesley shrugged, 'Not my fault. I didn't park her here,' he nodded to the two men emerging onto the cockpit deck. 'A fishing boat towed her here this morning – the onshore breeze blew her to shore, and they just tied her like this.'

Rosie sighed resignedly, 'Oh well, we'd better get started – it'll need everyone in the water to push her off. Where's Guran?'

'Er, that's the other thing. We can't go till after dark – that's when they load her up. Sunset's at ten-to-ten by the way.'

The Travel Agent

Rosie sighed and shook her head. 'Can't be done, Wesley. No-batteries means no lights. No-lights means we can't cross the Channel – if we try it, we'll get intercepted and arrested the minute we enter the TSS.'

'Ah, the guys thought of that. They tied torches to the forestays, red and green, coloured with a felt tip. And a white one on the stern.'

She stared at him. 'Bloody torches? Seriously?'

'The batteries should last a few hours. The forecast is Force-four easterly later, so we should be there by two.'

Rosie looked out at the catamaran, noticing for the first time that she was ancient and filthy – a near wreck, in fact. The two men on the cockpit deck were staring back. Like Guran, they were big men with Mediterranean complexions. One of them beckoned for the pair to come aboard.

Rosie shook her head again, 'This is bloody madness, Wesley. Who are you dealing with here?'

'As I said, we don't ask. How about I double your share, two-grand?'

She gave him a sidelong look, 'Oh yeah? Is that it - they made you an offer you couldn't refuse? How much, Wesley?'

A big sigh, 'Ten.' The Australian at least had the decency to blush.

'*Ten Grand?* What the hell are they moving - diamonds?'

Wesley simply shook his head.

'Don't tell me – we just drive the bus and look straight ahead.' Then, remembering her roleplay, she added, 'Well, I want half, Wesley, or I'm out, and you

2: The Traffickers

can try to do it on your own. And you'd better pray for a good offshore breeze after sunset.'

Wesley gave a mirthless chuckle and nodded towards the boat, 'I don't think they're going to let you back out now, Rosie.'

Rosie looked, and her blood ran cold. The first man was still beckoning, but the other was the more persuasive, pointing a snub-nosed machine pistol right at them.

The Travel Agent

2: The Traffickers

2/2

Dover Strait

Midnight: a clear, warm night in the busy Transit Separation Scheme and Rosie was nervous. It was not herself she was anxious for, but the sixty-odd young women packed into the two hulls. They would all be in enough trouble when they reached the Kent coast, but right now, Rosie's main concern was getting them all safely across the World's busiest shipping lane. Without navigation aids or proper running-lights.

Regulations required powered vessels to give way to those under sail alone. But to be identified at night, the sailboat needed regulation running-lights that only showed from specified angles. The makeshift lanterns swinging about on the forestays were both illegal and dangerous. Consequently, Rosie had for the past two hours, weaved her way perilously through a labyrinth of northeast-bound juggernauts - picture a pedestrian crossing several motor-carriageways at rush hour. The effort and stress had left Rosie mentally drained.

The Travel Agent

Now, in the relative safely of the central zone, Rosie had only the Channel ferries to worry about. It was much simpler to avoid oncoming ships than when crossing their paths at right-angles. But ahead remained the southwest-bound transit. According to the Marine Traffic app on her phone, that side looked even busier.

Getting the catamaran off the beach had been far more straightforward than Rosie had expected. The van driver, Guran, had come trudging over the dune walkway at dusk, leading the bedraggled captives, cajoling and bullying them into the cold water to wade out to the catamaran. The haunted, tear-streaked faces of teenage girls climbing up the transom-steps had moved Rosie almost to weep. If they only knew the life of secret slavery that was planned for them. Seeing the false hope in their eyes brought home to Rosie the importance of Mercury One's work, and filled her with a gritty determination to liberate these gullible and deluded young women.

Standing in chest-high water, Wesley and the three traffickers had held the vessel in place while the girls climbed aboard. With the tide on the ebb, Rosie had used the line to shore to prevent the boat from drifting out. As the girls waited in the water for their turn to board, snatches of conversation drifted up. In these subdued exchanges, Rosie thought she detected the inflectional tones of a Slavik language.

Once the captives were all aboard, Rosie simply released the rope and let the men push the catamaran off the sand before climbing aboard themselves. The gib sail and a helpful offshore breeze did the rest.

2: The Traffickers

In the last hour, the easterly wind had been picking up and, according to her Navionics app, was now driving them northwest at a useful nine knots. Wesley - who appeared to be as wary as she of the three men running the operation - had stayed with her up on the steering platform. There had been shouting below when some of the girls had attempted to come up for fresh air. But now all appeared quiet.

'I don't know about you, Wesley, but I'm parched' Rosie said in hushed tones. 'How about seeing if you can find us something to drink?'

The Australian grunted and flicked his cigarette butt arcing over the port bow in a shower of sparks.

'They brought some bottles of water on-board. I'll see if I can confiscate a couple.'

The moment Wesley disappeared below, Rosie fished the Blackphone out of her pocket and tapped in a text message to Harry:

> Heading for sandbanks at Winstanley Wetland Reserve. ETA 0230 BST. 60+ girls. Probably East-European. 3 x male traffickers (Albanian) – be advised, they have automatic weapons. I'll keep Wesley up here with me on the conning platform until it's over. Please don't be late. R.

She pressed Send and pocketed the Blackphone. Casting around in the darkness of the platform, Rosie noticed the locker where Wesley had sat. Lifting the lid and wishing for a torch, she rummaged around blindly among the assorted ropes.

'Ah! What have we here?' Rosie murmured and pulled free an eighteen-inch-long crowbar, a curved

The Travel Agent

nail-extractor at one end. She hefted the tool experimentally, then concealed it behind the compass binnacle - just in case.

Rosie turned her attention once more to the shipping ahead. They were approaching the northwest-bound traffic lane. Out to starboard, the red and white pairs of running-lights scattered out for miles into the inky blackness; the stern-lights to port resembled a crooked line of receding streetlamps. Beyond this jumble of transiting vessels, the Dungeness Lighthouse threw its commanding loom out across the Channel, still ten miles away but seeming much nearer.

Rosie would have to negotiate her way through the dense column of shipping at right-angles before turning westward in the Inshore Traffic Zone and their destination. It was not the shortest route, but to cut the corner would attract the attention of Dover radar. And that, in turn, would bring an unwanted coastguard interception. Rosie's job was to ensure this cargo, and their minders were safely delivered to those prepared and equipped to deal with them. She had no appetite to be caught in the middle of a firefight at sea.

Rosie pulled the hand-compass from her pocket and sighted on a ship to starboard that seemed to be closing at a steady angle: a possible collision. She memorised the vessel's compass bearing and repeated the process for three more ships whose angles seemed not to have changed much in the past ten minutes.

She spun around to a clunking of feet on the ladder.

'Fucking ratbags!' the Australian muttered, stepping up to the platform. 'They're charging those sheilas ten Euros for one of these.' He handed Rosie a small

2: The Traffickers

plastic bottle of water, 'Tried to make me pay too, but I told them to fuck off. Fucking Albanians. Strewth!'

He broke the seal on a second bottle, took a swig, and then stared out at the ragged columns of oncoming ships to starboard. 'Fucking hell, Rosie, how we going to get through that lot?'

Rosie took a long swig of water before answering. 'Don't worry, they look jam-packed from here, but the gaps will open up as we get closer. Think you can find some gaffer tape and make a better fist of securing those torches? Might help to avoid any misunderstandings when ships start approaching from starboard.'

Wesley had just started down the ladder when he swore and stepped up backwards.

'Where you go now, English?'

It was the man with the MP5. Rosie did not need to hear his voice. The air fizzing around him was enough to announce his presence; the guy was high on something, and that made him doubly dangerous, a fact to which Wesley seemed oblivious.

'Look, mate, I'm no more English …'

Rosie turned in time to see the big Albanian backhand Wesley viciously across the face; she caught him as he staggered backwards into her arms. She eased him down onto the deck-locker and glared up at his attacker.

'Was that necessary?' she snapped. She would like to have said more but held herself in check when she saw the man's unhinged expression.

'How long to landing?' demanded the Albanian.

The Travel Agent

Wesley groaned, and Rosie sat down next to him. 'About two hours,' she told the Albanian, pulling her backpack out from under the bench.

'Leave him and steer the boat,' growled the Albanian.

Ignoring the order, she tore open a pack of tissues and bunched a handful over Wesley's ruined nose, then tilted his head back. 'Here, hold this and keep your head like that,' she said quietly. 'And *please*, don't antagonise him again.'

The Albanian stepped forward and stood over her, gesturing threateningly with the gun, 'You, *shërbyese*, I said leave him, and steer.'

'Okay, okay,' Rosie said. 'Just don't hurt him again - I'm going to need him.'

She patted Wesley on the shoulder and stood up, taking the helm once more. They had drifted forty degrees to port, so she put on starboard helm to get back on course. The Albanian was standing close behind her now – she could smell him. And his breathing had become fast and ragged.

She glanced down at Wesley and saw he would be no help. There was no opportunity to reach for the crowbar, so she decided to bluff it out. Half turning, in a quiet, steady voice, she said: 'If you lay one finger on me, my friend, not only will I ruin your wedding tackle, but you'll have to sail this wreck yourselves. Furthermore, if this boat does not follow the rules exactly in this TSS, a UK Border Force Cutter will be on us like a shot. What will your buddies do to you if you screw this up?'

His eyes were still wild, crazy, but his shoulders had slumped. He pointed the MP5 lazily at Rosie's lower

2: The Traffickers

regions and sneered, 'We will talk again, *zuskë*, when we get to land.'

With a look intended to wither her, the man turned on his heel and disappeared below.

Rosie looked down at the Australian, still trying to stem his bleeding nose, 'Have you worked with these people before?'

Wesley lowered his head and dabbed his nose experimentally. 'Er, dow. A bate put theb onto me, why?'

'And this mate, he's worked for them himself?'

'I… I guess so … I duddo.'

'You didn't think to ask?'

Wesley looked back glumly and did not answer.

Rosie turned and watched the fast-nearing columns of running-lights – the nearest ships less than a mile away. The Albanian had frightened her. Her bluff had worked this time, but she was under no illusion about her chances if the brute caught her alone after landing.

Concentrate on the job in front of you, Rosie.

Rosie breathed out a sigh, put the rabid Albanian out of her mind, and began reassessing the bearings of the three nearest ships that were worrying her.

The Travel Agent

2: The Traffickers

2/3

Grounded

It was 0215 BST on a moonless night. According to Rosie's Navionics app, they were half a mile from the shore. The coast ahead was low and unlit, a barely discernible shadow against the clear night sky. So close to land, the light had become dim and suffused, the sea's surface betrayed only by the sporadic white ruffle of a breaking wavelet. The catamaran had just crossed the four-metre contour on the Navionics chart. Still, Rosie knew that this part of the Kent coast was treacherous with shifting sandbanks and sudden unexpected shoaling. They might grind to a standstill at any moment, and that could spell disaster. All she could do was press on and hope.

Wesley – who had cleaned up his bloodied face - stared out alongside her with the same anxious intensity – that of a yachtsman doing precisely the opposite of what was safe.

'Did they pay you upfront?' Rosie asked suddenly.

The Travel Agent

'Huh, half upfront – that money's safe. But now I'm not sure I'll…'

'Never mind. When we hit the bank, stay up here with me. Leave them to get the women ashore. Okay?'

Wesley turned and stared at her - his face made shrew-like by the dim light of her phone. 'What are you up to, Rosie?'

'I just want us to stay safe from those guys. I've got a bad feeling about this, so just trust me, okay?'

'Mm…'

Rosie looked down at her phone – two-metre contour coming up.

'Wes, we need to slow down. Furl the mains'l and shorten gib to the second reef.'

'Aye aye, Skipper,' grinned the Australian, chopping off a salute.

He seemed chirpier now that Rosie was taking the initiative, which she realised was out of character for the ordinarily pushy Australian. Perhaps the gaol term and the loss of his yacht had quelled his spirit. Briefly, she felt a stab of sorrow for the rogue. Feckless and corrupt as he was, he did not deserve what she now guessed these Albanians likely had planned for him - for them both.

The boat had almost lost way altogether when soft grinding sounds shivered through the twin hulls, and the catamaran scraped to a standstill. The two torches on the forestays were by now so dim they barely lit the prows of their respective hulls. Soft voices from the Albanians drifted up from the forward sundeck. Suddenly a bright column of light tore open the night, destroying Rosie's night vision. Slowly, the beam began traversing the ground, revealing monochrome

2: The Traffickers

sandbanks stretching out ahead like a rumpled blanket, dipping beneath the dark water in places but seemingly walkable. As the beam struck further out it came to rest on a high, grassy bank dotted with shrubs; an earth dyke, about two-metres high, with a shallow brick wall along the top. Only stars showed beyond the wall; it was like the edge of the world. The beam settled on a ramp of weed-covered steps leading up the side of the dyke, bringing a grunt of satisfaction from below. There was no sign of the Border Force squad.

The Albanians dowsed their searchlight. Shouted orders rang out; bumping and clattering and subdued cries as the Albanians harried the girls on deck and down the transom steps into the water. Panicked splashing - the water at the stern was too deep for some of them, distressed cries floated up; reassuring utterances from others helping them. And the harsh scolding of the Albanians urging quiet. An upsetting drama was unfolding in sound only. It was all Rosie could do not to rush down to help.

Wesley turned to head down the ladder, but Rosie grabbed his shoulder.

'Where are you going?' she whispered.

'To collect my dosh, of course.'

'You think they'll pay you now? Why should they, Wesley? Cheaper just to sow you up with 9-millimetre stitches, don't you think?'

'Nah, you're…'

'You need to trust me on this, Wes. These are not your normal druggies – they're the worst people - modern-slavers, for God's sake. No, I want us both to stay up here while they unload the women. When we get chance, we'll slip over the side and make our escape along the beach – they won't see us in the dark.'

'But there might be more work for me, for us, Rosie.'

Rosie pinned him back against the bulkhead, her elbow under his chin. 'You think?' she snarled into his face. 'Wise up, Wes. This boat's barely seaworthy, a hulk without even a name and they'll abandon her here for the coastguard to haul away. This trip is a one-off opportunity for them – with the money they must be making out of those poor sods, they'll upgrade to a motorboat they can drive themselves.'

With a grunt, the Australian pushed her away and hurried down the ladder.

'Wesley!' she hissed after him, but to no avail.

She stepped back out of sight and took out the Blackphone. No time for texting, she called Harry's number. He answered after two rings.

'Hi, Lassie. You okay?'

'For now. Where are you?'

'Aboot two-hundred yards south beyond the seawall from you. We saw yer light, and we're heading tae intercept them as they come over the dyke.'

Rosie peered into the gloom below where the line of young women sloshed through the water, faintly lit in green from the improvised starboard bow light. A girl began crying, and others joined in, setting off a pathetic caterwauling of fear and uncertainty. Angry male voices snarled in the darkness, calling in vain for silence.

'You'll need to hurry,' Rosie said. 'And I've lost Wesley – the idiot's down there with them now asking

2: The Traffickers

for his money – I'm worried they might decide to shoot him instead.'

'Ach! The wee daftie. Stay where ye are and keep the line open. We're nearly there, Rosie. And dunne fash yersel o'er that wee Ozzie shate.'

A great clamour of voices erupted as the Albanians harried the last of their captives into the water. From down on the sand, the powerful beam stabbed out once more, searching and quickly finding the steps. The lamp now swung around to the ragged column of girls, and back again to the steps, then went out. Albanians' shouts became increasingly strident through the moonless gloom as they steered their human cargo into line for the stairway.

In the brief moments that light had settled on the migrants, Rosie had only seen two of the Albanians. The guy with the gun was not one of them. Neither was Wesley in view.

'We're on the other side of the wall, hen. At the steps. Any news on yer pal?'

'No, but one of the…'

She stopped speaking at the sound of boots clumping rapidly up the ladder behind her. 'Someone coming,' she hissed, and dropped the Blackphone onto the locker-lid and reached behind the binnacle for her makeshift weapon.

Rosie turned just as the Albanian stepped up to the platform. Facing him boldly, she kept the crowbar down by her thigh and out of sight.

'Where's Wesley?' she demanded hotly, trying desperately to cap the sheer terror rising from her gut.

The Travel Agent

The big man leered and slowly drew a black-nailed finger across his throat. His grin widened at her dismayed expression.

'You've *murdered* him?' raising her voice for Harry to hear.

'And now, you, my little whore. I give you the fucking you want.'

Frightening as her situation was, it was not Rosie's first encounter with a would-be rapist. That recollection now came back at her, hot and visceral. She tensed for violence, knowing she would only get one chance, a chance she would have to create for herself.

The MP5 was a dangerous complication, but might also be an opportunity. Glancing down at the weapon she saw the safety was pointing up towards the barrel. She recalled from her short weapons course with the Royal Marines at Lympstone that Heckler & Koch labelled their weapons in German: 'S' for *Sicher*, 'E' for *Einzelfeuer*, and 'F' for *Feuerstoss* - the British Booties had re-dubbed them Safe, Economy, and Fun. She could not see the markings in the dark but was sure the top position was 'S'. Rosie readied herself - it was time to get creative.

'What you look at?' Suddenly grinning widely, the man lifted the gun to her face and touched the barrel to her chin. 'You like?'

She backed away until she felt the steel rim of the helm-wheel cold on her back.

'Have you ever fired an MP5?' she asked evenly.

The Albanian's brow furrowed. 'What you mean, bitch?'

2: The Traffickers

Rosie was gambling that an experienced shooter would never threaten someone with his firearm in Safe mode.

'Well, if you were serious about using it, you wouldn't leave the safety on.'

And sure enough, the Albanian seemed unfamiliar with his new toy. Instead of merely flicking the lever forward with his thumb, he lifted and turned the weapon sideways to check.

Rosie took her chance. Having created a distance between them, she swung the crowbar up and around, dealing her opponent a resounding blow on the left side of his neck. As he staggered sideways, Rosie reversed her grip on the crowbar. With all her strength, she dug the curved end into his exposed solar plexus, instantly doubling him over. A firm strike to the back of his head ended it.

Temporarily in shock, Rosie stood watching the Albanian sprawled face down on the deck, vaguely concerned she had hit him too hard. Quite sure she had not struck him a fatal blow, she reached down and felt his neck, then blew a sigh of relief to feel a faint pulse. Her hand came away sticky with blood, but she was relieved not to have killed him.

'You okay, hen?' Harry's voice hissed from the Blackphone.

Rosie picked up the handset, but her throat felt too constricted to speak.

'Rosie, talk to me!'

Swooning, she slumped down onto the locker and took deep breaths. Finally, she lifted the Blackphone to her ear.

The Travel Agent

'Yes, Harry. I'm okay.' She managed in a quivering voice.

'What in God's name happened tae ye, lassie?'

'I think they killed–' she broke off, still choked. After more deep breaths, she said, 'The other two Albanians are down on the sand – I can't hear anybody below so I'm going to find Wesley.'

'Rosie, be careful.'

Rosie kneeled beside her felled would-be attacker and eased the MP5's carry-strap from under him and transferred it to her own shoulder. Lifting the gun, she removed and checked the magazine, replaced it, cocked the weapon and switched it to 'E' for Economy. Thus, armed and ready, she picked up her backpack and stepped cautiously down the ladder to the cockpit deck.

'Harry, I need a medic here, urgently. Wesley's alive but in bad shape.'

'Where are you?'

'Down below in the starboard hull.'

'Okay. We're a bit busy here right now, but I'll get someone over to you when I can.'

'Thanks. And by the way, there's a shedload of what looks like cocaine down here too. That's why they left one of their guys onboard. Did you round the others up?'

'We got the two traffickers – most of the young ladies have scattered, but they won't get far. So what happened?'

'The idiot tried it on, so I tapped him with a crowbar. He's alive but out of it.'

2: The Traffickers

'Well done, Lassie. Now just stay on the boat until I come for ye, okay?'

'Hey, Harry, tell the guys to be nice to those girls, eh?'

'Rosie, I'm going to close the line now – call me back if you get problems. And make sure to secure yer Albanian – we don't want a hostage situation.'

Rosie patted her sequestered weapon and grinned.

'Don't worry, Harry. It's all under control.'

EPISODE THREE

Rosie's Doubts

3: Rosie's Doubts

3/1

Paella & GoT

McCaffey's flat was on the second floor of a town block above a row of modern, well-appointed shops.

'I take it you do *like* Paella,' he said, guiding her inside. 'I should have asked, really.'

Rosie swept past him into the narrow hall and immediately caught the pungent whiff of seafood cooking. She half-turned and smiled. 'Relax. I love Paella.'

'Go on through, then. Lounge on the left, toilet end of the hall on the right.'

Rosie walked into a bright, open sitting room; sunset light spilt in from a window framed at each side by two enormous areca palms.

'I should have brought wine,' Rosie said, looking down on the busy shopping street below, the noise of passing cars almost entirely silenced by the triple-glazing.

'No need, I've got plenty. You like Ribera?'

3: Rosie's Doubts

'Perfect.'

'Good. Grab a pew. I won't be long.'

Rosie plopped herself down on a wide, faux-leather corner settee. At the same time, McCaffey pushed through a pair of batwing doors, presumably to the kitchen. A coffee table and a large armchair matching the sofa completed the room's layout. The sky-blue painted walls were bare of hangings except the one holding a fifty-inch TV screen, which was currently showing the CNN News Channel with the sound muted.

She noticed Michael's iPhone on the coffee table. Still, she resisted the temptation to pick it up, guessing there would not be time to check his messages before he returned.

CNN switched to a news item about last week's terror attack on the Finsbury Park Mosque. The subtitles speculated that the 47-year-old perpetrator had been on a personal vendetta against all Muslims in retaliation for London Bridge.

'Stupid cunt,' said McCaffey, entering with two glasses, 'excuse the C-word, but that vigilante stuff boils my blood.'

'So I see,' said Rosie dryly, taking the proffered glass. She observed him and said, 'I wouldn't call it vigilantism, not when innocent people die. That's just plain terrorism, no matter who's done it.'

Her comment brought an ambivalent frown and a hint of colour to McCaffey's face; only a fleeting impression, but it gave Rosie a tingle of uncertainty.

'Don't you think?' she prompted.

'Yeah, well,' he picked up a remote control from the table and flicked off the programme. 'Let's forget the real world for a few hours. Dinner's in half an hour, what say we start the first episode and pause it halfway while I get the grub?'

The show began with a recap of the previous season's dramatic conclusion. But Rosie found herself unable to engage in the action, distracted by her new doubts about McCaffey. When the mark paused the video - saying he was busting for a pee - and left the room, Rosie grabbed his phone and activated it, only to find it was PIN-protected. With a frustrated sigh, she replaced the device. When, after a minute, McCaffey returned to the room, Rosie restarted the show.

Sometime later McCaffey's phone began sounding a klaxon-style alarm.

'Dinnertime,' he announced.

Rosie picked up the remote control and paused the show while watching sideways the four numbers McCaffey tapped in to cancel the timer. He drained his glass and then looked at hers, which remained untouched.

'You not drinking, Rosie?'

She wanted him out of the room before the security of his phone kicked back in. Hence, she took a big gulp, almost gagging, and handed him the glass with a forced grin and watering eyes.

'Just a top-up,' she croaked.

He took the glass, giving her an odd look, but left without comment.

As the door shut behind him, Rosie picked up his phone and found it was still active. She tapped the *WhatsApp* icon: with its point-to-point encryption, the most likely choice for secret exchanges. Scrolling down McCaffey's chats-list, she found a couple of

3: Rosie's Doubts

conversations recently with somebody called Julia. Mm, girlfriend or family? But there was nothing of interest there.

There was a contact called Astrid, and those exchanges looked more promising because some of the dates were recent. With an ear on the clunking and rattling from the next room, Rosie opened the thread. The most recent was from McCaffey:

> 15 July
> great news. yes, let me know.
> 1734

The one before it from Astrid read:

> 15 July
> all pax safely w thr their families. and-
> relax. Thank you, partner. ru ok for
> another run next mnth? xx
> 1654

Rosie felt her breath coming in short gasps - her first decent hit? Maybe. She scrolled up quickly, past a flight booking from LGW to LQA on 28th of May, one from McCaffey confirming a delivery job for a 44-foot Oyster ketch, and then, from Astrid:

> 19 May
> next assignment confirmed. 6 px this time
> so need a bigger boat (jaws? lol). They will
> be ready for pu end of month so get to
> work my captain x.
> 1438

The Travel Agent

Rosie's found her mouth had gone dry. From the kitchen came the sound of McCaffey scraping a skillet; he would be through any time with the food. She quickly closed the app, put the phone back to sleep, wiped the screen on her jeans, and replaced it. She noticed her hand was shaking and sat back just as the doors swung open - McCaffey backing in balancing two dinner-trays. Burning with guilt, Rosie jumped up to help him, her mind a jumble as she tried to figure out her next move.

After dinner and two episodes, Rosie checked her watch and made her excuse. 'I need to get home to Dad; he gets a bit maudlin around this time of year. Mum died five years ago this week.'

It was a lie, that was last month: June 17th, but what the hell? McCaffey was okay about it and walked her to the jeep.

Despite what she had discovered, she could not reconcile the idea of this guy involving himself in human trafficking. He seemed to Rosie too morally upright, too clear-sighted about wrongdoing in the world, too aware of injustices. It just did not add up.

By the time she arrived home, she had decided to keep to herself the evidence of McCaffey's exchanges with the mysterious Astrid. For the time being, at least.

Rosie was walking in the High Street the next day when her phone vibrated. McCaffey's number.

'Hey,' she said, stepping into a shop doorway, 'you okay?'

'Yeah, fine—'

'Listen, sorry I had to shoot off last night, I forgot to thank you for the meal, it was scrummy, and the wine.'

3: Rosie's Doubts

'No worries, you didn't drink much, still got two bottles whenever you feel like doing it again. I'm just phoning because there's something I forgot to ask you.'

'Okay, shoot.'

'It's my sister's birthday a week on Saturday, the fifth of August - the big Three-O, she's having a bit of an afternoon do at her house, a BBQ, weather permitting. Do you fancy coming?'

Shit! This was getting embarrassing. Still, it could not hurt to get cosy with the mark's family. Might learn something conclusive, then she could kick the loser into touch.

'Sure, I'm free. Where does your sister live?'

'Salisbury, you can park at mine, and we'll get the train, I'll pay.'

'Tell you what, I don't mind not drinking, why don't I drive us?'

'You sure?'

'Course I'm sure. When do you want to arrive?'

'Around noon?'

'No probs, I'll pick you up at ten-thirty.'

She ended the call, carried on into the paper shop and picked up the local paper with Thursday's Job Supplement. She stuffed the paper into her rucksack along with the things she had bought for tomorrow night's dinner with Dad – the two of them were sailing to Weymouth tomorrow. She wanted to cook him something special for his first night back on-board for over a decade. With a new spring in her step, she walked to where she had locked up her bike.

3/2

Julia

Rosie got to McCaffey's Guildford flat a few minutes late - but he was not out yet, and she had to go round the block because of the bustling shopping traffic. He was there when she came round again, and she double-parked to let him climb in.

'Sorry about that,' McCaffey said, reaching over and putting a small wrapped gift and card on the back seat next to the flowers Rosie had bought.

'No problem,' she smiled, 'you look flushed. Been busy?'

'One hell of a morning - typical, the one Saturday I have to be out early, and I get a short notice from my agent on a job. Been organising my flight and visa for Tuesday morning.'

Rosie drove on out of town and headed up to the M3. She did not speak until she was westbound on the motorway.

'So where is it you're going that you need a visa for?'

3: Rosie's Doubts

'Turkey, picking up a boat from Marmaris, bringing her home to Falmouth.'

'Oh, right. Long trip?'

He nodded. 'About six weeks.'

'And you'll be single-handed again, yeah?'

'… er, yeah, as always.'

Rosie glanced sideways: McCaffey's ear tips were glowing. He was a lousy liar.

'She's a fairly new boat,' he continued, 'well kitted out, so it should be a doddle.'

With a stop off in Libya? I don't think so.

'Well, be careful, Michael, stay safe, okay?'

They drove on in silence, transferring onto the A303 - which was busy but flowing smoothly. After an hour, Rosie turned left onto the A30.

'There's something you should know about Julia,' McCaffey said as they came to the Salisbury roundabout.

Rosie glanced at him, then concentrated on negotiating traffic.

'So, your sister's got two heads, or what?' she said, accelerating onto the city spur road.

'She's a bit burn-scarred, you know, around the face? Some people find it a bit of shock when they first meet her. And she's got a prosthetic left arm.'

'Whew, poor her. Thanks for warning me. Don't worry, though; I'm not easily shocked.'

Rosie got a five-year-old flashback to a legless, one-armed Afghanistan-veteran she had befriended during her confinement at Birmingham's Defence Medical Centre. She glanced again at McCaffey; he seemed relieved to have offloaded his news.

'So, what happened to your sister?'

The Travel Agent

'Mm, not a nice story, you sure you want to hear it?'

'Huh, I can't imagine anything like that being a nice story. I'm not squeamish, Michael, and I wouldn't ask if I didn't want to know.'

'You remember the London Bombings back in 2005?'

'Uh-huh, seven-seven, who could–' she inhaled sharply, 'Your sister? ...'

He nodded. 'Julia was on the Piccadilly Line with three schoolmates, heading for a day out shopping then off to a concert at the O2. They'd just got on at Kings Cross when it–'

Spotting a bus layby ahead, Rosie pulled in and stopped the jeep. She turned in her seat and laid a hand on her mark's bony shoulder. 'Michael, I'm so–'

'We lived in Watford then.' McCaffey was staring straight ahead, didn't seem to notice they'd stopped, 'I was twelve, didn't understand what was happening. My memories are kind of, you know, fragmented? Mum, bawling and screaming, Dad driving like crazy. They took Julia to the Royal London. We were sitting in the waiting room for hours; Dad, pacing up and down and pouncing on every passing medic for news. The place was chaos, people running around, beepers and phones going everywhere. Mum hugging me and crying.

'Eventually, a nurse came in and told us Julia had survived but was in ICU. We couldn't see her yet because they were getting her ready for theatre. They told us shrapnel had shredded her lower left arm, and they would need to amputate it at the elbow. Also, they were treating her for third-degree burns to her face and shoulder. Julia was my big sister and always took my

3: Rosie's Doubts

side when our father was having a go at me – which was often. We were close, so you can only imagine how it affected me.

'When we got to see Julia, she was still unconscious: gauze dressings from face to shoulder, tubes going everywhere. And the bandaged stump of her arm - it didn't seem real. It wouldn't sink in that this was my sister or something like this could happen to us. Why us? I kept thinking. What did we do to deserve this?'

He turned to Rosie with an expression so bleak it left her wanting to pull him into her heart, to take away his pain.

'Every time there's another terrorist attack, I relive that day in all its horror.'

She had no words, just swallowed and squeezed his shoulder. He came back to now with almost a jerk.

'Sorry, didn't mean to get so emotional.'

'Not at all,' she murmured. 'Thank you for sharing it. And your poor sister …'

'Ah, no. What I mean: it's only me now that's affected – Julia thinks I should man-up. You'll be surprised when you meet her how she's put the attack behind her. She's married a great guy, and they've got a lovely daughter. I'm quite proud of her for that, but I just can't find that same peace for myself.'

As she drove on, Rosie thoughts raced between confused and conflicted. Apart from the unlikelihood now that McCaffey deserved Mercury One's scrutiny, she had felt a signal change in her attitude towards him following that surge of raw emotion. For the first time, Rosie looked on the young man not merely as a mark, but a real person with real human feelings. Triage Officer Winterbourne abhorred such an unprofessional

The Travel Agent

lapse, but *Rosie* Winterbourne felt somewhat uplifted by it. Harry McAllister, Rosie's dour Scot's handler, was going to be furious.

Julia's home was a handsome old detached house in a pleasant tree-lined avenue away from the city centre. McCaffey had a key and let them in. Armed with flowers, Rosie followed him through a spacious hallway into a pleasingly large kitchen, where a man was dissecting lettuce behind a breakfast-bar. A pair of French-doors stood open; children's shouts and laughter drifted in from the garden.

The man looked up as the visitors entered and broke into a beaming grin.

'Michael, you made it!' he wiped his hands on a tea-towel and came around to greet the pair. 'Wasn't sure if you'd be off on another delivery,' he said, shaking McCaffey's hand with familial vigour, before casting an enquiring glance at Rosie.

McCaffey took his cue smoothly. 'Dan, this is my friend Rosie, Rosie, meet Dan, my Brother-in-law.'

'Delighted to meet you, Rosie, and welcome. Here, let me take those, I'll put them in water - freesias and lilies,' he sniffed deeply of the bouquet, 'ah, the fragrances just bounce off each other, don't they? Oh yes, she'll love these.'

'Good to meet you, Dan,' Rosie said. 'What a lovely home you have.'

'Hey, thanks, glad you like it. So, off into the garden with you both. Julia's out there with the kids and a few of our friends,' he leaned in and confided: 'They're all neighbours, and I'm afraid they started drinking a bit early.'

3: Rosie's Doubts

'We'd better catch up, then,' McCaffey laughed, 'C'mon Rosie, come and meet my mad sister.'

'I'll join you in a mo,' said Dan.

The doors led out onto an expansive patio furnished with white tables and chairs shaded from the noonday sun by two beautiful ash trees. Off to one side stood a red-brick barbeque enclosure, topped by a shimmering heat-haze and scenting the air with freshly lighted charcoal. Alongside that, two long covered tables bore glasses and wine-bottles and the beginnings of preparations for the day's comestibles.

McCaffey led her onto a well-tended lawn where stood a green-and-white striped canvass pavilion, two rustic bench-tables and a scattering of straw-bales. The garden led down a slope to where a cluster of children played on swings and a trampoline. A copse of apple trees and a greenhouse blocked any further view beyond.

McCaffey ushered Rosie towards the pavilion. Half a dozen adults stood or sat holding wine glasses and talking and laughing across one another. A woman looked around as the pair approached, and Rosie forced-on her brightly-unconcerned face. The woman had been beautiful and still had a perfect right-profile. But the long brown hair that swept over to the left did little to cover up the severity of her scarring.

Julia squealed with delight and rushed to greet her brother.

'Hey, Bro, you came.'

'Happy Birthday, Sis.'

As the siblings hugged, Rosie got her first look at the prosthetic left arm pressed against McCaffey's back. She was surprised at how uncompromisingly

The Travel Agent

mechanical it looked; a piece of precision engineering encased in high-quality white and blue plastic. Neat and functional, and a far less bizarre solution, Rosie realised than a false limb made to resemble what it replaced. She had once met an American yachtsman whose prosthetic leg had a shiny inox-bar for a shin bone. Dirk, aka Cap'n Ahab, had made that appendage a part of who he was.

'Sis, I want you to meet Rosie. Rosie, this is Julia.'

Julia beamed. Her smile was bright and lovely, unhampered by her disfigurement.

'Aw, little Bro, you got yourself a girlfriend,' she cooed with a wicked glint as her brother's ears turned a dark shade of pink.

'Well, actually, Sis—'

'About time too,' Julia went on. 'Hello, Rosie, hope my misanthropic brother's treating you well.'

'Er Jul …' McCaffey's ear tips had deepened to ruby,

'Pleased to meet you, Julia,' Rosie cut-across, taking Julie's proffered hand and throwing McCaffey a 'shut-up' glance.

'Why don't you go and get you and Rosie a drink, Michael. You'll find beer and fresh orange juice in the fridge and wine over there by the barbie. If you want anything else, ask Dan.'

'Just a coffee for me,' Rosie called after him.

When McCaffey had left, Julia lifted her hair with a mechanical finger. She said, 'I suppose he warned you about this?' She smiled at Rosie's startled expression and let the hair fall back. 'Truth to tell, he's more bothered about it than I am. I love him dearly, but it

3: Rosie's Doubts

was such a long time ago, it's just who I am now, and I wish he'd get over it like the rest of us.'

Before Rosie could find an apt response, a little girl ran up and threw her arms around Julia's legs and looked up pleadingly while another one looked on hopefully.

'Mummy, can Philly come up to my room and see my Hatchimals? *Please*, Mummy?'

Julia looked down the garden to where two boys were playing while another girl stood alone. 'Why don't you ask Elly as well, darling?'

'Okay! C'mon Philly.' Both girls ran off excitedly to collect the remaining girl.

'Come and meet the others,' said Julia, hooking Rosie's arm and heading back to the pavilion. 'They started a bit early, I'm afraid. Our friends are bigger piss-artists than us, and that's saying something.'

3/3

Evidence

It was past midnight when Rosie finally rolled down her street. She was approaching the house when headlights flashed up ahead. All the lights in the house were out - Dad had turned in. Rosie edged quietly into her driveway and parked. Getting out, she took care to close the door softly then walked up to Harry's Range Rover while rehearsing what to say. The rear door swung open at her approach, and she climbed in, pulling it closed behind her.

'How do we know he's not bringing home some of those jihadi brides that the ISIS bastards conned into going out there?' she said without preamble. 'I wouldn't blame him for that – it was outrageous to take away their UK citizenship. From fifteen-year-old girls? How fair is that?'

'Not drugs, then?' grinned Marcus.

Harry scowled at him briefly.

'So, what have ye learned, Lassie?'

3: Rosie's Doubts

'I learned there's a sister who got badly hurt in seven-seven.'

...

'We didnae have that on our radar,' Harry said, 'but it doesnae change anything. From what yer said when you got in, you must know he's trafficking people in some way or other.' He moved his face closer to her, his eyes, cold. 'What are ye nae telling us, Rosie?'

Rosie turned away and exhaled heavily but did not speak. Harry did not scare her, but his doggedness was exasperating. And now she had to finesse her way out of incriminating a man she knew in her heart to be innocent - at least of what Harry was alleging.

'If you could have seen him, heard him telling me about his sister ... well, you'd just know he wouldn't get mixed up in slave-trafficking. I'm sure we've got this – no, I *know* we've got this wrong, and I'm going to prove it.'

'Ata girl–' Marcus began.

'Don't you dare patronise me,' she snarled.

'Oops,' said Marcus, abashed.

Harry stared at her a moment, then said in a softer tone, 'Hey, hen, we're all on the same side here.'

He added, 'Don't tell me yer've grown a soft spot fer yer mark? I'd consider that extremely unethical, Lassie.'

Rosie opened her door, 'No, Harry, McCaffey's just another mark. Give me a week. I'll message you when I've got to the bottom of this.'

Rosie could not sleep. She had to find a way of getting to the truth without alerting McCaffey and his accomplice that they were under surveillance. The

The Travel Agent

conundrum rolled around in her head into the early hours when a strategy began to work itself into her tumbling thoughts. With a determined sigh, she threw off her duvet and got up. While her laptop was starting up, she crept downstairs and made herself a cup of tea. For the first time in six years, Rosie felt the craving for nicotine. She cursed the old addiction back into its dark corner and took her drink upstairs.

A search for flights to Turkey pulled up lots of available seats - unsurprising given the country's current unrest. Five seats were available on a Turkish Airlines flight leaving Gatwick at 1045 on Tuesday for Dalaman, the nearest airport to Marmaris.

Rosie stared at the screen, asking herself what the hell she was thinking. After an epiphanic moment, eyes wide in shock at her audacious plan, she picked up her phone and tapped in McCaffey's speed dial.

'Hey, what's up?'

'Sorry to call so early, I want to ask you something. You awake?'

'Well yeah, I am now. Go on then, ask.'

'This delivery, I want to come with you.'

...

'You still there?'

'Yeeeaah, erm— Look, are you sure? Because you know I can't pay you?'

'Sorry if this is a bit random and spontaneous - but you got me hooked on the idea of sailing on a long voyage. I'm not a sailor, but maybe you can teach me? I mean, won't it help pass the time a bit quicker, or something. You said it could be quite boring.'

3: Rosie's Doubts

Along with McCaffey's anxious breathing, Rosie imagined she heard his mental cogs turning. After an age, he spoke.

'It's not that simple, Rosie. I need to check with my agent. There's an insurance issue. And the owner needs to approve it as well.'

'Look, I'll pay my way, I'll even pay any extra premium on the insurance. Can you call your agent and see if you can make it happen? Please, Michael, I'd just so love to come sailing - it might be just working to you, but to me, it's the adventure of a lifetime.'

There was another long pause, then a sigh.

'Okay, I'll see what I can do and call you later. Meanwhile, you'd better check the flights for Dalaman on Tuesday morning.'

'Already done. Ready to hit the Book Now button as soon as you call. What flight are you on by the way?'

'1045 - Turkish from Gatwick.'

'Wow, karma! Don't take too long, Michael; there are only five seats left.'

She had no sooner ended the call when the Blackphone buzzed on her bedside table. Harry. She picked up.

'What do yer think you're doing, Lassie?'

'Collecting evidence to prove my theory. I think it's called the scientific method – consider it a field trip. I'll see you in about six weeks.'

'You're not allowed to follow leads outside the country, Rosie, you know that.'

'So, Morocco last year, and last week in France was what?'

The Travel Agent

'Those trips were different, one-offs, with prior approval from our leaders.'

Rosie sighed heavily. 'So, don't pay me – I'm off on my holibobs.'

…

'I want this, Harry, for my peace of mind.'

'Nothing to do with infatuation fer yer toyboy?'

'Please, Harry, don't insult me …'

'Anyway, I thought you had an interview coming up - you'll miss it.'

Oh, shit! In her excitement, she had overlooked her interview at FCO.

'Er …'

'Okay, Rosie, for me, I think it's a way to go. So, I'll talk to Mrs Easterwood. If she approves it, she can get yer interview delayed. Just don't book a flight until you hear back from me.'

'What about a visa, can I do that now?'

'I expect our boy needs one because he's going there tae work. You'll go as a tourist, so you'll no need one.'

As she ended the call, a sparkle of anticipation came into her eyes.

EPISODE FOUR

Michael's Mission

The Travel Agent

4: Michael's Mission

4/1

Mediterranean

Rosie stirred to the soft beeping of her phone - her wakeup alarm telling her she was on watch in fifteen minutes. She rolled onto her back and watched the shivers of light on the vinyl head-lining. Since leaving Marmaris, the start of the fifth day at sea, though the constancy of a six-hourly watch routine rendered the passing days almost meaningless.

The boat was heading for Libya, just like on Michael's previous trip. Sometime after passing Malta, the young skipper had taken the fuses out of the GPS navigation system, telling Rosie it had broken down. To keep up her cover, she pretended the subterfuge had fooled her. Her feigned ignorance included acting oblivious to Michael's failure to record their position. Not in the logbook or on the paper chart, which made Rosie wonder just how stupid he thought she was. Most likely, he was using a navigation app on his phone when Rosie was not around.

The Travel Agent

Because that was what Rosie was doing. Before leaving home, she had bought the Mediterranean maps for her Navionics app. Rosie had been secretly tracking their progress since Marmaris. Yesterday, she had challenged him about his change of course, but he refused to tell her why: saying she would have to wait until afterwards.

'Afterwards of what?'
'Patience, Rosie, just enjoy the trip.'
She was going to try to find out today before something irreversible happened. She was also finding it increasingly difficult to play the ignorant landlubber in the cockpit: she was just itching to trim those sails properly. Her skipper, she had discovered, was an adequate sailor, but well short of brilliant.

A slow whistle from beyond her cabin door told her a cup of tea was in the offing. Rosie sat up and swivelled around to swing her feet down onto the carpet. She stood, steadied herself against the shifting heel of the boat, and stepped to the washstand. Throwing off her thin nightshirt, Rosie dampened a flannel under the tap and gave herself a thorough wipe down - a spray of deodorant where needed, then pulled on a tee-shirt and shorts. Checking her face in the mirror, she mussed her mousy bob into some sort of shape, then opened the door and stepped into the saloon.

'Morning,' Michael greeted her, handing her a mug, 'another day, another dollar.'

'Do you know that could get quite irritating? Got anything else in your store of inane aphorisms?'

Michael snorted. 'Sleep okay?'

4: Michael's Mission

'Apart from someone gabbling on the radio,' Rosie replied as she climbed the ladder to the cockpit with her tea.

'Oh, yeah,' said Michael, following her up. 'We almost ran into a bunch of Maltese fishing boats. Spread out for miles, they were. I had to give them a wide berth.'

A newly risen sun stood incandescently on the horizon, making it impossible to face to port. Rosie sat with her back to it and enjoyed the warm breeze ruffling her hair.

'All quiet, apart from the fishing boats?' she asked.

'Yeah, like the grave. We're nicely on track: broad reach, no reefs, seven knots. Barometer's steady at 1016. AIS in silent mode.'

'Was that even English?'

Michael gave an injured frown, 'I taught you all about points of sail a few days ago. Reefing we've been through - and the significance of pressure rise and fall on forecasting weather. What don't you get?'

'Er, AIS is in silent mode?'

'Means other ships can't see us.'

'Wow, an invisibility cloak, who knew?'

Michael's his hawk face reddened - not amused. 'You said you wanted to learn about sailing, but all you've done so far is take the piss and make a joke out of everything. When are you going to start taking it seriously?'

'Now, let me see,' she said, putting a finger to her lips. 'How about, when you take me seriously enough to tell me why we are going towards the world's most dangerous country, and what you intend to do when we get there? Just talk to me, Michael.'

The Travel Agent

Michael sat down on the banquette opposite and stared at her. He looked shocked.

'When did you know?'

'When did I know what, that we turned south after Gozo?' She jerked a thumb over her shoulder. 'Well, that great ball of fire rising over there could be a clue. And I think most people would know that south if you're in the Med, means Africa, while the Strait of Gibraltar is where the sun goes down. So, are you going to tell me why?'

He said nothing for a moment, ears glowing and a frown that made his countenance even more birdlike.

'We're going to pick somebody up,' he said at last.

'Okay, I get that. Go on?'

'A nurse, working for UNICEF, we're giving her a lift to the UK.'

'Okaaay... so why doesn't she go home on a UN flight?'

'Because she's cut off, because of the fighting. She can't get back to Tripoli.'

'Er ... and you found out about this, how?'

'She phoned me. I know her, you see, from Rwanda. Her name is Astrid.'

Finally! Enter the mysterious Astrid.

'So why the big secret, Michael. You could have told me this before.'

'No, I couldn't. Astrid said not to tell you anything until she was safely on-board - she's ultra-careful about her security.'

'It sounds like you've done this before, picked her up, I mean.'

Michael sighed, and his bony shoulders slumped, 'A couple of times... Look, can we park it for now?

4: Michael's Mission

Astrid will fill you in on everything tomorrow, I promise.'

The young skipper's ears tips were burning, so Rosie decided to push no further. She might not have all the answers - particularly the WhatsApp message that talked about needing a bigger boat because there were six passengers. Still, at least she knew who Astrid was: a UNICEF nurse, eh? Interesting.

'Okay, so now you can stop treating me like an idiot and put the fuzes back in for this map thingy…' tapping the pilot-chartplotter, '…so we can see where the hell we're going.'

It was mid-afternoon, and Rosie lay reading on the banquette cushion opposite Michael, who had relieved her at noon. She had tried to sleep in her cabin. But the anticipation of their midnight rendezvous filled her with nervous wakefulness. So, she lay shading under the bimini trying to lose herself in R.E. McDermott's *Deadly Straits*, which - given the novel's theme of maritime terrorism - really was not working.

'Uh-oh, looks like we've got company,' muttered Michael.

Rosie sat up and looked out to port where Michael's was sighting his binoculars. Converging towards them at speed, almost lost to view behind a huge bow-wave, was the sleek, dark grey shape of a patrol craft. This gave Rosie a surreal moment of connection with the fiction in which she had immersed herself.

The Travel Agent

4: Michael's Mission

4/2

Coastguard

The pair watched with growing tension as the vessel cut across the yacht's wake. The cutter flew a Libyan flag at the stern, 'COASTGUARD' emblazoned in big black letters on the hull. Just as Rosie thought the cutter was going on past, the surging vessel suddenly swung hard over towards them.

Michael glanced worriedly at Rosie, but she needed no prompting - she knew what the inveterate Libyan officials would make of a woman's naked legs and a skimpy top. She swung down the companionway and went in search of something modest to wear. As she entered her cabin, the rumble of powerful diesel engines sounded alongside.

'Good afternoon,' came a heavily accented voice on the radio, *'what please, the name of your vessel?'*

'Good afternoon, sir, we are *Bluehound of London*, over,' came Michael's reply.

'Thank you, Captain, now please state your last port of call, and your destination.'

The Travel Agent

After a frenzied ransacking of her holdall, Rosie pulled out a rumpled pair of jeans and a cotton shirt with sleeves.

'Our last port was Marmaris, Turkey, and we are heading for Djerba, Tunisia, over.'

'Captain, how many person on-board your vessel?'

'Two persons, over.'

'Are you carrying any weapons or ammunition?'

'Negative, no weapons, no ammunition.'

'Are you carrying any drugs or illegal contraband?'

'Negative.'

Feverishly, Rosie pulled on the jeans and tucked in her shirt then looked around for something she could use as a hijab.

'Captain, what is your business in Djerba?'

Sod it, she thought, we're under a British flag, they would just have to suck it up. She hurried up to the cockpit to find the Coast Guard cutter stationed close on the starboard quarter. Two uniformed officers stood by the pilothouse door looking the yacht up and down, while a third hunched inside, a radio mic in his hand.

Michael stood staring back at them awkwardly, apparently stuck for a response.

'I say again, Captain, what is your business in Djerba?'

'Tell them we're visiting Houmt El Souk,' Rosie hissed.

Michael's eyes locked with Rosie's in frozen terror. She stepped up, grabbed the mic from Michael's hand and spoke in Maghrebi Arabic:

'We are visiting the ancient fortress and market at Houmt El Souk for tourism, water and provisions.'

4: Michael's Mission

There followed a long pause, the two men on deck eying Rosie with what looked like suspicion. Perhaps because she had addressed them in Arabic, or disapproval that she had not covered hair. Rosie watched the man inside the pilothouse keenly studying his console. She knew he would be checking where *Bluehound's* current heading would take her. She also noted that the two men on deck were wearing business-like sidearms.

The officer inside stared out of his window at Rosie, then lifted his mic and spoke in Arabic: *'Your present course is for Zuwara.'*

'We have to sail with the wind,' Rosie explained, sweeping a hand up to the mains'l. 'We will turn to the right in one hour.'

The man now looked back at Michael, and said in English, *'You must not enter Libyan waters, Captain, you understand?'*

Rosie handed the mic back to Michael.

'Yes, sir,' he replied. 'We will stay clear.'

'Just one more thing, Captain, you have seen small boats?'

'Negative,' Michael replied. 'We passed some fishing vessels in the night, but nothing since.'

The three men continued staring at Rosie for a long moment. Then they went inside, and the cutter peeled away in a smoky roar, causing the yacht to roll heavily in her wake.

'And bon voyage to you too, mate' muttered Rosie.

'Whew!' said Michael. 'Thought for a moment, they were going to board us. I didn't know you spoke Arabic. What did you say to them?'

The Travel Agent

'I just told them we're picking up provisions in Houmt El Souk and then going sight-seeing. They were bothered that we were heading for Libya, so I explained about the wind and that we'd be altering course for Tunisia soon.'

The young skipper blinked and shook his head. 'You're full of surprises, Rosie Winterbourne. How did you know about Houmt El Souk? You been there or something?'

'There's a big book downstairs, all the ports and that? I read it when I was bored one night. And as you know, I remember stuff.'

He looked at her in disbelief. 'You memorised the Med Pilot, all of it?'

She grinned. 'The night shifts are pretty boring.'

'Well, thanks for digging me out of the shit.'

'No problem, Captain.'

4: Michael's Mission

4/3

Rendezvous

It was half-past midnight. Having taken a circuitous route to the west before doubling back under cover of darkness, *Bluehound of London* now approached her mark under a shortened headsail in a light northerly breeze. A clear night, a thin sliver of moon had just appeared over the eastern horizon casting a sharp glitter-path towards the port bow. A line of yellow lights to starboard marked the coast road from Tripoli to the small town of Zuwara: visible as a cluster of lights far to the west.

Michael checked his depth. Four metres, and almost on the final waypoint.

'Okay, furl it in as I showed you,' Michael murmured.

With a flick of the wrist, Rosie whipped the headsail-sheet from the winch and hauled in on the furling line until the remaining sail disappeared around the forestay. As the boat lost steerage way, she began to slew to the breeze, her bow turning shorewards.

The Travel Agent

Michael switched the AIS back to silent mode. It had been transponding for the past ten minutes: plenty of time for Astrid to have picked up the boat's signal. *Bluehound* was now a little more than a mile from shore. With the flood tide and wind pushing her inshore at around 0.2 kts, they had about thirty minutes before the water became dangerously shallow. Using the engine was not an option, and neither was dropping anchor. Either action would make too much noise and risk alerting the authorities ashore.

Michael activated his phone, its soft glow lighting his face. He touched the call icon and put the phone to his ear.

'Stand by with the lamp,' Michael called quietly.

Rosie lifted the portable searchlight onto the counter and located the switch.

'Yes, we're here,' he said into the phone. 'Are you ready?'

He listened, then said, 'Rosie, give them a two-second flash.'

Rosie complied.

'Good, they see us. Won't be long now.'

A few moments later there came a faint splashing of oars then a shape appeared out of the darkness, several hunched figures silhouetted against the glow from shore. As the boat neared, Michael moved forward to take their bowline while Rosie sat by at the stern.

Dark-coloured burqas covered three of the boat's occupants, one of whom was at the tiller, the other two rowing. Two women in long dark abayas and hijabs stood in the prow: one exceptionally large, the other much smaller. The larger one threw a rope to Michael, and then another line came sailing over to Rosie, this

4: Michael's Mission

thrown by the person steering. Rosie caught her rope and, as the nearside oar was lifted clear, heaved the boat's stern close alongside before snagging it onto a cleat. When she looked up again, the big woman was already on-board and making for the companionway. At the same time, Michael helped the smaller one aboard.

Before going below, the big woman turned to look at Rosie - a middle-aged, careworn face etched with compassion. Astrid was a long call from the Scandinavian beauty Rosie had imagined. The nurse allowed her the ghost of a smile then disappeared down the ladder to the saloon.

The anonymous figures in burqas now began passing large bags up from the boat, Michael taking them and handing them to the smaller woman who placed them carefully along the deck. She stepped forward to lend a hand, but Michael shooed her back into the cockpit.

'We've got this, Rosie,' he called quietly. 'Just keep a good lookout.'

When all the bags were aboard, six in total, the smaller figure slipped silently below, and Michael began passing them down the companionway hatch. Rosie could now see these were identical white holdalls bearing a large red cross in the light spilling from the saloon. After passing all six holdalls down, Michael returned to the side where two of the burqas handed him up a large suitcase; this also disappeared down the hatch, followed by Michael.

Was the other woman coming along as well, Rosie wondered? And what was with all the baggage? Intrigued, she went forward peered into the saloon.

The Travel Agent

She saw Michael and the two women fastening small rope nets to the overhead grab rails.

'Is someone going to tell me what's going on?' Rosie called.

Astrid and Michael ignored her, continuing to adjust the nets. The small woman looked up at Rosie: a girl no more than twenty years old, middle-eastern; a beautiful face apart from the livid empty socket where her left eye had been. She looked about to say something, but Astrid turned the girl, took her in a hug, kissed her forehead, and then spoke to her: *'Gå nu, Greta. Ta hand om dig själv, så ringer jag när de alla är säkra med sina nya familjer.'*

The girl mumbled something back, turned and came up the ladder, a sad smile on her face.

'Hello, you must be Rosie.' The girl said in heavily accented English, 'I am Greta. Thank you for helping. *'Iinah eamal Allah* - it is God's work.'

Before Rosie could answer, Greta had slipped like a wraith over the side and into her boat.

Suddenly Michael came stomping up the ladder at a run.

'Slip the boat, Rosie, we're in less than two metres - we need to leave - *now!*'

The rowboat had no sooner pulled away when an ominous grinding sounded beneath the hull, and the yacht lurched to port.

'Shitshitshit!' hissed Michael, running back to the cockpit. 'We're fucking aground! Means we'll need the engine to drive off. *Fucking hell!* They'll hear us in fucking Tripoli.' He stooped to turn the starter key, but Rosie smacked his hand away.

'Wha—'

4: Michael's Mission

'We can sail her off, Michael, you need to trust me now. Take the helm and turn slowly to starboard when I say, not before.'

'What the fuck, Rosie?'

Rosie took up the port genoa sheet and leaned back on it, pulling out the sail in one swift wallop and hauling it taught before turning up expertly on the cleat.

'What are you doing?' Michael gasped. 'Rosie, we need... Fucking hell!'

The yacht suddenly heeled to the wind, bringing the keel clear of the sandy seabed. Slowly, *Bluehound* began to inch forward, parallel to the shore.

'Now, Michael,' Rosie instructed. 'Ease her to starboard, not too fast, steady as she goes. That's it. Well done.'

Rosie now turned her attention to the mains'l, and as the yacht came up to windward, she hauled back on the main halyard, hoisting the sail smoothly up the mast. She turned up on the winch and tightened down with the winch handle, then turned back to an astonished Michael.

'Sorry about that, *Captain*, she's all yours again.'

Before Michael could reply, a sound came from the saloon that was the last thing Rosie ever expected to hear. A baby was crying.

The Travel Agent

4: Michael's Mission

4/4

Kindertransport

It was the strangest sight. A vision so incongruous it caused Rosie to stop halfway down the ladder and just gawp, speechless. The purpose of those string nets was now clear because tiny infants in pink onesies occupied two of them. One baby, with beautiful brown eyes, tracked its tilting surroundings with mild curiosity. The other hammock's occupant lay at rest, delicate eyelashes unmoving despite the squalling cries from the infant in Astrid's lap.

The nurse, now divested of her Arab robes and wearing green scrubs, was tucking the child's chubby brown legs into another onesie. Next to her on the banquette was a jar of ointment and an opened pack of disposable nappies. Rosie now saw why the three of them had handled the six holdalls so carefully. Three laid emptied on the sole boards, but the others stood on the lee banquette, their invisible occupants croaking and shuffling like Gremlins hoping for an after-midnight feed.

The Travel Agent

Rosie could see she would have to shelve her curiosity. Astrid looked up as Rosie stepped the rest of the way down the ladder.

'Hi. I guess you're Astrid. I'm Rosie. What can I do to help?'

Just as they had all six babies settled quietly into their hammocks, the first child, who had been asleep, awoke and began crying. In no time, all six infants were caterwauling noisily. Michael stayed on watch at the helm.
Astrid wasted no time getting the first child guzzling greedily at a bottle.

'You want to help?' she said to Rosie, nodding towards the galley sink, where five more filled bottles stood in a bucket of warm water. Rosie lifted one of the screeching bundles from its hammock and sat down next to the nurse. As she did so, the child fell silent and gazed up at Rosie with a look of trust and curiosity. At first, the infant would not take the teat; her little mouth pressed stubbornly closed, but at the first dribble of milk on her lips, she latched on like a suction pump.

It took almost an hour to feed the six infants, and by then, the first two babies were again howling from their hammocks. After a pause for the cup of tea that Michael popped below to make them, the two women began the noisome circuit once more, this time wiping shit and changing nappies.

By two-thirty, Rosie felt shattered while Astrid seemed inexhaustible. As the pungent smell of milk and wet wipes and baby-shit filled the saloon and the

4: Michael's Mission

reality dawned on the difficulties this novel situation presented, Rosie grew increasingly despondent.

Finally, peace reigned once more as the last of the little darlings dropped off. Astrid went around the saloon dowsing most of the lights while Rosie put the kettle on then went to change her tee-shirt, which was dribbled and stained and stank of infant detritus.

When she came out of her cabin again, all was silent and serene. The six little nets with their precious cargoes swinging in the dim light were achingly cute. Just as the kettle threatened to whistle, Rosie turned off the gas and made three cups of tea then ferried them to the top of the ladder where Astrid took them from her.

'So,' said Rosie, settling back on the cockpit cushion with her tea. 'Who's going to tell me what's going on?'

An awkward silence ensued.

Michael was still at the helm, the red glow from the compass up-lighting his avian features. Astrid sat opposite Rosie, cutting a somewhat heroic figure staring out astern at the sea's empty blackness, like the mannish warrior, Brienne, in Game of Thrones.

'Astrid?' Michael prompted.

The nurse gave a little shiver, then picked up a tablet computer from the bench and patted the seat beside her. 'Come, Rosie, sit here, please,' she said, opening the tablet, 'I have something to show you.'

As Rosie swung across with her tea and sat next to her, Astrid began tapping the screen.

'This footage was uploaded to YouTube but was taken down soon after.'

The Travel Agent

A scene appeared, a bonfire burning on a rubble-strewn street of war-damaged buildings. In the foreground stood three black-clad and thickly-bearded militiamen armed with Kalashnikovs. One of the men held his rifle aloft. Impaled on the end of his bayonet was a filthy bundle stained with ominous dark patches.

Rosie gasped as she realised what was happening. She wanted to look away, but the scene held her transfixed in horror. There was no audio, which was fortunate: the spectacle silently playing out on the screen told its own ghastly story. A woman rushed forward, only to be clubbed to the ground with a rifle butt. Beyond the flames, and shimmering in the heat haze, a dozen women in niqabs stood witnessing with undisguised terror as the bayoneted bundle was lowered onto the fire. A fold of cloth dropped and caught alight, flames licking around a tiny, feebly waving arm. The man turned the bundle so that more of the infant was exposed, a glimpse of a little face, eyes and mouth wide in a silent shriek.

Rosie looked away, 'Turn it off! For Christ's sake, that's disgusting.'

Astrid shut down the player and laid a hand on hers. 'I'm sorry, Rosie, I did warn you. But you had to see that to understand.'

Rosie sat for a moment swallowing rapidly, then dashed across the cockpit, knelt on the counter and stuck her head between the guardrails. Into the swirling dark water went the tea she'd just drank, the remains of last night's chicken stew, and when she had nothing left, bitter bile and dry-retching.

4: Michael's Mission

When at last Rosie slumped back down into the cockpit with her eyes streaming, Astrid was there with a handful of tissues.

'That's what I did when I saw it,' Michael murmured from the helm.

'Where did that come from?' Rosie asked after she had cleaned up.

'From Greta,' said the nurse. 'The girl who came on-board.'

'Jesus *Christ* that was awful. Who *were* those animals?'

'Militia forces escaped from Syria. This happened just outside Benghazi - the video came from Greta's phone last October. She managed to upload it to her Cloud account before she was caught. The phone went on the fire with the little babies.'

Rosie shook her head, 'Ugh, don't. I can't get those images out of my head.'

'Imagine how Greta feels. She had to witness such things many times over. She almost died for taking that footage.'

'Is that why…' Rosie pointed to her own left eye.

Astrid nodded. 'She is the wife of one of the fighters. Her name is Greta Maloof, ethnic Palestinian but a second-generation Swedish national. When she was fourteen, she was persuaded to join the caliphate in Syria to "live a more fulfilled life". When she was caught videoing that incident, her husband beat her up, then gauged her eye out with a bayonet. She managed to escape.'

'And why those poor babies—' Rosie dry-yacked again.

The Travel Agent

'All baby girls, the daughters of the men who burned them.'

She stared at the nurse, speechless, then up at Michael at the helm.

He nodded. 'You'd better believe it. They treat their women like baby factories, but they only want boys: boys to fight for the caliphate. One girl in the family is usually tolerated. Any more, well, that's just a waste of resources. Girls are trouble - eventually, they need to be married off, and that costs money.'

'Doesn't say much for the caliphate's long-term strategy,' Rosie observed dryly. 'Why don't the mothers run away like Greta did, with their kids?'

Astrid said, 'Greta was lucky, she was married to a jihadi commander and used her influence and privileges to escape. Most of them have no such opportunity. Their boys are kept together in a creche and taught the Quran and Allah's ways until they are old enough to fight. Caliphate wives are like any other mothers: devoted to their children. They would rather die than leave them, even if they are little trained killers.'

'Jesus!' Rosie said, leaning back and looking up at the cold frozen universe. 'What a world.'

Astrid closed her tablet and took it below, returning a few minutes later wearing a fleece over her scrubs.

Rosie asked, 'So what happens now to our six little survivors?'

Astrid smiled and said, 'So now our babies grow up as English ladies in nice families. They will have a British birth certificate and a valid National Insurance Number. They will never know their true origins.'

4: Michael's Mission

4/5

Passage

Within a day, the three of them had fallen into a routine that Rosie dared hope was sustainable in the weeks ahead. And sustainable it was, after a fashion. Astrid took to sleeping in the saloon with her charges, establishing a four-hour feeding cycle, changing and resting. Rosie or Michael helped after coming off watch. But they too needed rest: too much shipping and too many fishing fleets around to risk leaving the cockpit unattended for more than ten minutes at a time.

During calm days the forepeak became a nursery for a few hours, with lee-cloths rigged either side of the double bunk. The babies were laid to gurgle and grin at one another, Astrid tickling and cooing and rattling toys she'd brought along in her Tardis-like suitcase.

Rosie found the whole business of baby management strangely unsettling. She thought of them as alien creatures, wondering vaguely if she lacked the maternal instinct with which all women were

The Travel Agent

supposedly endowed. She had mentioned it to Michael one night at watch change.

'No, I don't suppose you are the maternal type,' he snapped. 'Your expertise is more in the sailing department.'

She looked at him sharply. She had not expected such bitterness. It was time to come clean, she realised, this could not be left to fester.

'Michael, I have something I need to tell you, only some of it has to stay a secret between us, you can't tell another soul…'

After her charges had been fed and changed on calm evenings, Astrid would come up and sit in the cockpit, bringing a hot drink to whoever had the watch. On one such evening, Rosie asked, 'Why does Greta do what she does? I would have thought after what she's been through, she'd be keen to just get home to her family.'

The nurse stared out at the moonlit sea for a long moment before answering. When she turned back, her eyes were glistening. 'There is no easy way back for girls like Greta.'

'Why ever not?' asked Rosie, 'I thought the Swedes were enlightened about that stuff.'

'Yes, Sweden has a reputation for religious and cultural tolerance. But it also has an extremist faction of the Right who hate it that Islamic migrants are being allowed to settle in our country. That attitude extends to the government and the judiciary, not all, but an influential few. If Greta had returned home before her sixteenth birthday, she would have been deradicalized and returned to her family. But after sixteen she is a

4: Michael's Mission

criminal in Sweden, a terrorist, and will face charges if she returns.'

'But why stay in Libya, can't she escape to somewhere safer, find a new life for herself?'

'Ah! Now that is another question. Remember, Greta was a Jihadi bride, married off to one of their leaders. She had her first child at fifteen, a little boy who died, and a year later, a daughter taken from her. Only when her husband moved the group to Libya did she discover about the baby girls. And now Greta believes her little girl was also murdered. It is mainly compassion that drives her, but I think she is also trying to atone for her complicity.'

'So how did you get involved?' Rosie asked.

'Greta turned up at our clinic in Benghazi one afternoon, begging for water. The staff on duty took her in and put her on a rehydration programme. She tried to tell them what happened to her, but she only spoke a little Arabic, and no English or French. When they realised she was speaking Swedish, they called me to come and talk to her. What a terrible state she was in; her poor face battered, one eye missing. And whipped, oh the lash marks on her back! It was unbelievable. The poor child walked across twenty miles of desert to escape the monster who did this to her.

'And so we devised our Kindertransport for baby girls. I knew a man in London willing to help find homes for them, he is an old friend, a Doctor I met in Rwanda working with the UN. He is an obstetrician and has a private practice in Harley Street, specialising in IVF for the filthy rich. Ha! No, I should not be unkind. A childless couple is a childless couple, eh?

The Travel Agent

They pay well for our babies and give them a good life. Without their money, we could not do this.'

4: Michael's Mission

4/6

Arrival

The weeks passed with remarkable swiftness until one bright Saturday afternoon found *Bluehound* entering the Western Approaches. That night, the yacht made her rendezvous with the fast motor launch, *Sarirnaqal*, which would take Astrid and the infants to a secret destination on the Devon coast.

By midnight it was just the two of them again, sitting in the cockpit sipping hot cocoa and watching *Sarirnaqal's* stern-light drawing away to port.

'Who owns her?' Rosie asked.

'Truthfully? Not a clue. I know one thing, though. *Sarirnaqal's* not her real name. They've got a pirated AIS transponder.'

'I gathered that much, or she would have come up on the Ship Register. By the way, do you know what *Sarirnaqal* means?'

Michael grinned. 'No, but I'm sure you do. Tell me?'

'I didn't know myself until I worked it out this morning. It's an Arabic word, well, two words, really,

The Travel Agent

that's why it fooled me: *sarir naqal* means "Carry-cot".'

For the first time since Libya, Michael's laughter sparkled with genuine mirth.

'Oops, her stern-light just disappeared,' observed Rosie.

'That's them gone silent, then,' Michael said.

'So where do they land?' Rosie asked.

'Oh, just a little bay on the Devon coast. The new parents will be there in their posh cars ready to take them home.'

'You sound kind of wistful, missing them already?'

He laughed. 'Not really, you?'

Rosie spluttered. 'You're joking. I'm just basking in the silence.'

An overcast first-light the next morning found *Bluehound* sailing past Pendennis Castle. It was impossible to sail into Carrick Roads with a north-westerly wind, so Michael started the engine while Rosie dowsed the sails. They would motor the last five miles to Falmouth Marina.

With Michael at the helm, Rosie made them tea. She sat in the cockpit, taking in the picturesque scenery of the Penryn River.

'Not a bad trip,' commented Michael.

'No, it was okay,' Rosie said. 'But I'm really looking forward to a good old English breakfast.'

For the last two weeks, they had been eating dried and tinned provisions – the inevitable consequences of a non-stop six-week passage.

But Rosie was distracted by more than mere food. Since Astrid's departure with her small charges, Rosie

4: Michael's Mission

realised that her relationship with Michael had undergone a subtle change. She no longer thought of him as her 'mark': a mere subject for investigation. The young skipper was certainly no Adonis. Had he not been her assignment, she would not have looked twice: he was bony and gawky, with unattractive angular features. But something was engaging about Michael, not least because he was essentially a good and kind-hearted man. Naïve at times, that was true, and he could be annoyingly lackadaisical in his seamanship, but nevertheless …

Michael interrupted her thoughts, 'Do you realise, this is the first time we've motored since Marmaris?'

'And?'

'Saved me loads in fuel.'

'You pay for the fuel?'

'Mm, goes with the contract. The skipper pays all normal cruising expenses, food, fuel, water, additional crew.'

'Phew! A bit harsh.'

'It's priced into my fee: any savings are a bonus.'

'Michael, I never asked you this, and tell me to butt-out if you want, but are you seeing anyone? I mean a regular girlfriend?'

Michael's reaction was to stare straight ahead with compressed lips, a little colour shading those tell-tale ears and a slight whitening of knuckles on the wheel.

'Sorry,' Rosie said hurriedly. 'I didn't mean to embarrass you. Let's forget I asked, eh?'

Had she just made a terrible mistake? Was her young skipper gay? Maybe he had yet to come out of the closet with his family. It happened.

The Travel Agent

Rosie looked out to port where a big P&O cruise-ship lay alongside the wall at Pendennis Docks. Suddenly the boat's engine note dropped as Michael throttled back to idle. Standing up to look ahead, Rosie saw the reason they had slowed: a small motor launch, crossing the bow left to right.

'St Mawes ferry,' said Michael. 'I seem to catch her every time I come to Falmouth.'

Rosie sat down and sipped her tea. Jesus, this was awkward. Stupid, stupid!

After a time, Michael gave a quiet harrumph.

Rosie looked up at him, 'What?'

'It's no big deal, really,' he said. 'You may as well know. I haven't *'seen anybody'*, as you put it, for more than three years. I had a girlfriend - Sara. We worked together on VSO in Rwanda. We were going to get married when we got home. Sara didn't make it. I never really go over it.'

'Ooh, I'm so sorry.'

'Don't be. I'm only telling you this because …'

'Go on - because?'

'Since you came into my life I've been feeling, you know? Like there could be something going on between us - am I making sense?'

'Perfect sense, Michael. I appreciate your frankness.'

'And you, Rosie? How do you feel about that?'

Rosie had no response to give – things had just escalated out of her control. Instead, she asked him: 'What happened to Sara – you say she didn't make it?'

'She got shot in Kigali - machine-gunned to death one afternoon by a pissed-off Hutu with a Kalashnikov.'

4: Michael's Mission

Rosie inhaled sharply, 'Oh, *Michael!* That's … that's just appalling.'

'Mm'

After berthing alongside, Rosie and Michael began the onerous task of removing all evidence of their erstwhile cargo: scrubbing out spots of vomit and detritus from the seat cushions, cleaning the sole-boards, and spraying vast quantities of air-freshener.

After the work was done, Michael went to the broker's office to arrange a time to hand over the boat. He took his wash-gear with him to take a shower in the shore facilities.

Meanwhile, Rosie took her shower in the after-cabin suite – a long, hot one - now that shore-power was connected. She came out into the cabin to find Michael returned, his back to her, carefully packing his holdall.

'When is the owner coming?' she asked, padding softly around the double bunk.

'Not till four; my money's in the bank though, so I reckon we can book into a hotel tonight and get the train in the morning. I think we could both use a good night's–'

'Boo!'

Michael gave a start to find she had crept up behind him. He turned.

'I beg your..?'

'Just shut up and kiss me,' she said, dropping her towel.

The Travel Agent

4: Michael's Mission

4/7

Thank You

'This is all a bit romantic,' Rosie said, looking around the softly-lit room and glittering silverware. 'I do hope you're not going to propose.'

Michael snorted, 'You should be so lucky. I just thought you deserved a treat after helping us out. We never tried six before, and frankly, I don't think we'd have coped without you.'

'Well don't try it again, buddy, because this crew ain't volunteering. Don't get me wrong, I wouldn't have missed the experience for the world, but for me, that was a one-off.'

He shook his head, 'We won't be doing it again, it's getting too dangerous, with ... you know who everywhere now. Anyway, I'm taking a nice long break. We'll look at it again next year.'

Rosie nodded and raised her wine glass. 'Glad to hear it, let's drink to that.'

They clinked and drank.

'What will you be doing instead?' she asked.

The Travel Agent

Before he could reply, the waiter arrived with the food. They had both ordered the grilled turbot, which came whole and formidable. Dishes of accompaniments began to fill all the remaining space on the table.

'Hope you're hungry,' Michael grinned when the waiter had finally left.

'Starving, actually,' Rosie said, peeling back the soft skin of her fish with a fork and savouring its steaming aroma. 'I skipped lunch when you said we were coming here.'

They ate in silence for a time, then Michael said, 'I might take a holiday - Lanzarote, maybe.'

She stared at him. 'Er, why? I mean, you must have been there on deliveries.'

He shook his head. 'Never had the pleasure. I've only ever done Med to UK and points between.'

'Well it's no different to the Costa del Sol; boozy all-inclusive's and beaches full of screaming kids and bored dads. Not my idea of a holiday.'

'You said you enjoyed your time there.'

'That was different. I was mostly in Arrecife, away from the tourists. I learned Spanish there and did a bit of cruising. Las Palmas was stunning.' Then she grinned impishly, 'Hey, you could hire a bareboat yacht - a busman's holiday.'

Michael gave her a sour look and went back to dissecting his fish. For the next half hour, they chatted about favourite destinations and picked at the various vegetables and devoured chunks of succulent fish and laughed and teased one another and giggled and drank wine.

4: Michael's Mission

Finally reducing her turbot to a fan of bones - head still attached, staring at her through a frosted eye - Rosie sat back and sighed. 'That was terrific.'

'Their fish is always a hit,' Michael said, lining up his knife and fork.

'Pudding?'

She pouted, patting her flat stomach. 'How dare you!'

He chuckled. 'I mean, can I tempt you to something to absolutely ruin that athletic figure?'

She smiled. 'Thanks, but I'm stuffed. Just a coffee, I think.'

'Now,' Michael said after the table was cleared and the coffees arrived, 'I've got something for you.'

He slid a thick white envelope across the table.

Rosie eyed it suspiciously. 'What's that?'

'Your share from the last trip.'

She shook her head and pushed it back. 'I can't take that, Michael.'

'Just put it away,' he said, sliding it back, 'you earned it.'

'Look, can't I just donate it to the baby fund or whatever?'

He shook his head. 'Not needed, and we're having a break from that, remember? Just take it, Rosie, and stop embarrassing me.'

Sighing, she slipped the envelope into her bag. 'There. Happy now?'

Michael smiled. 'Delighted, thank you. So, what's next for you?'

'Funny, you should ask. I've got a chance to start full time with the Foreign and Commonwealth Office. I'm taking the train up to London tomorrow first thing. My interview appointment's at ten in Whitehall.

'An office job? Yeah, right.' He shook his head. 'Sorry, Rosie, I can't see it.'

'No, not an office job. The FCO covers a whole raft of departments. If I get the job, I might be away for a while.'

EPISODE FIVE

The Interview

# The Travel Agent

5: The Interview

5/1

Sammy

Entering the Foreign & Commonwealth Office from King Charles Street, Rosie walked across the opulent Durbar Court, up an imposing stairway and into a wonderland of imperial architecture and fine art. The ceiling high above was festooned with heroic paintings and finely decorated domes and arches filled with gilded coffers. A grand, red-carpeted staircase wove around three flights up to splendid columned balconies overlooking the entrance hall. The walls behind them were filled with classical scenes in rich, vibrant colours.

Rosie followed the directions in her letter to the reception desk, manned by a dozen headset-wearing receptionists looking incongruous amid the nineteenth-century grandeur. As Rosie approached the desk, an immaculately turned-out woman looked up from her computer and raised a haughty eyebrow.

'Hi. I have an appointment with a Janet Brown? My name's Rosie Winterbourne.'

The Travel Agent

'May I see your letter of appointment and some photo identification?'

Rosie dug into her bag, and pulled out her purse, drew out her Driving Licence and slid it across the counter with her letter. The woman skimmed the letter then made a show of comparing the picture on the licence to Rosie's face.'

'That's fine, Ms Winterbourne,' she slid both documents back across the desk. 'Please take a seat. Janet Brown will come to fetch you shortly.'

Rosie had no sooner sat down on the plush leather bench than a young woman entered through a set of double doors and crossed the floor towards her, heels clicking on the polished marble. Her elegant stride made her wide trouser bottoms flap from side to side.

'Rosemary Winterbourne?' she asked in the kind of plummy accent coached in 'exclusive' ladies' schools.

'Yes, that's me.' Rosie stood up. 'But it's just Rosie. And you're Janet Brown?'

With a playful glint, the girl leaned in conspiratorially, 'That's a sort of FCO euphemism – awfully dull.'

'Oh?'

'I'm Sammy, merely a foot-soldier come to take you to where you need to be. Come, it's this way.'

Sammy led the way back from where she had come and held open one of the doors for Rosie.

'It's a dreadful hike, I'm afraid,' Sammy said as Rosie moved past.

Sammy fell into step beside Rosie as they entered the long corridor. The décor here took a nosedive: brown linoleum tiles, simple dadoes on the walls, dull magnolia above, institutional green below.

5: The Interview

'So, Sammy…'

Sammy stopped and half-turned with an apologetic smile. 'Sorry, frightful bore, but no chatting in the corridors.'

'Fair enough, lead on.'

They walked on in silence, past a pair of doors, 001 to the left, 002 on the right. Every ten paces, a set of doors: odd numbers left, even numbers right. Rosie smiled as she passed 007 on the left. After an age, they came to a junction where Sammy steered them left into an identical corridor: door 125 on the left, 124 on the right; doors every ten paces. After 231 (on the left) a narrow stairway opened on the right. Up they went, twice turning left, reaching a landing at the top with a door onto yet another corridor. Doors left and right: four-figure numbers now: 1091 left, 1092 right… A hundred doors glided past in a monotonous blur until Sammy finally stopped.

'Here we are,' she said brightly, 'OSCT Recruiting: better known as Room 1305.' Sammy knocked and opened the door but did not enter.

'Just take a seat inside, Ma'am,' she said, 'the SIO's team will be here shortly.'

Ma'am?

As Rosie stepped past her, Sammy whispered, 'Don't take the red pill.'

Rosie turned with a startled look - the pretty civil servant winked a long eyelash, shooed her inside and pulled the door closed.

The floor inside was ancient polished parquet. A row of five wooden chairs lined one wall. There were no windows: the light was from a quartet of lamps hanging from an ornate rose that matched the moulded

The Travel Agent

cornice surrounding the ceiling. A portrait of the Queen hung on one wall. There was nothing else in the room except another door. Rosie crossed the room and tried the handle. It was locked. She sighed and sat down on one of the chairs and reached into her bag for her Kindle. She was just getting back into the story she had started on the train when the door swung open, and a tall man entered.

'Rosemary Winterbourne? My name is Herbert,' terse and officious.

Herbert looked every inch the superannuated civil servant. He was totally bald and dressed in an immaculate broad pinstripe suit and what looked like a regimental tie. Rosie stood up and took his proffered hand.

'It's just Rosie, actually. Excuse me for asking, but is Herbert your given name or your surname?'

Herbert smiled but offered no reply. Two more people entered the room, one of whom Rosie immediately recognised.

'Ms Winterbourne,' said Herbert, 'let me introduce Lucy Broacher, and of course you have already met Erin Easterwood.'

Rosie had last seen the olive-skinned Intelligence Officer more than four years ago whilst recovering from a brain aneurism in the Azores. With raven hair worn in a shoulder-length bob, Erin Easterwood was more attractive than a mother of three teenagers had any right to be.

'Yeah, we've met,' Rosie said, grinning as she crossed the room to shake her hand. 'Hi, Erin. It's been a while. How are you?'

5: The Interview

'Hello, Rosie, I'm well,' she gave a grin and added, 'You look a lot better than when I last saw you.'

Rosie almost guffawed, 'No, lying in a hospital bed with a bandaged head isn't my best look. How are Philip and the children: Sara, Frances and Henry, as I recall.'

Erin's grin widened, 'Impressed! They're all fine, thanks.'

Erin half turned to admit the second woman, 'And this is Lucy Broacher. Lucy, meet Rosie Winterbourne, the young lady who recently apprehended sixty-four illegal's and three, armed cocaine smugglers.'

Rosie spluttered. 'Hardly. I think my handler and forty-odd Border Force agents might have had something to do with it.'

Lucy was short, no more than five-feet-three, blonde ponytail and a stern face, maybe in her early thirties. She had a firm handshake and a confident manner, neither friendly nor hostile. Rosie's instinct was to like her. But she had to remember she was here for an interview and could not take anything for granted - not even Erin's friendship was a given.

'Ahem, when you're quite ready, ladies.' Herbert had unlocked the door to the next room and now ushered everybody through.

The Travel Agent

5: The Interview

5/2

Room 1305

Herbert took up position behind a long wooden desk, with Erin to his right, and Lucy to his left. The desk was bare except for Herbert's briefcase.

Rosie stood by the solitary wooden chair facing them.

'Sorry about the inquisitorial layout, Ms Winterbourne,' said Herbert. 'But please, do take a seat.'

He began removing papers and documents from his briefcase while the two women took out notebooks and biros. A knock came at the door, and Sammy walked in with a tray containing a jug of water and four upturned glasses, placed it on the desk, and left without a word.

'So, Rosie, how was the trip from Malta?' Erin asked.

'Er, okay. Why do you ask?' Rosie wondered if they had found out about the babies.

The Travel Agent

'Well, your Triage Report was pretty skeletal, the detail noticeable by its absence, I would say.'

'Yes, well…'

Herbert looked up. 'Right ladies, are we ready to start? Good. Now, Rosie, let us begin with you telling us something about yourself. Start where you like, anything you'd *like* us to know, anything you think we *ought* to know, and what you can offer the Secret Intelligence Service.'

Rosie took a deep breath. She had been expecting this and had rehearsed what she was going to say, but now it came down to it she decided to wing it a little, starting with The Accident.

'Okay, well I assume my departure from the Navy will come up, so I may as well start there. I used to believe I could get to be a high-ranking naval officer,' she began.

'I was ambitious and good at my job and was getting great commendations. Then there was an accident, a car crash. My mother died, and my father was in a coma for eighteen months…'

Rosie looked down at the dull green carpet. The sudden rush was unexpected – she usually found she could talk about it. But now, of all the stupid times, she found herself fighting a great wave of emotion.

'Ms Winterbourne if you want to take a moment…' Herbert began.

Rosie held up a palm while she steadied her feelings and after a few deep breaths, looked up and met their worried frowns.

'Sorry. I'm okay now,' forcing a gritty smile. 'Anyway, I started getting these flashbacks, hallucinations, and narcoleptic seizures.'

5: The Interview

Rosie paused, studied the three faces for glazed looks, then continued. 'I was sent for psychotherapy and was eventually kicked out of the navy with PTSD. So much for the master-plan. Nobody could fix me. When they started talking about sectioning me under the mental health act, I did a runner in my Dad's yacht. I sailed the Atlantic for a year: Caribbean, Florida. And Bermuda - where I first met Erin.'

Herbert glanced at Erin, 'That's where you first approached her?'

Erin gave a wry grin, 'That was the plan – Christmas Eve – but Rosie eluded me, sailed off the next day before I had the chance to talk to her sober.'

'She came to see me again in the hospital,' Rosie explained. 'That was in Sao Miguel where they took me after an accident at sea. Erin said there might be a job for a woman with her own boat and my er … my special gift.

'I was intrigued by the offer, but I also wanted to finish the degree I'd started before I joined the mob… I mean the Navy. I'd been studying the Classics then, but Erin persuaded me it would be useful to switch to Arabic and Islamic studies.

'So, I started again at Bristol University in 2015 and finished this year. I'm still waiting for my results. Any chance of a glass of water?'

Lucy poured her a glass and brought it over.

Rosie took several mouthfuls and placed the glass on the floor. 'Thanks. What else do you want to know?'

'What about your work as a TO with Mercury One,' said Lucy, sitting down again.

'Mm. I triaged five yachtsmen and one woman in the three years. I got one hit: Wesley Corcoran, a few weeks ago.'

Herbert said, 'Did you enjoy the work with Mercury One?'

'Well yes, I did. I enjoyed the subterfuge, the role-play, and of course, the opportunities for social interaction with seafarers. That was the one thing I was missing at Uni. But I never really felt I was being stretched in Harry's team – it was pretty mundane stuff, looking for human-traffickers. I knew I had more to offer, and that was frustrating.'

Lucy asked, 'Did you ever have sexual relations with any of your marks?'

Rosie had not expected that one. She took a moment, then said, 'Not while they were under investigation. The last guy, Michael McCaffey, and only one time – and that was after I'd cleared him. We're still good friends but not exactly lovers.'

Not yet, Rosie thought.

Erin now interjected, 'Rosie, you've sailed most of your life, you sailed alone for more than a year, but in the last four years, you haven't sailed alone at all. Why is that?'

Rosie pressed her lips together. They wanted a sailor - she knew that much. It was the main reason for this interview.

'I enjoyed the six-week passage from Malta with Michael. But do I want the sea gipsy's life again? I honestly don't know - and won't until I sail alone again.' She paused, let the silence settle, then said, 'Want me to leave now?'

Herbert said, 'Do you *want* to leave now?'

5: The Interview

'No.'

'Good,' said Herbert. 'Now, you mentioned earlier your special gift. I understand you have what is called a photographic memory, is that right?'

Rosie sighed softly. This, she knew had been on the cards, but it did not make it any easier.

'When I was a little girl,' she began, 'my Grandmother told me it was a gift from God. But Granny Bee believed in ghosts as well. It was my shrink at RDMC, Professor Hardy, who finally nailed it.

'I have a condition called hyperthymesia: a form of mental illness to do with sleep disorders. It's not that I memorise stuff, it's just that I can't forget. Apparently, I don't have proper dreams like most people, so the memories don't get filed and sorted into my hippocampus. But the good prof assured me that the brain is such a wonderful mechanism, that it can compensate for its own deficiencies. So happily, I can expect a normal life with no side-effects. Which really goes without saying, because I'm thirty-two and I'm sure I would have noticed by now.'

Herbert handed each of his colleagues a sheet of paper, then asked Rosie, 'Do you mind if we test your memory with a few random questions? Say if it disturbs you.'

'No, go ahead. I was kind of expecting it. Just bear in mind I'm not a stage magician, and I don't do party tricks. If you ask me something I never knew in the first place, then I won't have an answer.'

Herbert looked to his left, 'Do you want to start, Lucy?'

The Travel Agent

Lucy checked her sheet and said, 'We'll start with things you might have come across in your Islamic studies, is that okay?

'Go ahead, I'll give it a try.'

'So, where, in the Quran would you find the words: "God does not burden a soul beyond that it can bear."?

'That would be in *Sulah Baqarah*, Verse 286.'

Herbert looked at his own sheet, stuck out his lower lip and nodded.

Erin said, 'According to Ali Imran's words in 3:51, what is "the Straight Path"'?

Rosie paused a moment, then answered, 'Indeed, Allah is my Lord and your Lord, so worship Him. That is the Straight Path.'

Herbert said with a lop-sided grin, 'I'll ask you the only question to which I happen to know the answer: what tribe did the Prophet Muhammad come from?'

'The Quraysh,' Rosie answered.

'Who is the president of Surinam,' Lucy quick-fired.

'I haven't a clue,' said Rosie. She frowned, then grinned. 'Their first president was Johan Ferrier, though, 1975 to 80.'

'When did Mozambique become independent from Portugal?'

'Twenty-fifth of June 1975 - a Wednesday.'

'Who was alleged to have assassinated Swedish Prime Minister Olaf Palme in 1986?'

'Mm, let's see.'

Rosie laid a finger on her lower lip and stared upwards. After a moment she returned a blank look, perversely enjoying their growing disappointment.

Finally, Herbert sighed.'Well never–'

5: The Interview

'26th of February - a Wednesday,' Rosie interrupted, 'Christer Pettersson was convicted in 1988 but was acquitted a year later. Pettersson died on twenty-ninth of September 2004 - that was also a Wednesday, by the way.'

'Extraordinary!' said Herbert.

Rosie grinned, 'Yeah, they're all Wednesdays. Funny that.'

Erin did a double-take of her answer sheet and then grinned hugely at Rosie. For fun, Rosie had changed Palme's assassination date to make it a Wednesday.

'Okay, last question,' Erin said, still smirking. 'Four years ago, when we first met in Bermuda, and I helped you into your dinghy because you were drunk, I whispered a set of three numbers in your ear. What were they?'

'How should I know? I don't even remember getting into the dinghy. Oh, wait… Christmas Eve 2014. Wow! *Another* Wednesday. Three numbers? 76091 56023 56109.'

Erin slid a crumpled piece of paper to Herbert, who looked at it and smiled at Rosie. 'Even when drunk, eh?'

Rosie shrugged with a self-effacing eye-roll.

Erin said, 'That number sequence has particular significance, Rosie. You had not remembered it until I prompted you with context. Please keep it to yourself from now on.'

Rosie did not understand but suspected she wasn't supposed to, so she nodded anyway, keen to move on. Herbert opened one of the files from his briefcase. 'Now, let us proceed to the formal interview.' He

The Travel Agent

looked at his watch, then at Lucy. 'Shouldn't the coffee be here by now?'

'I'll check with Sammy, Sir,' Lucy said and left the room taking out her phone.

'Now, Rosie, there are about fifty standard questions I have to ask. Some of them you might find a bit personal, a bit tricky to answer, or even a little uncomfortable. But for a successful interview, an Intelligence Officer candidate must make a good stab at answering frankly and honestly. Is that clear?'

Rosie nodded.

5: The Interview

5/3

Recruited

Rosie took the steps down to King Charles Street in a state of mild euphoria. London looked brighter in the afternoon sunshine: multi-coloured cars and multi-coloured people; bright red buses and brightly dressed tourists; fancy cameras and shiny black cabs. The pavement of Parliament Street felt oddly springy and light underfoot - like the rubber they used on playgrounds - a sensation which continued as she crossed the road and headed for Westminster Bridge. It was less than a mile to Waterloo Station, but she would have walked it if it were ten.

'An impressive interview,' Herbert had told her. 'I expect you'll be contacted very soon with a job offer.'

A fresh start! A new life of excitement and intrigue. New challenges to stretch her underused capabilities. How it would all begin, she could only guess.

'I think you know better than to ask,' Erin had chided gently over coffee in the staff café. 'I don't

The Travel Agent

even know which department they have in mind for you.'

Perhaps a mysterious phone call inviting her to a rendezvous at a particular park bench, Rosie thought.

Look for someone wearing a blue carnation and carrying The Times.

She grinned to herself. Probably just a letter in the post.

Crossing Westminster Bridge, she walked on past Belvedere and hung a left on York Road - the small one-way section that changed to a two-way after a hundred yards. Her usual shortcut to the station on visits to the capital - less traffic and fewer people.

She was halfway up the narrow road when a car entered from the other end and cruised down towards her - a dark blue Insignia. It gained her attention purely because it had just driven over giant white letters saying: 'Local Buses Only'. She shook her head as the car approached her.

That's a thousand pound fine on your doormat tomorrow, my friend.

That was a dead certainty - this part of the city boasted more live recording cameras than parking-meters. Rosie could see two of them right now on the County Hall building to her left, and at least one more on the Park Plaza Hotel opposite.

Shit! Was he stopping to ask her for directions? Double red lines, for Christ's sake!

The car had tinted windows rendering invisible those inside the vehicle, but she waved him on urgently.

'Don't stop here,' she shouted at the vehicle. 'You'll get arrested.'

5: The Interview

The car cruised slowly alongside her, and the driver's window slid down. A man in sunglasses and baseball cap called her over.

'Excusa me, can you helpa me, plis?'

Rosie walked over – a foreign visitor, poor sod. The armed response cops were probably on their way.

She leant down with her left hand on the window ledge. 'Do you know you're not allowed… hey!'

The man had snapped a handcuff-bracelet onto her left wrist. She pulled away but found the other bracelet secured to the car's roof grab handle.

'Listen to me, Rosie,' said the driver, no accent now. 'If you come willingly, you'll not be harmed. If you struggle my colleague here will sedate you and we'll take you anyway. Your choice. Make it now.'

Rosie noticed the passenger had got out and was coming around the front of the car. She allowed the tension to ease out of her, took a breath and said, 'Okay. First, who are you, and what do you want with me?'

The passenger spoke; tall - well over six foot, sunglasses and black cap, like the driver.

'We're friends, Rosie. Someone wants to talk to you, only it's a wee bit sensitive, hence the extreme measures.' As the man spoke, he reached inside the car and unlocked the cuff. Before she realised what was happening, found both her wrists cuffed in front of her. Her captor had a firm grip on the links - there was no getting away. With his free hand, her captor opened the rear door.

'Do you want to do this,' he asked politely. 'Or shall I?'

The Travel Agent

'Okay, alright, I'll get in. I just hope you can explain this to the cops when they stop you in about two minutes from now.'

The tall guy smiled, pushed her onto the back seat, followed in beside her and closed the door. The car squealed away, Rosie casting about left and right for the alerted police vehicles as the Insignia merged with the upriver traffic towards Lambeth Palace.

'You're hoping in vain, Rosie, said the tall man, the York Road cameras have all decided to break down for an hour. And now, I'm afraid it's blackout time.'

'Wha…'

Quick as a snake, he threw a hood over her head, loose and soft, but elasticated so it snapped tightly around her neck.

'Aaaargh - what the fuck?'

'For your own good as well as ours. You really don't want to know where we're going because that would make you an unacceptable risk. Is that clear or shall I spell it out?'

'N…no, that's clear. Can you at least tell me who you are?'

'Not now. Later maybe. Will you play nice if I take the cuffs off?'

Rosie grinned to herself at the irony. *Wise up, Mister, would I tell you otherwise.* She held her wrists up and felt his big capable hands take hold, felt the cuffs fall away.

'Thank you,' she said.

'Leave the hood alone, or they'll go back on, okay? Just sit back and relax for the next hour or so and we'll have you home in time for dinner with your Dad.'

5: The Interview

5/4

Firegate

Despite the peril of uncertainty and loss of control, Rosie found herself more curious than afraid. The men were undoubtedly professionals - the way they had anticipated so precisely her every move during her abduction on a city street was impressive. The tall guy had acted with such skill that any attempt at resistance would have come too late.

She had listened out for sounds she might recognise to try and work out where they were going, had attempted to gauge the car's speed, in stop-start traffic, or speeding along freeways. At one point a large jet had flown close overhead - Heathrow approach, maybe? Slough, perhaps.

But for the last twenty minutes they had been on a motorway; steady high speed, lane changes to overtake trucks, traffic on both sides. They could have been anywhere, travelling in any direction, a dozen motorways to choose from. Impossible to know. And the heavy beside her was giving nothing away. He had stopped responding entirely to her oblique questioning. Eventually, she just gave up and let her mind drift in pointless speculation.

She became so removed from reality in her dark world that it was a while before she noticed there was no longer any traffic noise. The car had slowed down and came to a gradual halt. There came a brief buzz outside, followed by the squeak and rattle of what sounded like a wheeled gate sliding open. The car moved forward again. The sounds changed, the grinding of tyres reflected from surrounding walls - a tunnel then, a tunnel going downwards.

The room was like a regular hotel room, but without windows or a bed. A spacious room. A settee and two armchairs, coffee table, big TV screen, dining table with chairs, beige carpet. Two steel thermos flasks stood on the sideboard - one labelled coffee, the other, hot water – along with a jug of milk and a sugar bowl. A box contained teabags of various flavours. Another had a selection of biscuits.

'All very civilized,' Rosie murmured, pouring herself a coffee. She sank into an armchair and waited; thought about getting out her Kindle, but would be unable to concentrate on fiction when the real-life drama was so close at hand.

However, Rosie did not have long to wait and gave a little start when the door clicked open.

'Good afternoon,' a rasping voice - a forty a day voice. 'Rosie, is it?

Rosie stood up, refusing to be intimidated. 'What?' she snapped. 'You're not sure you kidnapped the right person now?'

5: The Interview

The woman stopped and stared at Rosie a moment - a hard, humourless face unmitigated by any attempt at makeup - then walked over to the flasks on the sideboard. She even walked like a man. She was tall and rangy, could have been fifty or sixty, dark green jacket and skirt, black, no-nonsense shoes.

While the woman made herself a cup of tea, she spoke. 'You are Rosemary Winterbourne, born third of October 1986 at your Grandmother's house in Guildford. Your Mother was Margaret Winterbourne nee Brenton, now deceased. Your father is Peter Winterbourne, only he isn't your biological father, that was prob–'

'Where did you get all this?'

The woman sighed deeply and carried her tea and briefcase to the settee. 'I'm sorry if this has upset you, as I can see it has. Digging into your past was a necessary precaution, as was how you were brought here today.'

'Who are you exactly?'

'I can't tell you that, not yet - maybe not ever.'

'Yeah, right,' she said with a casualness that belied her anxiety. That last remark had sent icy fingers reaching down Rosie's spine, but maybe she was reading sinister intent where there was none.

'So, why am I here, can you at least tell me that?'

'You attended an interview this morning, and you passed muster. Consider this part-two of that process.'

Rosie stared at the woman suspiciously - her knowledge of the interview was convincing but not conclusively reassuring.

'You have a most extraordinary recall ability,' the woman went on. 'Three-and-a-half years ago you were given a sequence of three numbers. They were: 76091, 56023, and 56109. Am I right?'

'Mm, okay. So I'm here because … ?'

'You are here to be offered a place on a counter-insurgency training course.'

Rosie sighed. 'Okay, so, I kind of guessed that. But why couldn't they just have told me that at FCO this morning – like: "you have to be taken to a secret location blindfolded and meet some nameless people". I could have lived with that. Instead, your heavies accosted me in the street: I was handcuffed, threatened with sedation, and generally scared shitless.'

The woman was smiling now – a smile which sat somewhat unpleasantly on that severe countenance.

'Unfortunately, there is nobody in SIS who could have told you. We operate very much off-grid. If a stranger pulls up alongside and asks you politely to get in, what do you do? Probably run away while dialling 999 on your phone, correct? The way my two agents acted ensured minimum fuss and no witnesses.'

Rosie gaped. 'So, SIS doesn't know I'm here? Wherever here is.'

The woman shook her head regretfully.

'So, what happens to me if I don't want to play your games?'

'You will be taken home tonight and never hear from us again. You'll probably be offered a job as a cypher clerk at GCHQ. But we both know that is not going to happen, Rosie. Because everything I've learned about you in the last few months tells me you want what I have to offer with a passion. Otherwise, you would not have made it this far.'

5: The Interview

Rosie was silent for a long time, digesting the implications of what she was hearing. The woman was right; for Rosie, it was always about the perverse thrill of doing vital and dangerous work to protect the public without anybody ever knowing. It was not something she could easily explain, even to herself. The prospect of working and travelling undercover on important secret missions gave her the goosebumps - including right now.

'So, what will SIS think has happened to me if I end up working for you?'

'Let us just say, there are well-established protocols for secret secondments.'

Rosie relaxed, finished her coffee, pleased that her hand remained steady, feeling oddly relieved. The woman watched her intently, not speaking, not smiling now, but with a palpable air of expectancy that seemed to crackle around her. Suddenly Rosie realised the cause of her own sanguinity; because she, Rosie, now controlled this situation. Everything that had happened in the past four years had seemed to be pulling her toward some nebulous purpose. Now it stood clear before her. But it was not in her nature to submit without at least a token protest.

'So, you want me to come and work for your secretive little outfit, she sneered. 'Actually, your *illegal*, secretive little outfit because in a democracy that's what it amounts to. You must be pretty sure of yourself to have brought me here, expecting me to be grateful.'

But the woman seemed unfazed. 'I'm sure of *you*, Rosie, that's what matters. Yes, I do want you to work for me, but I'll never ask you to do anything illegal, at least, not without your full consent.'

Rosie sat back and stared at the ceiling, shaking her head and smiling mirthlessly. She sat forward and looked at the woman's brittle, unsmiling face. 'And what is it, exactly, that makes you so keen to recruit me?'

'Alright, one,' she began counting off on her fingers. Nails trimmed short, Rosie noticed, like her own, a slight nicotine stain on one index finger, no rings or wrist adornments, not even a watch.

'... a quick, analytical mind and high mental agility.

'Two, cool under pressure, which is supported by the citation for a Queen's Commendation - you drove a boat to intercept cartel drug-runners while under fire.'

Rosie gasped. 'That was seven years ago, and anyway, that citation was bullshit – we were shot at by a zoned-out junkie with a handgun from a bouncing speedboat.'

'Three, you display a natural empathy, able to read people and respond to best effect to get what you want.

'Four, a grasp of languages and an extraordinary memory - you taught yourself Spanish and became fluent inside a month. And you learned Arabic at University.

'Five, independence and proven self-reliance. Great job with those Albanians, by the way.'

'You know what? ...'

'Six, you're exceptionally fit with rudimentary judo skills.

'I hope you don't mind me saying …'

5: The Interview

'Finally - and here's the real curtain-raiser - you're an accomplished single-handed sailor with your own oceangoing yacht.'

'… I think you're full of shit.'

'Okay, I exaggerated. You're none of those things.'

Rosie stared at her. The woman stared back, po-faced, but a slow twinkle came into her eyes.

Rosie spluttered into laughter.

The woman looked quite human now, Rosie thought, almost attractive when she dropped that harsh veneer.

'At least you've got a sense of humour,' Rosie ventured, 'unlike those two *gamberros* of yours?'

'Gamb—? Oh, I see,' her laughter was a hoarse cackle, and Rosie wondered how many cigarettes it took to get such a fucked-up larynx.

'So, what you really want is me *and* my boat. Whatever for?'

The woman sighed, but the recent laughter still etched her face, 'All in good time. Do I take it you're interested?'

'And if I say yes, what happens next?'

She leaned forward, 'Rosie, understand this; recruiting you is not without risk for me - if I didn't have confidence in you, this interview wouldn't be happening. I need your answer before we can move on.'

'A girl called Sammy at the FCO told me not to take the red pill – is this what she meant?'

'I have no idea, but it's an apt allusion. Well?'

Rosie sipped her coffee, thinking hard, contemplating her clandestine future, and yes, the idea still excited her.

'Okay, when do I start?'

The Travel Agent

The woman beamed at her then, taking an envelope from her briefcase, became business-like.

'This is a letter from the Office for Security and Counter-Terrorism - where you had your interview this morning - thanking you for your application and offering you an aptitude test. You will be away for one month, after which you may or may not be offered a permanent post. This is your cover. OSCT is not your employer, I am. But it's close enough to the truth to explain your absence. You can tell friends and family you've applied for an intelligence monitoring position, basically a safe office job.'

Rosie took the envelope and studied it, her name and address, Her Majesty's Government postmark, dated yesterday. 'So, you knew I'd say yes?'

The woman flashed a smile then continued, 'There's a kit-list in the envelope, things you need to take with you. It doesn't mention electronic devices - that's because they're not allowed. Switch your personal phone off before you go and leave it at home. You still have a Blackphone I understand?'

Rosie nodded, patted her side pocket.

'Bring that with you, it will be reprogrammed. You can take a book or two, but paper only, no eReaders. You'll be picked up from your home at 6.30 on Sunday morning. Don't ask where you're going, and don't talk to your driver.

'From now on you'll refer to me as The Housekeeper and address me as Ma'am. You will never use your own name with colleagues. Your codename is *Galene*.'

'Galene? The Greek goddess of calm seas?'

'Let us hope so. Welcome to Firegate, Galene.'

5: The Interview

On the way home, Rosie was told she could remove her hood and found they were on the A3 leaving Guildford. The *gamberros* introduced themselves as Gauntlet (the tall one) and Hammer, the driver. They also welcomed her to Firegate and wished her luck on her training course.

The Travel Agent

5: The Interview

5/5

Farewell

Early the next morning, Rosie called Michael from her bedroom.

'Hey, how did it go?'

'Complete waste of time. But that's not why I'm calling. What are you doing tonight?'

'Nothing much. Watching a–'

'Fancy dinner at mine? My Dad's been wanting to meet you, and I've got an announcement to make.'

'An announcement? That sounds dramatic. You off to climb Everest?'

'Don't be an idiot. Are you on?'

'Sure, what time?'

'I'm driving down to Mullhaven this morning to work on *Pasha*, so I'll pick you up on my way home, say around six?'

'Great, see you then.'

Ending the call, Rosie hurried downstairs and found Dad in the garden tidying the borders.

'You get the mystery job?'

The Travel Agent

'Sort of. I'll tell you later. But what I want to tell you: Michael's coming to dinner tonight, so you get to meet him at last. Will you cook something special?'

'Delighted, my dear. Tell you what, pork tenderloin stuffed with haggis ... Er, the lad's not Jewish is he?'

'No, that's perfect, we'll get some wine on the way home, got to go.'

'Later then, drive steady.'

'Always. Love you, Dad.'

'You too, Sweetheart.'

Getting in the jeep, Rosie gripped the steering wheel and grinned. *'Galene,'* she murmured and found the sound of her codename curiously pleasing.

Michael was waiting outside his apartment door when she drew up in the jeep.

'Sorry I'm late,' she said as he climbed in and reached for his seat belt. 'Friday traffic.'

'Get the boat sorted?'

She pulled away and accelerated down the street, negotiated a badly parked truck, then turned right on the Cobbingden road before answering.

'Yeah, bills all paid. Still got the varnishing to finish on the coachroof rails.'

'Well I'm free Tuesday, want me to come down and lend a hand?'

She cleared her throat, meaningfully, 'I'm not going to be there - I was rather hoping you'd be available to finish it for me next week. Do you mind?'

'Why, where are you off… oh, is this the big announcement?'

She nodded, 'Something like that. So, can you do it? You'll have my jeep.'

5: The Interview

'Wow, that'll be a first! Is the world about to end?'

'You'll have her for a month. Just take good care of her. She's insured for any driver, so you're covered.'

'Come on then, out with it.'

'You'll have to wait. My Dad doesn't know anything yet either, so I'll tell you both over dinner.'

Despite her business-like manner and outward sanguinity, Rosie had the uneasy feeling she was about to jump into the deep end of a *very* deep pool.

EPISODE SIX

The Training Course

6: The Training Course

The Travel Agent

6/1

Departure

Sunday morning. The car came at 6.30 - a white Octavia with a taxi sign on the roof. Rosie felt as if she were leaving a part of herself behind. And in a way she was. For Rosie Winterbourne, after this day, would become Galene. She would return a different person.

Last night had been hard; hard for Dad too. After Michael had left in the jeep, she had Rosie sat down with her father and told it all. Because there had to be somebody in her life she could confide in, or else the pressure of maintaining a crypto-existence would become unbearable. Sod the Official Secrets Act - this was her Dad.

With a final hug, she picked up her rucksack and walked quickly to the cab and slid into the back, waving and smiling sadly at Dad as the car pulled away.

The driver was a small man, perhaps in his seventies. His wizened face stared at her briefly from the rear-

6: The Training Course

view mirror, bony knuckles gripping the wheel at ten and two. Rosie's cheery 'Good Morning' won only a disapproving scowl.

The car headed north then west, roughly in Basingstoke's direction but avoiding the main trunk routes that would considerably reduce the journey-time. Rosie had brought along a Val McDermid paperback filched from Dad's bookshelf. But she found herself unable to concentrate for long. The excitement of a fabulous new career and anticipation of a tough month ahead vied for supremacy in her supercharged imaginings.

The car was gliding along a single-track road somewhere on Salisbury Plain. It suddenly struck her that she was in a car with a stranger and had no idea where they were going.

'You're not a real taxi driver, are you?' she ventured slyly at the wrinkled brow that was all she could see of the driver's face in the mirror.

He glanced up then, a sharp, ice-blue stare, but made no reply.

Rosie sighed. 'So, can I at least know where we're going?'

'An airfield.' was the terse reply. The oddly high-pitched tone was as sharp as the old guy's stare and brooked no further questions.

But Rosie was undeterred. 'So, I'm going on by plane, I guess. Where to, exactly?'

'Sparta, and no more questions, Miss. I'm not supposed to talk to you.'

Sparta!

The Peloponnese? Surely not. Or was Sparta just another codename for some isolated hideaway in

The Travel Agent

England? She decided to go with that; the idea of flying to Greece was too ludicrous.

Twenty minutes passed, Rosie watching for gaps in the high hedgerow to catch a glimpse of some clue, some landmark that might indicate where they were. The car slowed, and the hedge gave way to a high chain-link fence. Turning right, the old man stopped the car in front of a pair of closed gates, each bearing a garish red sign:

> DANGER
> Army Firing Range
> Unexploded Ordnance
> Keep Out

The driver got out and unlocked a colossal padlock, allowing the tall gates to swing ponderously inwards.

'Really?' breathed Rosie, as the driver got back in.

'Long as we stick to the track,' he assured her. 'Wander off and—' he mimed a mushroom with his hands, 'Kerboom!'

So, there was humour in the old iceball after all.

The short airstrip - a concrete rectangle in the middle of a broad expanse of moorland festooned with bright yellow gorse bushes - was another mile or so inside the range. On it stood a ridiculously tiny aeroplane, a four-seater, for Christ sake, with a single, flimsy-looking propeller! A man in white coveralls stood alongside the plane watching their approach.

Within ten minutes the Cessna 150 was accelerating towards the end of the rapidly dwindling airstrip, Rosie seated rigidly next to the pilot, gripping the overhead

6: The Training Course

grab bar with white knuckles. Just when she thought they were going to plough into the yellow furze, the aircraft nosed smoothly skyward, and the bushes fell away beneath.

As they climbed into the cloudless sky, Rosie watched the pilot adjust his controls, throttling back slightly, checking instruments, and levelling out at two-thousand feet. He then banked sharply to starboard before steadying on course. Rosie glanced at the compass: they were heading north. Okay, not Greece, then.

'How long is the flight?' she said into the intercom.

'About three hours - you feeling okay?'

'Mm, fine thanks.'

She scanned his instrument panel and located the GPS; ground speed 110 knots. So, 330 miles.

'That puts us in Scotland, right?'

'It would if we were taking the direct route. We need to detour around the Manchester and Leeds Traffic Zones - then we'll be heading for the Northumbrian wilderness. Ever been?'

'No. Wilderness, eh? Sounds kind of remote - crap nightlife, I suppose?'

His laugh was a jarring sound in the headphones, 'Doubt you'll have any energy to spare for night-clubbing. Yeah, it's remote, about as remote and desolate as it gets anywhere south of the border.'

It was just after 2pm when the destination came into view: a grass landing strip barely visible amid a vast, dark and brooding pine forest. The pilot brought the Cessna down close to the treetops, and as he circled the small clearing, Rosie saw an old-style Landrover next to the grass strip. She gasped as the pilot suddenly

The Travel Agent

banked and then, throttling back, threw the plane it into a horribly steep dive at the grass strip. Barely clearing treetops, the plane flared out and thumped down heavily, bouncing twice and then rumbling along to the end of the strip.

'Can we go back?' said Rosie. 'I think I left my stomach up there.'

'Always a bit tight, landing here,' said the Pilot. 'Sorry, I should have warned you.' His supercilious grin looked anything but sorry.

Rosie gave him a sour stare and removed her headphones. She opened her door and climbed out just as the Landrover pulled up alongside. 'Thanks for the ride,' she shouted, sliding her backpack out of the rear door. 'Fly home safe.'

As the plane trundled away, a short, stocky man wearing a brown lab coat climbed out of the vehicle and opened the tailgate for her bag.

'Hi,' she said brightly.

'Hello.' He sounded nervous, ill at ease, offered no handshake and made no eye-contact. He seemed to be looking somewhere over Rosie's left shoulder. She thought of Doctor Frankenstein's assistant, Igor.

'And where are we going?' she said, sliding onto the front passenger seat.

'Camp Sparta,' said the driver, looking straight ahead as they pulled away.

'Oh, *Camp* Sparta. And how far is that from here?'

'Five-point-seven-three kilometres.'

Rosie sighed and sat back and wondered about her creepy driver. Was it too late to change her mind? As if in reply, there came a sudden roar outside as the Cessna took to the sky once more.

6: The Training Course

Steady girl. You can do this.

6.2

Camp Sparta

The driver aimed the car at the clearing's edge, where a line of silver birch trees fronted the dark tumble of dense pine beyond. A narrow track opened the route up into the forest. The Landrover bumped and rocked its way upwards on the unmade surface for what seemed an age until at last, the trees thinned and then opened onto a grassy plateau. Igor stopped the car beside a long, narrow, single-story building of ancient brick and timber. Behind this stood a vast, windowless structure of olive green, corrugated steel.

'Is this it, then?'

'This is Camp Sparta,' confirmed Igor in his odd monotone. 'And this is called the Lodge.'

Rosie jumped out and retrieved her rucksack from the back then stood for a moment surveying the Lodge while Igor fiddled with a bunch of keys at the door.

Ivy snaked up the black timber frames and spread into the narrow eaves, while patches of green and yellow lichen stained the overweathered brickwork; a

6: The Training Course

smell of leaf-mould hung in the still air. What stood out most, were the three windows evenly spaced along the wall on either side of the door. Their faux-wood frames and double-glazing seemed monstrously incongruous in the dilapidated but oddly romantic Lodge.

'Home for the next thirty days,' she murmured.

'If you last that long,' came a growl from behind her.

Rosie turned to find an Olympian figure standing by the Landrover. Wearing white shorts and white tee-shirt, he was a man of middling height, but bulging with such latent power, it was hard for Rosie not to stare. He had a face carved from granite, eyes of ice-blue, cold and penetrating.

'Go on in,' muscleman ordered. 'Turn left, and down the passageway - yours is the end room. Dump your bag and change into running gear. *Move.*'

Determined not to be intimidated she said, 'And you are?'

'Gardener,' he snapped. 'Your trainer.' He motioned her on with an index finger, 'Go on, in you go.'

Rosie turned to find the door open. Igor was nowhere to be seen.

'Who was the joker in the brown coat?' she asked.

'Don't worry, you'll soon get used to Moth.'

She sighed and picked up her bag. The door was out of step with the rustic old building: the mortice locks top and bottom, the same heavy-duty veneer as the window frames. Rosie entered a passageway where soft light filtered from glass ovoids in the ceiling. Despite a faint smell of disuse, the interior looked recently remodelled. A new-looking rope-fibre carpet covered the floor, while the walls were smooth and

The Travel Agent

painted a neutral shade of beige. The passageway led to the back of the building then split left and right to form a 'T'. The rear wall was windowless.

Rosie's door was at the very end, but since Gardener hadn't followed her in, she checked out the first room. It was a kitchen cum dining area, clean and utilitarian, all shiny steel and white wood: fridge-freezer, dishwasher, cooking range with two ovens – enough to cater for an army. Plenty of light from the two large windows once the blinds were opened. Red quarry-tiled floor. An electric kettle. A nice cuppa was on her mind. The three other doors before her own - numbered six to eight - were locked. Rosie's door was number nine.

Her room was, well, spartan. In contained a single-size bed against the far wall under the window, cream-coloured mattress with a fresh bedsheet and a thin quilted duvet folded on top of a single pillow. With a resigned sigh, Rosie dumped her bag on the floor and sat on the bed - at least the mattress was firmly sprung. She reached over and turned open the Venetian blinds to let in more light and took in the bedside table with reading lamp, the small fitted wardrobe, the chest of drawers.

And a door.

Rosie stood, stepped forward and opened it. An on-suite bathroom, tiny and again, windowless. She pulled on the light cord to reveal a walk-in shower, a sink with a mirror, and a toilet. All in all, she had lived in worse places.

'Hope you're feeling fit, Galene?' It was Gardener, standing at her door.

'Already? I've only just got here.'

6: The Training Course

'It's not a holiday.' he said, walking away, 'Outside in running gear in two minutes. And take that stud out of your ear – no jewellery allowed.'

'Shit,' she muttered, pulling open her backpack, 'there goes my cup of tea.' Still muttering, Rosie took out the offending stud, put it in her pack, and then changed hurriedly into shorts and tee-shirts.

'Two minutes warm-up,' Gardener said as she came out into hot sunshine, 'then we go.'

Rosie looked around the site; in one direction, the track they had driven up leading down to the forest, everywhere else was scrubland leading uphill to a few exposed rocks.

'Go? Go where?'

He gave her a cold stare. 'You don't get to ask questions. Warm-up, go!'

'Blimey, you're no fun,' she muttered, catching her ankle behind to begin her usual stretching routine.

She had barely finished when Gardener said, 'Right, that's enough, let's go.'

The trainer slung on a rucksack and began jogging up the hill. Rosie ran to catch up, then fell in alongside, breathing steadily, finding the pace well inside her limits. The physical part of this course was going to be a walk in the park. Rosie was pleased when, after about twenty minutes, Gardener increased the pace. He led them into an area of woodland, dodging around trees and jumping narrow streams. Reaching a wider watercourse, they turned downhill where the fir trees crowded close. A thick carpet of pine-needles was springy underfoot. The sharp perfume of pine mingled with the odour of fungus was not unpleasant. And now there was a track to follow,

The Travel Agent

Gardener increased the pace once more. And just when Rosie thought she had had enough, the trainer pushed her harder.

They had been running for about ninety minutes, Rosie now beginning to flag, soaking wet, her breathing ragged and laboured, calf muscles burning. And now the downhill sprint was starting to tell on her thigh muscles. At last, Gardener began to slow and brought them to a halt at a gate in a high fence. Producing a key, he unlocked the gate and shepherded her through.

'Follow the track,' he said, pulling chain back around the gate, 'I'll catch you up.'

Ten minutes after catching up, Gardener slowed the pace and then pulled up by a big fallen tree. He produced two bottles of water from his rucksack. 'Well done,' he said, handing her a bottle, 'you're fitter than I thought.'

Rosie felt anything but fit: head pounding, pulling in great lungs full of air - for a moment, she could not even take a drink. And worst of all, Gardener was not even breathing hard.

'Take five minutes,' he said, 'drink some water. I'm going to take a piss over there behind those bushes.'

Gratefully, Rosie sank down onto the fallen tree and shortly began sipping her water and wondered what the hell she had got herself into. Somewhere nearby, she heard running water and was tempted by the idea of dangling her naked feet in a cold stream. Five minutes passed, and Gardener had not returned. Ten minutes, and she began to get uneasy.

6: The Training Course

'Gardener?' she called in the direction he had gone. No reply, just the sighing of the breeze in the trees and sporadic birdsong. She walked towards the bushes.

'Gardener, you okay?'

She walked around the bushes where he had supposedly gone to relieve himself, then not seeing him, scouted around in a circle back to the fallen tree. Then she saw he had left his rucksack behind. She sat down, thinking. Was this some sort of test? Had he left her to find her own way back? She could think of no other reason for his sudden disappearance. The route they had taken had changed direction many times, and blindly following her trainer, Rosie had not really noticed. Except for their general direction of travel: roughly southwest. But without knowing the starting point, she had absolutely no idea where she was.

Rosie reached down and lifted the rucksack onto the trunk beside her. After a moment more, she unzipped it and peered inside. The trainee pulled out a plastic shopping bag and was about to open it when something else in the rucksack caught her eye. Laying the shopping bag aside, she reached in again and pulled out a pair of high-heeled sandals in white leather and a petite matching handbag. Mystified, she set them aside and drew out a folded sheet of notepaper and a small, laminated map. Opening the note, she skimmed what was written there, then stared at the message in bewilderment.

'Fuck ... Off!' she breathed.

6/3

Gadfly

Rosie reread the note, slowly this time, shaking her head in disbelief. She opened the shopping bag and found clean panties, a silver-grey cotton dress and a short blue jacket. The dinky handbag - not at all her style - contained a pink lipstick, a vanity-mirror, a comb, a handy-pack of tissues, and a purse containing forty pounds and some loose change. And a small lady's watch which told her it was now ten past four.

The last three items in the rucksack were a paperback anthology of short stories, two high-protein cereal bars and - almost predictably - a pack of wet-wipes.

Rosie sagged and put her head in her hands. She was hot and stinking and knackered from what must have been at least a twenty-mile run. And now a six-mile hike through a forest to turn up at a restaurant in this rather fetching outfit looking fresh as a daisy?

'Hell's bells!'

6: The Training Course

Rosie was more tired than she could ever remember feeling. It was twenty past six, and she had reached a place where the stream disappeared into a culvert under a road. The embankment here was overhung with dense elder brush; good cover to transform herself from a filthy, sweat-streaked wreck into a slinky Mata Hari.

However, the intriguing image soon faded as attempting to sit down on the grassy bank her thigh-muscles turned to jelly, and she landed painfully on her bottom. Even taking off her trainers and socks was agony to her tortured muscles. Grunting like an old woman, she shuffled out of her shorts and lowered her feet into the pebbled streambed, sighing ecstatically as the cold, shallow flow enveloped them. She tugged off her vest and began her improvised ablutions, carefully cleaning every part of her exhausted body, finding the caress of the perfumed wipes oddly sensual, reviving, cooling her skin and even easing some of the pain.

Ten minutes later, Rosie stood at the roadside, dressed for dinner except for her trainers that she had put on to climb the embankment. She now flipped them off, scrubbed her feet with the remaining wipe, and stepped into the dainty white sandals. Dropping the muddy trainers into the shopping bag, Rosie stuffed everything into the rucksack then set off down the empty road to find the hotel. The stiffness in her legs, combined with the unfamiliarity of elevated heels, gave her an ungainly and robotic gait.

The Reservoir Hotel overlooked a large body of water. Several expensive cars were the exclusive occupiers of the carpark. Her jeep would have been

The Travel Agent

entirely out of place here. Passing through the front entrance, Rosie headed for the Ladies.

Dressing under the trees, Rosie had not thought much of the outfit Gardener had provided. But checking her appearance now in the full-length mirror, she concluded it was not bad. A little too spicy for her liking, perhaps - it made her legs look long. She applied a touch of lippy, ran the comb through her hair, washed her hands, and she was ready.

Rosie asked for a table for one in a discreet corner. She kept her head firmly front and centre as she followed the waiter through the half-full room, acutely aware of eyes following her. Yes, perhaps the outfit was a little too racy.

She sat with her back to the wood-panelled wall where she could see most of the other diners.

The waiter handed her a menu. 'Can I bring you a drink, Madam?'

'A glass of house red and some water, please.'

Taking stock of the other diners, Rosie met a hostile glare from a woman two tables away. She quickly broke eye contact and studied the menu. Some jealous wife who had caught her husband ogling, no doubt. Not a good start.

As she scanned down the dinner menu, Rosie noticed her hands were trembling and felt a cold sweat beginning to break out on her brow. Signs of low blood sugar: it seemed like hours since the last of the cereal bars. The single slice of toast this morning at breakfast seemed a hundred years ago.

Rosie also felt terribly alone. Solitude on her boat at sea was one thing, but here, surrounded by strangers,

6: The Training Course

people out of her social experience, was depressing beyond words.

Come on, Rosie – don't fall at the first hurdle.

Glancing up, she saw the waiter returning with her drinks and quickly searched the starters menu for something quick and easy.

The waiter placed her drinks carefully at their assigned stations, 'Are you ready to order, Madam?'

'Er, what's the Soup of the Day?'

'Cream of Asparagus. It comes with bloomer bread and–'

'Yes, I'll have that, and don't go away.'

Rosie flipped to the Specials page and zoomed-in on the first item that looked edible:

'Er, the Butteryhaugh Roast Duck with Blueberry and Juniper Jus. A bit of a mouthful but yes, that sounds great. Thank you.'

As the waiter left, she took a slurp of her wine. It felt warm and reviving, but insufficient to sate her gnawing hunger. She needed to concentrate, but hypoglycaemia was sapping her ability to think clearly.

She glanced around the room and found only one set of eyes watching her: a lazy smile from a man of around seventy. Rosie glared at him until he looked away, then snatched up two sugar cubes from the cruet and popped them into her mouth. The taste of sugar melting on her tongue was sheer heaven; it was all she could do to not close her eyes, or worse, roll them up into her head. The relief was immediate, and gradually, the shakes subsided. Her brain began to function once more.

The Travel Agent

Rosie took out her book, opened it at a random page and began to read. She was a girl on her own, not wanting company, happy with her book. However, after a few minutes, stifling yawns as the words became blurred and unreadable, Rosie realised she was becoming dangerously tired. The arrival of the soup saved her. She set the book aside and began eating.

Looking around while eating felt more natural - what everyone did. Rosie began by giving names to the other diners to help her recall later when she would eliminate the unlikely ones and mark up those who seemed off or out of place. This was a new experience for Rosie - Gardener's terse note had contained no advice on how to proceed.

As a Triage Officer, Rosie knew the identity of her mark in advance. There was a description to work with, and a convenient place to meet him or her. And more importantly, she could be herself, Rosie Winterbourne, student. Here, she had to identify him or her from body-language alone while acting out an unfamiliar role. Impossible!

Rosie finished her meal and sat back with a satisfied sigh, then catching the waiter's eye, signalled for the bill. It was now 8.40 and 'Lily', three tables to Rosie's left, looked to be getting ready to leave.

The other candidate on her shortlist of two, MG (Mister Grumpy), was nearing the end of his meal. He had a female partner, but that did not rule him out.

Nothing much to look at, Mister Grumpy was thirtyish, short dark hair, open-necked blue and white striped shirt (short sleeves, no tattoos), grey slacks and brogue-style shoes. What marked MG out for Rosie was his fastidious focus on his partner. He seemed

6: The Training Course

inordinately attentive, with an apparent disregard for his surroundings. He was a man in a vacuum, while his lady-friend seemed always to be looking around for an escape route, clearly uncomfortable with MG's overbearing attention. This to Rosie seemed to qualify him as the possible mark, the woman merely a reluctant prop.

There were quite a few other occupied tables, mostly couples of varying ages. But all, it appeared to Rosie, were behaving naturally, chatting and drinking and laughing. There were a couple of twenty-something guys sitting just beyond Lily who were probably a couple.

A strikingly good-looking young woman - of possible Caribbean origin - sat alone at the far corner of the room. Her table was littered with what looked like her business accoutrements: phone, tablet, notebook, pen, and throughout her meal she had been texting, tapping and writing with such frenetic industry that Rosie had long since ruled her out.

But Lily - so named for the flower-pendant she wore over her roll-neck sweater - was looking good for the mark. She was an attractive forty-something, light brown hair worn in a neat bob, white trousers tucked into knee-length suede boots.

Lily had arrived a short time after Rosie's roast duck and had flowed into the room. She moved so gracefully into her seat that her performance seemed practised, even rehearsed. For a woman alone, she seemed somehow too calm, too relaxed: she might have been in her own sitting room. Once, Rosie had caught Lily looking her way: a passing smile that held a hint of amusement, a knowing kind of smile that

The Travel Agent

Rosie found disconcerting. And suspicious. Yes, Lily was the mark, the joker in the pack, she was sure.

The waiter arrived at Rosie's table with her bill, which she paid there and then, ready to follow Lily. MG and his partner seemed to be having a spat, whispering angrily at one another, unpleasant but certainly not uncommon behaviour.

Lily stood to leave, and Rosie looked away towards the entrance to let her pass but then was startled when ...

'Hello, all alone, then?'

Lily! Standing by Rosie's table gazing down at her with a look of such directness that Rosie felt her blood rising hotly. She knew at once she had made a terrible mistake.

'Er, no, I'm meeting someone,' she improvised, looking at her watch. 'He should be here soon.'

Lily leaned closer with an air of mischief, her voice low and husky. 'I think you're adorable. If your beau doesn't show, come and find me at the bar. I have a room here.' She gave a brazen wink and walked on.

As Lily's elegant figure sashayed out of the room, Rosie reflected that in other circumstances, she might have been tempted by the audacious proposition. Even now, as she forced her attention back to her mission, the thrill of the encounter continued to stir her lower regions.

With the vampish lesbian ruled out, Rosie turned her attention back to MG, who was already standing impatiently waiting for his partner to gather up her coat and handbag. Rosie waited until they had left the room, then picked up her rucksack and followed. She stopped at the hotel entrance and watched the couple

6: The Training Course

traverse the carpark to a gleaming red Mercedes. No. It couldn't be MG either. Now what?

'Not so easy is it, Galene?'

Rosie whipped around and came face to face with a stunning coffee-coloured girl. It was the woman who had been using the hotel restaurant as her office, a bulky business bag slung on her bare shoulder.

Rosie opened her mouth to speak.

'Shh, not a word,' said the girl, walking quickly down the steps. 'Come on.'

The woman led Rosie around the back of the hotel to a red Honda CR-V SUV.

'Yes, it was me,' the girl said when they were inside the car, 'The last person you suspected. I'm Gadfly.'

Gadfly started the car and moved out of the carpark. Rosie was too bewildered by the rapid turn of events - at her failure remotely to have considered this beautiful biracial girl as her mark - to say a word.

'Let me guess,' said Gadfly, 'Gardener told you he needed a pee and left you in the woods.'

'Mm. And I screwed up.'

'Don't worry,' Gadfly said soothingly, 'You weren't expected to get this one right. But you will. Now, let's get you back to the Lodge so you can crash – you must be shattered.'

At least Rosie had been right about one thing; there was a faint but detectable West Indian accent there.

6/4

The Tunnel

An urgent banging jerked Rosie into dazed wakefulness. She searched her fuzzy brain for a clue as to where she was and how she came to be in a strange bed.

'Galene! Briefing in twenty minutes!'

Gardener's brusque tones brought her back to the now. She wondered again if he was even human, maybe he was an android. If so, his protocol module needed an upgrade.

Dawn light fell in grey strips through the blinds, her backpack in the middle of the floor, clothing spilling out where she had rummaged for a t-shirt to sleep in. The silver-grey dress and blue top draped carelessly over a chair.

After the drive back up to Sparta with Gadfly, Rosie had returned to her room so exhausted she had the energy barely to make up her bed. Undressing and collapsing onto it, she had fallen immediately into a deep and untroubled sleep.

6: The Training Course

She checked her watch and groaned—five a.m. Rolling stiffly out of bed, Rosie hobbled to the bathroom for a long, hot shower.

As the high-pressure water pounded Rosie back to life, she found herself humming a tune. A random earworm – no idea where it came from. Then she realised it was one of Dad's favourites from the sixties. Delighted at how the lyrics summed up her feelings, she began singing the words:

> We gotta get outta this place,
> If it's the last thing we ever do,
> We gotta get outta this place,
> Girl, there's a better life for–

'If that's how you feel, Galene, you can go home today.'

Rosie whipped aside the shower curtain to find Gadfly, grinning. She handed Rosie a towel. 'Come on, we need to get started. No time for daydreaming.'

'Jesus, is there no privacy in this place?' Rosie said, taking the towel.

'Don't worry, the men won't come in here. I just wanted to chat about last night while you get dressed. I've washed your running strip - it's laid out on your bed. Then we can join the others for a briefing over breakfast.'

Rosie quickly dried herself, then stepped out into her bedroom, pleased to note that her muscles seemed to have lost their earlier stiffness. Her visitor had taken a seat on the chair where the dinner outfit had been, said outfit now stuffed into the bin with the white sandals.

The Travel Agent

'You won't be needing those again, I'm sure you'll be glad to learn.'

Rosie slipped into her clean shorts and pulled on her singlet, then went to the bin. 'I quite like the sandals,' she said, pulling them out.

Gadfly shrugged, 'Take them, with our compliments. So, how did last night go, do you think?'

Rosie plonked herself on her bed and sighed heavily, 'I was completely hopeless, didn't have a clue what I was doing. Got the whole thing wrong−' she let out a guffaw, 'only succeeded in picking up a dyke ... oh sorry, you're not−'

Gadfly laughed, 'No, I'm certainly not. But thanks for asking. Now, tell me who was in that room and what criteria made you reach the conclusions you did.'

Gadfly listened without comment as Rosie described, table by table, each of last night's diners, recollecting her thought processes at the time.

Reaching the end of her inventory, Rosie grinned ruefully. 'You looked like some buzzed-up high-flyer getting ready for a Monday morning business meeting, so obviously, it never occurred to me you were the mark.'

'As I told you last night, those skills will come. But what you need to work at is your own cover. You gave a couple of tells that would have made you the observed rather than the observer, and that's a dangerous position to be in.'

'Tells?'

'Gestures, expressions, body language. Didn't they train you about that at Mercury One?'

Rosie shook her head, 'Our training was pretty basic.'

6: The Training Course

'Tells are what betray your cover to anyone with reason to think they were being watched or followed. From the self-conscious way that you entered the room, not daring to look at anybody, to your show of reading while taking sneaky looks around the room. And the rucksack? Uh-uh. You should have checked that in at the cloakroom.'

Rosie winced. 'Pretty crap spy, eh?'

Gadfly nodded, but smiling, said, 'Yeah, pretty crap. In a few weeks, though, you'll look back at this and laugh, trust me.' She stood up as Rosie finished lacing up her trainers. 'Now, let's get breakfast and get to work.'

The two men were already seated at the table, Gardener halfway through a mess of bacon and eggs, Moth spooning up milky heaps from a bowl of muesli. Trays offering a wide selection of comestibles lined the kitchen worktop: fried and poached eggs, bacon, beans, tomatoes, warm croissants, a rack of toast, preserves in miniature jars, a flask of coffee, and various fruit juices.

'Wow! All this food for four people?'

Gadfly tapped a chart on the wall, where each offering in the trays was marked with its calorific value.

'Two-thousand calories minimum for breakfast, another two-thousand at dinner tonight, two-hundred in fresh fruit and energy bars to get you through the day.'

Seeing Rosie's look of horror, she smiled, 'Don't worry, Galene, nobody gets fat at Camp Sparta.'

The Travel Agent

'Who cooks all this stuff?' Rosie said, sitting down with her 900-calorie plate of beans on toast and two poached eggs.

'We all do,' said Moth, dribbling milk down his chin. He pointed at Rosie with his spoon. 'Except you.'

Moth still seemed unable to do eye-contact.

'Why am I excused, I *can* cook, you know?'

'Because you'll be busy,' grunted Gardener without looking up from his meal.

'For you, and one of us two' explained Gadfly, nodding towards Gardener, 'each day starts with a fifteen-mile run before breakfast. Today is the only exception.'

'Why all the running?' asked Rosie. 'I mean, it's not as if I'm unfit or anything. I thought I was here to learn counter-terrorism.'

'The daily runs serve two essential purposes,' said Gadfly. 'First, to build up your stamina for the physical demands on your body that come later in the course. But most importantly, to prepare your muscles and joints to perform in ways they've never done before: in martial arts and self-defence.'

'It's not all running, see,' Gardener added. 'There'll be stops to work on your upper-body strength and your ability to process data and solve problems while under physical stress.'

'Okay,' said Rosie, 'so when do we get to the interesting stuff, you know, the spook training?'

Gardener blew down his nose, shook his head despairingly but said nothing.

'Well for a start,' Gadfly said, 'we don't use that term in Firegate – we're not SIS. But to answer your

6: The Training Course

question: development of your cognitive, analytical and field-craft skills will form around 75% of the course. It will run alongside the physical training and conversational Arabic. We begin this morning with a tour of the Training Hall - just as soon as you've eaten another 1100 calories.'

6/5

The Wall

Invariably for Rosie, Code Red passed without too much fuss; a spot of blood, slip in a tampon, life goes on. Until now. The pains started on the Tuesday morning of her third week after the Daily Run with Gadfly - a grinding ache with excruciating spasms deep in her lower abdomen.

'You're looking pale,' Gadfly said, taking her aside after breakfast. 'Are you okay?'

Rosie shrugged, 'I'll be fine, a touch of the ragtime blues, that's all.'

'Ah, thought so.'

'Stupid, really. I never get it this bad. So *painful!*'

'Menstrual cramps. It's the change in diet and intensive training. I'll get you something that'll help.'

The dam broke the following morning as Rosie sat on the toilet.

'What the hell is happening to me?' she muttered, scowling into the toilet bowl. At least, with the discharge of so much clotting blood, the dragging pain

6: The Training Course

had eased, but now she felt nauseous. The Daily Run with Gardener this morning was not a pleasant prospect.

A slight drizzle had been falling throughout the night, leaving the fir trees sparkling with diamonds in the sunrise. The five-mile warmup-run passed with its usual silence. Rosie had long since ceased expecting any human warmth from the cold cyborg.

A dull ache had started up in her lower back, adding to her general feeling of unwellness. When Gardener pulled up and ordered: 'Right, give me a ton,' Rosie's mood was already verging on rebelliousness.

Nevertheless, she dropped obediently onto the damp forest floor, the matted pine-needles giving slightly under her palms and wafting up the sharp scent of pine. Rosie took a deep breath, then began a hundred push-ups, a number she had grown into from twenty on the first day until a hundred seemed too easy and left her itching to do more. But today was different. After ten, she began to feel a deadening in her shoulders, unusual tensions and protestations from her abdominals.

'Three-five-one-seven,' Gardener called.

She filed the number away with the twelfth sit-up, a technique she had practised until it was automatic. It was merely an extended way of using her memory, just a development a skill she had had all her life. By fifty, Rosie had four more random numbers matched with stroke-numbers.

At the upstroke of sit-up number seventy-four, the will to continue finally deserted her, lethargy numbing her nervous system and draining the strength from her musculature.

The Travel Agent

'Keep going, Galene, fight it, FIGHT IT!'

'Sod off!' Rosie gasped.

Then, without warning, her muscles turned to liquid, and her face flattened onto cool pine-needles. Vaguely the thought penetrated that Gardener's attempt at motivation had seemed to contain a trace of emotion. But Rosie was past caring.

'Just−fuck−off!' she gasped, 'I can't do this anymore.'

Suddenly his granite face was down next to hers. For the first time, the light from those cold eyes seemed to soften. 'If you give up now, you go home today, is that what you want, Galene, failure?'

Rosie rolled over and sat up, pulled up her knees and hung her head between them. Gardener stood up, 'You've hit the wall, Rosie, but you can get over it. You really want to fail?'

'Yeah, I want to go home.' she looked up. Gardener stood with legs apart, staring down at her like she was a piece of broken machinery he could not figure out how to fix.

'You were right,' she said, 'I'm not good enough for this.'

Gardener hunched down in front of her and frowned. 'When did I say that?'

'Gadfly told me, of course, who else here talks to me like I'm a person? Anyway, she thinks the same, and I get the same vibes from Moth, so ... well, I guess you're all three right. I'm just so hopeless.' She hung her head again.

The trainer reached over and touched her elbow, 'C'mon, let's take a walk back.'

6: The Training Course

For a mile or so, they walked in silence, until Gardener said unexpectedly, 'I have absolutely no idea why you're here. You're The Housekeeper's pet project, and she's keeping your mission under wraps. That's the way we work. But I have to tell you, Rosie, it normally takes at least three months to get an agent into shape. Even with the appropriate background, which you certainly don't have. That was my objection, but it was overruled. So, we are where we are.'

Rosie did not speak, found herself floating on a rare cloud of happiness. She would be going home, giving up this ridiculous dream of being a glamourous undercover agent tracking down the bad guys and keeping the world safe. The pressure was off - normality could now return. The cyborg had just called her *Rosie*, hadn't he? So, Galene was a dead duck. Welcome back, Rosie.

'As for Moth,' Gardener continued, 'well, he doesn't really have a view, at least not one that he shares. You must have noticed he's quite a way up there on the spectrum. It's true. When you first came here, I didn't think you'd make it. But–' He snapped his fingers, 'Fifth Number?'

'Three-seven-five.' said Rosie, without thinking. She glanced sideways at Gardener and found him grinning. He looked almost human.

'So, I can remember stuff. I always could. Hardly a qualification for superspy.'

He laughed then, which almost made her miss her step.

'I'm sure you were never going to be that, but you know–' He lifted the sleeve of his tee-shirt to reveal a livid bruise in blue and yellow on his shoulder. 'That flying kick you delivered last week still hurts.'

Rosie let out a tearful guffaw. He had kept quiet about that, which had reinforced her view of him as impervious to feeling.

'If you'd followed through like you should have,' he continued, 'instead of standing there gawping, I could have been in real trouble.'

'Yeah, right.'

He shook his head, then stopped walking and took her by the elbow, turning her to face him.

'I'm not patronising you - I'm telling you how things stand. This morning you hit the wall, the same wall nearly everyone hits on this course at some stage. What matters now is what you do about it.'

'What I do about it?' she snarled back, tears of rage blurring her vision. 'What I do about it is go home, that's all.' She pulled her elbow from his grasp, 'I just want to go home,' she sobbed and walked on.

Presently, Gardener was alongside her once more, but maintained a tactful, and, it felt to Rosie, an empathic silence.

Rosie was so absorbed in herself, she failed at first to notice when Gardener had dropped behind. Turning, she saw him standing looking up into the trees. He silenced her with a finger to his lips and beckoned her back.

'Up there,' he whispered, pointing to the top spread of a tall pine tree.

Squinting up, Rosie saw a flash of white through the denseness of the canopy. As her eyes adjusted, she realized the untidy mass of twigs wedged into the tree's topmost branches was, in fact, a nest: an eyrie!

6: The Training Course

She breathed in sharply as a large raptor stood and cocked an eye at them.

'Is that an osprey?' she whispered.

'Uh-huh, a nesting pair; and they've got fledgelings.'

'Really? How do you know?'

'All those small feathers floating around the nest. That pair come back to the same tree every year. The young ones will be quite big by now. Come October they'll be off to Africa.'

6/6

Decision

Rosie sat on her bed, contemplating failure. It was mid-morning. Since returning from the aborted Daily Run, she had been isolated in her room, the rest of today's programme cancelled. Transport was being arranged, apparently, for her trip home this afternoon.

The euphoria that had followed her declaration to quit now felt not quite so uplifting. Yes, she looked forward to going home, getting her life back, and hopefully her job with Mercury One, if Harry would have her back. But giving up did not sit well; she had never thrown in the towel on any project, it simply was not in her nature.

Too late now.

There came a soft knock at the door, and Gadfly entered.

'Here, you'd better eat something.'

'Thanks,' Rosie said, taking the bowl and spoon with a rueful smile. 'Guess you saw this coming, eh?'

6: The Training Course

Gadfly lifted the chair close to the bed and sat. 'Not really. We all thought you were getting on surprisingly well.'

'Well, I didn't. I'm just not cut out for this work.' Rosie jabbed her spoon listlessly at the milky mush in the bowl. 'What is this?'

'Muesli, 200 calories, including the milk.'

Rosie grinned through her despondent mood. 'It'll be good to get back to sensible eating.'

Gadfly grew serious, 'If that's really what you want.'

Rosie shook her head sadly. 'I'm− Mm, I'm not happy about flunking this, but then, I haven't really been happy here at all. It's so ... I feel ... not lonely exactly, but ... like I'm removed from the human race. I don't think I like the person you're turning me into. I feel like I'll never be able to talk to anybody openly or honestly again. It's hard to put into words, but all this stuff I'm doing, this room, the Training Hall, it all seems so unreal− Do you know what I mean?'

Gadfly nodded. 'Alienation from society at large. And to be honest, that's really the point. I'd be worried if you didn't get those feelings from time to time, we all do. Only a psychopath would *enjoy* some of what you've been through. You've been learning just how evil and nasty humans can be: your evening case studies, the Dark Web, it's drummed into you, day and night that the world is a bad place. But trust me, it does not affect who you are. Nothing can change that, and when we leave here, we all drop back into the real world, the world of normal.'

'And what about in the field, on a mission. What then?'

The Travel Agent

'A trained agent in the field is disciplined and unemotional – like Gardener. And when the mission's over, you go home and maybe have a cry. And when you're all cried out, you revert to your other self.'

'That sounds bleak. Is that what it's all about, acting the part?'

Gadfly smiled, 'It's what life is about. When you're at work, you're ice; when you're not working, you're whoever you want to be. Our codenames and protected identities reinforce the boundary. The guys here know nothing about your private life, where you live. That's how it works. Simple and effective.'

'And you?'

Gadfly smiled, 'It is my job to know everything about your past, Rosie Winterbourne, and I mean everything.'

For a moment, Rosie sat in silence. Eventually, she asked, 'Why do you do it? I mean, what do you get out of this secret other-life?'

'Okay, I'm not a field agent, not anymore. In Firegate I'm just what you see here, a Civil Service Training Officer.' Gadfly grinned and circled a finger around her face, 'The wrong complexion for our type of fieldwork.'

'Oh, I see. And before Firegate?'

'I was a drone pilot. I still am, as a matter of fact: the only one in the agency. I'm also a trained psychologist. As for previous employers, I can't tell you. But then, as now, I believe in what we do. All those news reports of foiled terrorist attacks? They're only the tip of a massive iceberg. Most of our targets simply 'disappear' before they become a public story. In an ideal world, these people would face justice and due

6: The Training Course

process. But it's almost impossible to produce admissible evidence without jeopardising our own operations and compromising agents. Our less-conventional approach saves countless innocent lives. And that's what floats my boat. It also prevents murderers from becoming martyrs.'

'Those case studies I've been reading?'

Gadfly nodded. 'All neutralised. No story there.'

'What about relatives, friends. Don't people ask questions?'

'Sure, they get reported missing. But these folk are radicals, extremists, caliphate activists. What would you naturally assume?'

Rosie nodded. It made sense. But ... 'Gadfly, are you completely comfortable with killing people just because they m–'

'Don't go there,' Gadfly interrupted, shaking her head. 'That's not what we do. We only investigate known returnees who have been members of Daesh or have been trained by them. The burden of proof remains the same as in the judicial system. Every Cleaning has to be approved at the highest level.'

Cleaning!

Rosie shivered at the chilling euphemism.

'Look at it this way,' Gadfly continued, 'if you put them on trial for planning an act of terrorism, they win anyway. Their business is, after all, fear and disruption of our daily lives. They don't care what dead people think, so the success or failure of a mission is irrelevant. The threat of what they are *prepared* to do is what counts. Firegate sees to it that the threat gets no publicity at all. And what can they say? "It is not fair.

The Travel Agent

We are sending people to kill you, and they keep disappearing."'

Rosie snorted.

Gadfly stood up to leave.

'Here,' she said, handing her an old-fashioned Nokia phone, 'make some calls. The phone is secure, but don't say anything about where you are or what you're doing. Just keep it bland and sociable.'

'But why?' said Rosie, 'I'm going home today, aren't I?'

Gadfly opened the door, then turned back. 'You have a visitor this afternoon, then you can choose.'

Rosie sat on a tree stump on the ridge overlooking the Lodge. Her eyes wandered with her attention over the vast emptiness of the forest; shadows flitting like spectres across the pine canopy in the cloud-occulted light. A warm breeze soughed back and forth through the trees; a rhythmical oscillation like the breathing of some giant brooding creature. Strange, she had not until now considered the arboreal beauty of her surroundings.

She had tried Dad on the home landline, but he had not picked up - and then she had remembered he went to the Bowling Club on Wednesday mornings and would not be home till after two.

She dialled Michael's number.

'Who is this?'

'How's my jeep and my boat?'

'Hey! Rosie, so glad you could find the time. Where the hell you been?'

'Where I still am, of course. Told you I'd be away a month. Is everything okay?'

6: The Training Course

'Yeah, the planet keeps turning. Listen, I called you loads of times, and your phone is always switched off. Can't you even make phone calls?'

'Er, this is a phone call, right?'

'Yeah well, I was about to bin it like I do with all withheld numbers. Must've been a bit of telepathy, I guess. Anyway, how are you?'

'I'm alright. Can't say too much. I saw an osprey this morning, in an eyrie with chicks. Thrilled to bits.'

'Er, is that supposed to help me guess where you are?'

'Michael, stop it now, or I'm hanging up. How's *Pasha*?'

'Bobbing on the pontoon, happy as a sandgirl. Your varnishing's all done. I went down and checked her for leaks again yesterday. She's dry as old bones.'

'Thanks. I hope you're taking good care of my Jeep?'

'I think I'm in love. You ever think of selling her, I'm your man.'

'In your dreams, sailor. I guess you're getting around more, now you're on wheels.'

'Yup, been up to Watford to see my folks - first time in a couple of years. And spent last weekend in Salisbury; Julia says hi, by the way. Seems you made an impression; she asked when you'd be over again.'

'That's nice. Maybe when I get back, but I might be busy.'

'So, what's the job about.'

...

'Okay, I get it.'

'Sorry, Michael. So, you got anything planned for next month?'

The Travel Agent

'Funny, you should ask. We've been asked to do another run in October. I'm looking for suitable delivery jobs now.'

'Just the two of you again?'

'Yep. I didn't really want it, but Astrid's been badgering me like hell; you know what she's like. Easier just to go with it. Hey, I don't suppose—?'

Rosie cut across with a laugh. 'Don't even ask.'

'No, didn't think so. Anyway, I've got another job before then. Flying to the Azores on Saturday to pick up a Contessa 28, taking her to Largs. Twelve days, weather permitting.'

A sound that had been playing on the edge of Rosie's perception now took on a more insistent note - a distant thwocking of rotor-blades. She looked down the valley and saw a speck rising above the forest canopy.

Registering Michael's last words, she said, 'Oh, that's a nice trip, but do take care. Oh, and take my car back to Dad's before you go because I'll probably be back before you. Listen, Michael, I have to go now. I'll try and call you again before Saturday but can't promise, okay?'

'Er, okay, bye, then.'

Rosie ended the call and watched the helicopter skimming the treetops on its approach to the Lodge, where Gadfly and Gardener stood waiting. Swooping low overhead, the aircraft nosed into the air, stall-turned into the wind and touched down smoothly on the open ground in front of the Lodge.

'Here we go,' Rosie murmured, then rose with a sigh and ambled down the slope to face the music.

6: The Training Course

She had got halfway down to the Lodge when, with the rotor-blades barely stopped, the left-hand door swung open and out jumped a figure she recognised. Green jumpsuit, commando boots and a baseball cap.

'I'm sure that woman's a transexual,' Rosie muttered.

Waving a dismissal to Gardener and Gadfly, The Housekeeper made straight for Rosie, turning her firmly around by the elbow.

'C'mon, dearie, let's take a walk,' she growled, 'I'm gasping for a fag.'

Rosie kept her silence as the woman lit up and took a deep pull on her cigarette. They continued up to the ridge to where Rosie had been sitting then on down into the forest.

'You've come to give me the Blue Pill,' Rosie said at last.

The Housekeeper glanced sideways at her before blowing a stream of smoke up into the trees. 'It was always there for the taking, Galene. The question is, do you want to take it?'

'I bottled it this morning. I can't do this anymore.'

'Can't or don't want to? Gadfly thinks you can make it. So does Gardener. Gadfly tells me even our misanthropic genius seems to have taken a shine to you.'

Rosie laughed, 'Moth! Tell me, is the guy really autistic, or is it just an act?'

'No, he's autistic all right, but the most extraordinary surveillance technician in his field. That's why I poached him from GCHQ. And as I said before, I believe in you too, or I wouldn't have taken the chance.'

The Travel Agent

Rosie did not reply. She felt the liberty of her failure being eroded by this persistent woman.

'Why do you think I sent you here?'

Rosie gave a wry chuckle. 'You wouldn't believe how many times I've asked myself that. To be trained as a Firegate agent, obviously. But I found out it's supposed to be a *three*-month course, not one. Apparently, I don't even have the necessary prerequisites.'

The Housekeeper shook her head. 'No, you don't. And trust me, you will never be a first-echelon agent, even with *six*-months training. I want you as yourself, I want your essential qualities, and, as you so acutely observed at your interview, I want you and your boat. This course is just to develop the skills you might need to keep you - or indeed get you - out of trouble. It's a necessary safeguard, that's all.'

Rosie stared her. 'You want to hire *Pasha* as a skippered charter boat?'

The woman laughed her hoarse laugh. 'Don't worry. You won't be smuggling agents behind enemy lines. In fact, virtually nothing will change. I want you, sailing alone on your boat as you do now, the perfect cover for your mission.'

'Which is?'

The Housekeeper shook her head again. 'Get through the next ten days, and you'll find out. Still want the Blue Pill?'

6: The Training Course

6/7

Run-down

Rosie emerged from her shower and quickly dried herself down. Pausing at the mirror, she examined her new hair. After this morning's Daily Run, she had dug out the clippers Gadfly had loaned her and gone for the full buzzcut.

'Mm, not bad,' she murmured, grinning at herself. She had always had a somewhat boyish look. The severe haircut had enhanced it.

'I could quite fancy you myself,' she murmured.

Thankfully, the scar from her operation barely showed; the Portuguese surgeon had done a fine job. She dropped her hand to her newly exposed left earlobe and sighed. Maybe one day she would put it back in, but the Grav Maga classes had shown her how dangerous that little jewel could be to the wearer. Yup, she could live without the stud.

'Sorry, Mum, needs must.'

She stood back a little and swung her torso from side to side, noticing her shoulders had filled out, her

6: The Training Course

biceps too. She felt her boobs and grimaced. Always on the small side, they seemed now to have shrunk to little more than muscular mounds, hardly more prominent than the twin-row of muscles beneath.

A six-pack!

She snorted a laugh. 'Carry on like this, lady, and you'll grow a dick.'

It was the Monday of Rosie's final week at Camp Sparta, and the end was in sight. However, she had to admit she was beginning to enjoy herself and would probably miss the new skills and personal challenges. She was still high on this morning's performance. Two-hundred sit-ups while Gadfly had barked out telephone numbers at random intervals. She had successfully recalled each one in the order given. She could do likewise with vehicle registrations, names, street addresses, emails. Rosie had come a long way from naming the days of the week of given dates.

Inspection complete, Rosie slipped into her jumpsuit and padded barefoot to the kitchen.

'Hope you've left me some,' she said, making straight for the bacon and eggs.

'Whoa!' exclaimed Gardener, staring at her hair.

Gadfly looked up, startled. Moth stared too, but blank-faced, turning away when Rosie looked at him. She ran a hand proudly over her furry scalp.

'Well, I like it. And whatever anyone else thinks is irrelevant.'

As she began piling food onto her plate, Gadfly, seated at the table, gave a meaningful cough.

'What?' Rosie said, looking back at her.

Gadfly nodded at the wall chart.

'Oh, you've reduced my calorie intake. How come?'

The Travel Agent

'You're in your final days, time to re-accustom your body to normal eating and normal physical activity.'

'What, no more Daily Runs?'

'We wind 'em down with the calories,' explained Gardener, 'fifteen-k tomorrow, ten the next day, and so forth. Sunday will be the last.'

'And the gym work?'

'Ah,' said Gardener, 'that's gonna intensify. You've made good progress on the Krav Maga and Silat. It's time to hone those offensive techniques – time to introduce knife and firearms skills.'

'Firearms? No way. Whatever my mission is, it is not going to involve shooting people. I've made that quite clear.' She looked at Gadfly for support. The woman merely shrugged.

'So, you overpowered your assailant,' said Gardener, 'disarmed him, or her. What are you proposing to do with the AMT Hardballer now in your hand, ask to see the manual? Ask your assailant how it works?'

'What's an AMT..? Oh, I see.'

'Oh, indeed,' said Gadfly. She held out a hand, palm up, 'Reality, meet Galene. Galene, say hello to Reality.'

'Okay, okay. I get it. So, what's on the agenda this week?'

'Everyday-spoken Arabic,' said Gadfly.

'Electronic improvisation,' said Moth.

'Zero Profile, theory and practice,' said Gadfly.

'How not to die,' growled Gardener.

Rosie grinned, shaking her head. 'You three are wasted here.'

EPISODE SEVEN

Galene's Mission

The Travel Agent

7: Galene's Mission

7/1

Reunion

The crowds filtering through the arrivals barrier had thinned by the time Rosie spotted Michael's spider-like frame struggling with his boat-bag. Spotting Rosie, he grinned his gawky grin and waved, and it was not until then Rosie realised how much she had missed her young skipper.

'Thanks for coming,' he grunted, dropping the bag and leaning in to kiss her chastely on the cheek.

Rolling her eyes, Rosie folded him into a tight hug, then kissed him lightly on the mouth, which seemed to take him by surprise.

'Good timing,' she said, picking up one handle of the boat-bag while he took the other, 'I only got home yesterday.'

Michael paused and studied her. 'You look ... kind of different,' he waved a hand over his head, 'and what's with the hair?'

'I thought I'd try radical. You like, or no?'

The Travel Agent

'Kinda sexy, I guess, but maybe a little er– how shall I put this, tomboyish?'

Rosie laughed. 'You mean, I look like a dyke. Well, don't worry, I haven't come out.'

'And what happened to the ear stud?'

'Change of image.'

'I quite liked it.'

'Tough,' Rosie grinned. 'New life, new look. How was the trip?'

'Oh, not too bad. At least up to fifty-one north. Then I got a right hooley up my arse: three days of sou'westerly Force Nine pushing up past Ireland,' a wry chuckle. 'Nearly shaved the corner off Donegal.'

'Oops!'

Michael glanced sideways at her, 'I take it from the ebullient mood you passed?'

'Uh-huh, knocked 'em dead.'

Rosie grinned inwardly. She pictured Gardener's granite features staring up at her from the gym mat as she gripped his iron-bar wrist in both hands, heel poised a hairbreadth from crushing his windpipe with a *cap kaki*. It was the first and only time she had comprehensively taken down her powerful trainer.

The Saturday morning traffic out of Southampton's Eastleigh Airport was light. In no time the jeep was speeding towards Guildford on the M3 Motorway.

'How's your Dad?' Michael asked.

'Pretty good. The old man's getting out more now; bowling on Wednesdays, AA meetings on Monday nights, RNA weekends away–'

'I didn't know he was– you know ...'

'Say it, my Dad's an alcoholic.'

'Sorry.'

7: Galene's Mission

'Off the booze for five years, and I'm proud of him for it, so don't be sorry.'

'Okay.'

Rosie shifted uncomfortably in her seat. Something had changed between them, something she could not pin down. He seemed no different on the surface, but the bond that had existed before felt somehow more fragile. Perhaps it was her. She reached across and touched his knee.

'It's good to see you, Michael.'

He gave her hand a squeeze and smiled back at her, 'You too, Rosie.'

Rosie!

This would take some adjustment.

Ten minutes drifted by in silence, then Michael said, 'When do you start work at er…' he sighed heavily, 'when do you start work?'

'A week on Monday.'

'So, it's a daily commute to where, London?'

Rosie compressed her lips. She had not thought of an easy way to handle this.

Michael must have sensed her dilemma. 'Okay, you can't say. Will you be home at weekends?' He sounded resentful.

'It's not really that kind of work. Think of it as one of your delivery jobs. I'll be out of contact until the job's finished, however long it takes. And there's likely to be longish breaks between mis– er, between jobs.'

'Missions! You were going to say missions. Jesus, Rosie, just what are you into here?'

Rosie glanced sideways at him. The Housekeeper's chilling words blarped an alarm.

The Travel Agent

Knowledge makes them both useful to the enemy and a threat to us.

But against that was the fact that Michael had trusted her with the baby smuggling. Moreover, he had proved himself capable of the utmost discretion. He was good at that stuff. Coming to a decision and seeing a service area ahead, Rosie indicated left. Her current best friend deserved to learn at least something of her new role, even if not the whole truth.

'It's no big deal,' she told him after she had killed the engine.

She had chosen a spot at the car park's furthest end, well apart and facing away from other vehicles.

'Just a bit of covert surveillance in Gibraltar, that's all.'

'Covert! Looking for what, exactly?'

'Drug smuggling, mainly.'

He stared at her. 'How, exactly, did that happen? You went to train as a codebreaker, you said, a nice safe office job, you said.'

'Er, yeah. I wasn't q–'

'And now you tell me you're some kind of undercover cop mixing it with the Gibraltar Mafia? Fucking hell, Rosie!'

'It's really not like that. And stop talking to me like I'm your daughter.'

Michael breathed in profoundly then blew out. 'Okay, sorry. but–'

'I know, you're worried about me,' she put a hand on his knee and gave it a squeeze. 'And that's sweet of you. But really, it's nothing dangerous. I won't be confronting any gangsters or breaking into drug warehouses. I'm just a girl on a boat laid up in the

7: Galene's Mission

marina and minding my own business. My brief is just to be extra vigilant and report anything suspicious.'
Three dark, bearded faces arraigned on the screen. Housekeeper: 'You know these from your homework at Sparta, British Daesh foot-soldiers, you realise they re-entered the UK undetected, and you know they're terminated. You don't know that these three were last seen in Libya and came in together, possibly via Gibraltar. They weren't the first, and they won't be the last. Where's the back door, Galene, and who's their travel agent?

'So why couldn't you tell me before?'

'Well, firstly, I didn't know before. And even if I had known then, my employers are quite paranoid about security; I've already told you more than I'm supposed to. So not a word, okay? Not even to my Dad.'

'He doesn't know either! Don't you think he should?'

Rosie shook her head. 'Definitely not. My Dad's been to hell and back and needs his life to be blissfully calm.'

That was another lie, right there. Dad knew the real version of what she was getting into, and in his case, she could tell from the new sparkle in his eyes that pride and excitement trumped all the worry and fear. After all, he was a fellow adventurer, *carpe diem* and all that, and knew that his daughter would always choose the road less travelled.

Michael was no shrinking violet when facing danger but lacked the spontaneity that so often gave rise to Rosie's seemingly irresponsible choices in life. So, it

The Travel Agent

would be imprudent to burden him with knowing her real mission on the Rock.

But there was a more critical motive. By misdirection, Rosie hoped to prevent any discussion of her work between Dad and Michael, should they cross paths during her absence.

Later, as they approached Guildford, Michael said, 'What are you doing after you drop me off?'

'I'm going to come up to your flat if that's allowed.'

She glanced at him, fascinated that his ear tips had turned bright red.

'Then what?' he almost croaked.

'Well, Sailor,' she purred, running a thumbnail up his inner thigh, which made him squirm, 'That would be up to you.'

7: Galene's Mission

7/2

Sea Trial

It was one of those crisp September mornings when the sun, climbing into a clear sky, seemed to cool rather than warm the world. Flipping her rucksack over the quarter-rail, Rosie strolled along the pontoon to take stock of the boat's condition.

The work crew had made an excellent job of polishing the hull, removing all the rust streaks and bringing the white Gelcoat to a high gloss. The deck and coach-roof too bore evidence of serious elbow-grease, and the stainless-steel fittings gleamed like new.

'Not bad, for an old girl, eh?' she said. Once upon a time, she could have expected a terse response from *Pasha.* Thankfully those psychotic delusions were far behind her.

The two bagged-up sails on the coach roof were a reminder of her first job this morning. A light breeze from astern would mean turning the boat around before the sails could be rigged, and Rosie began to

The Travel Agent

regret turning down Michael's offer to come along for the sea-trial. But she had wanted to do this first one alone, a re-bonding thing between her and *Pasha* she could not explain, even to herself.

By the time the Mullhaven town hall clock was striking one, *Pasha* was ready for sea. An hour later the yacht passed the breakwater heading for open water. The south-westerly breeze had gradually strengthened throughout the morning, and a scattering of whitecaps dotted the Channel, promising a lively first outing for boat and skipper.

With the wind looking like strengthening further, Rosie decided on two reefs in the main and let out only two-thirds of the genoa. A familiar fear filled her as *Pasha* heeled from the wind, not the fear of imminent danger, but the visceral thrill, the vulnerability of being alone in a potentially hostile environment.

Rosie headed south initially. When the Normandy coast appeared - a thin black line on the horizon - she tacked starboard and pointed for the Isle of Wight. By now the wind was gusting Force 7, still south-westerly. *Pasha* was bucking and bouncing close-hauled into a short and choppy sea while her skipper whooped with the sheer joy of sailing free and solitary once more. Yes, Rosie, the seafarer, was back. And no, she had *not* lost her nerve.

At six pm, with the Coastguard forecasting Force 9 imminent, *Pasha's* captain set course for home, reaching the Mullhaven breakwater at sunset.

'It's a cat this time,' said Michael, 'a Lagoon 44, so it'll be quicker and more comfortable.'

7: Galene's Mission

'Not so good upwind, though,' said Rosie, absently twirling a swizzle-stick in her glass. 'You'd better time it right for the weather, coming north. A deep Atlantic Low is what you need, and right now the Azores High looks quite stable.'

Michael looked at her drink 'Amazing what you can see in a swirling glass of orange.'

Rosie stared at him a moment, looked at her orange juice, then snorted.

'Stupid sod,' she laughed, punching him playfully on the shoulder. 'I'm heading south myself over the weekend, remember, so naturally, I've been watching the weather. Where are you picking up the cat?'

Michael wiped a beer-moustache from his lip. 'Lefkas and this is definitely the last run, thank God. We won't be able to do it after Brexit anyway, not if they stop free movement.' Michael shook his head and pulled a tight smile, 'I still keep thinking about that Libyan gunboat intercepting us, bloody nightmare, so it was.'

Rosie sniggered, 'Hardly a gunboat, but I know what you mean. Is Astrid hanging up her tabard then?'

'Better than that,' he looked around the half-empty pub and lowered his voice, 'No little ones this time. Greta's coming home with us instead, and without her there the whole operation collapses.'

Rosie looked at him, horrified. 'Is that wise? I mean, officially she's still a jihadi bride. You smuggle her into the UK, and you could be in−' she trailed off. Michael was shaking his head.

'No, it's all above board. Astrid's arranged for her to be repatriated to Sweden. They've got this new de-

The Travel Agent

radicalisation programme there; apparently, she could be back with her family in a few months.'

A sudden unaccountable shiver ran up Rosie's spine. She reached across the table and placed her hand on his. 'Be careful, Michael, won't you? Don't do anything stupid, and make sure you've got a good cover story in case the Coastguard find you again.'

'Don't you worry, Moneypenny, barring any unsheen difficulteesh, I'll be back.'

She shook her head, smiling. 'Don't give up your day job, Sweetie.'

'No, seriously, I learned that lesson. I've bought my own Imray Med Pilot, and I've got a week to memorise the North African yacht havens.'

'And the tourist places of interest. You need a reason for visiting.'

He nodded grimly. 'And the plaishes of interest.'

7: Galene's Mission

7/3

La Linea

The stiff October north-westerly that swept *Pasha* briskly across towards La Linea brought a stink from the Spanish oil refinery at the head of Algeciras Bay. Off to starboard rose the overpopulated pile of limestone that was Gibraltar, its upper escarpments and clinging greenery still in deep shadow from a sun struggling to rise above the ridge.

The Andalusian hills to the north brought back memories of Rosie's last visit. The handsome Mateo had taken her on a romantic horse-ride and then ensnared her in a bizarre sexual fantasy. It was not *all* him to be fair. Mateo's was a predilection in which Rosie had collaborated, even encouraged. Until the afternoon the Spanish vet had almost killed her.

His house was up there somewhere, and for a fleeting moment, a strange thrill of that old vulnerability ran through her as she imagined the Spaniard with binoculars watching her approach.

The Travel Agent

But that was five years ago when Rosie had been in a bad place emotionally. This was now, and she was Galene. It was true: reinvention *was* liberating.

An hour later, with the boat tied up at the Reception Quay at Alcaidesa Marina, Rosie booked in. She then motored on to her allotted berth. As she nudged alongside, a skinny figure with a frizzy mop of blonde hair ran along the finger-pontoon to take her lines.

'Thanks,' said Rosie, tossing over the bow-rope before stepping over the rail with the stern-line.

'Welcome back,' said her helper, 'Rosie, isn't it?'

Rosie did a double-take on the woman. 'Oh, erm− Kate?'

'Well remembered. Took you long enough to get back here.' A toothy grin, 'You get lost?'

Rosie laughed. It had been more than five years since she had sailed away following a drunken night with Kate and Bill on-board their Westerly. God, it felt so good to be back among liveaboards.

That afternoon - following her boat's washdown and stowing sails - Rosie let herself into the marina's washhouse. She stuffed her stale bedding and dirty clothes into one of the washing machines. She then lingered a luxurious half an hour under a hot shower, washing off the salt and sweat accumulated over the two-week passage from Mullhaven.

That evening, Rosie met up with Kate and Bill at the marina bar on the quayside.

'A book!' exclaimed Kate, 'I didn't know you were a writer.'

'Neither did I until I finished Uni and realised I would need to earn a living.'

7: Galene's Mission

'Ah, welcome to the club,' said Bill, a broad-spoken Geordie, 'we're all slaved to the mighty lucre.'

Bill, Rosie knew, freelanced as a boat renovation specialist. At the same time, Kate, a lively Essex girl, worked for a Gibraltar property agent.

'What kind of book are you writing?' asked Kate.

Rosie chuckled, recalling that the woman was a keen devourer of romantic fiction and chick-lit. 'Not your kind I'm afraid. It's a thriller, an idea I had when I was here last. It's about drug-smuggling on the Rock. That's why I came back; to do some research.'

The pair exchanged uneasy glances.

'I know,' Rosie said. 'It's dodgy to ask questions, especially over there,' she nodded toward the Rock. 'But don't worry, I'm not planning to do any kind of exposé of real people or events. I just want to learn about the coastal security arrangements over there, I thought maybe talk to someone in the Border and Coastguard Agency, just for accuracy, you know? The rest will be pure fiction, invented up here.' She tapped her brow.

'All the same, pet,' said Bill, 'you need a be careful. It's common knowledge that the BCA could put an end a drug-smuggling tomorrow if they 'ad a mind. Wheels within wheels, ya knaw. 'Who ya thinking of askin' laike?'

Rosie grinned and gave a shrug. 'Well, you two, for a start.'

The following morning Bill knocked on *Pasha's* hull.

'Good timing,' said Rosie, poking her head out of the hatch, 'I just finished breakfast. Want a cuppa?'

The Travel Agent

'No, it's okay, pet, I just wanted to give you this,' Bill handed a scrap of paper across the rail. 'It's a bloke ah know in customs, he might be able to help with ya book. The phone number's where he works, so ring him in working hours. He likes a drink, does Albert, so take him to a pub.'

She looked at the note; Albert Astevaras, a Gibraltar phone number. 'Thanks, Bill, I'll call him later.'

'And a word to the wise, Rosie. The fella's a bit of a one for the ladies, a tad touchy-feely if you know what ah mean. Just saying, laike.' He gave a grin and sauntered off along the pontoon whistling.

After washing up her breakfast things, Rosie manoeuvred her bike out of the forepeak and onto the pontoon, where she re-attached the front wheel and gave the spindles and moving parts a squirt of WD40. After her shower she donned her running gear and a small rucksack. After two weeks at sea, Rosie was severely in need of a workout.

Pedalling her leisurely way along the Avenida toward the Frontier, Rosie reflected once more on her personal history with this place. The memories were poignant. On this same road, for example, had come the nightmare incident that had led to her mental breakdown and consequent departure from the navy. Before all that, there were the frequent visits during her navy years: riotous drunken nights on the town with shipmates; cheap booze, all-night clubs and bohemian tapas bars.

Her initial response to the idea of being sent here had been a kaleidoscopic mixture of nostalgic joy and regret. But now she was Galene, with a job to do. This time she felt in control, part of the security

7: Galene's Mission

establishment of her country. This time she was five years older and a hundred years wiser. This time her sanity was intact. All in all, it felt good to be here.

Although not yet ten-o-clock, it was already comfortably warm. Over the Rock hung the Levanter, thinning away to the west: precipitating out of the moist Mediterranean air and melting in the updraft of Algeciras Bay.

The usual traffic queue tailed back from the Frontier, but cyclists could make their way unhindered to the gate, where they were waved through with barely a glance at their passports. At the runway, waited patiently among a knot of pedestrians and other cyclists as an EasyJet plane taxied to the western end then turned for its take-off run. She was in no hurry because today was purely self-indulgent—a spot of me-time before she started work.

At Victoria Stadium Rosie locked her bike to a steel rail, crossed the road to Casemates Square and up into Main Street, enjoying the crowds and the sunshine. In one of the many duty-free electronics boutiques, she bought four local SIM cards with prepaid data packs. Finding a pleasant street café where she ordered orange juice. With one of the new cards activated as default, she dialled Albert's number to arrange a meeting.

An hour later found Rosie running strongly up the steep, winding road leading to the Jew's Gate. Already, she had her second wind, breathing evenly and deeply, her leg muscles zinging hot and every sinew tingling with limitless energy. Her body was working at full capacity, and it felt good.

The Travel Agent

As she passed the gatehouse above the Jewish Cemetery and the morning sun cast it's first beams over the ridge above, Rosie caught a sudden glint of light off to her right. She glanced around and saw it again: a flash of sunlight and an indistinct shape withdrawing quickly behind the gatehouse wall. Curious, the agent slowed her pace and looked back, but the figure was gone. After a moment more she dismissed what she'd seen as probably a bird hopping about in the cemetery. But still, that flash of reflected sunlight…

From Jews Gate, the path took her around to the eastern side of the Rock. The track petered out at the foot of steps carved into the rock. Here she paused to take in the stunning view across the Strait; a shining sea dotted with ships, the mountains of Morocco melting into the desert haze.

Now the real effort began. After donning a sweatband, Rosie started running up the precipitous zig-zag route on the crumbling stairway to the topmost ridge. This was the formidable climb known as the Mediterranean Steps. The last time she had taken this challenge, six years ago, it had almost beaten her, and she recalled slowing to a walk for the last two flights with legs like blancmange. The consequent stiffness had lasted nearly a week.

But the gruelling month at Camp Sparta had taken her to new levels of fitness and stamina. Rosie ran up those six-hundred steps now like a young mountain goat, surprising apes at leisure who, in the main, scuttled out of her way. One alpha male, however, eyed her balefully, steadfastly refusing to move.

7: Galene's Mission

Carefully, and avoiding eye-contact, Rosie sidestepped past him.

Throughout the climb, Rosie's breathing continued even and steady. She powered on by stages, ever faster, tirelessly: thrilling to the sensation of thigh and calf muscles being stretched to their limits.

At the top of the ridge, she paused, gazing out on a spectacular view of the Costa del Sol, the resort towns of Estepona and Marbella glistening in the clear sunlight. She had seen these views often, but they never ceased to take her breath away.

On the WW2 battery - between two gigantic guns pointing out across the Strait – the agent dropped down to two-hundred brisk press-ups, fifty squat-thrusts, and a hundred sit-ups. Sparta's instilled habits had become so automatic it was now part of her daily routine, even at sea.

Continuing past the Skywalk - a glass platform rewarding the adventurous tourist with a daunting but majestic all-round view - Rosie ran northward along the rocky, undulating ridgeway. The descent - past the Siege Tunnels and Moorish Castle - called on her lesser-used frontal thigh muscles which soon began to twitch.

By the time Rosie reached the top of the town, her legs felt like rubber sticks that she could barely control. She slowed to a walk and checked her watch. A shade over an hour, not too bad. The total distance had been a mere four miles, but the steep climbs and descents made it seem much farther. Thoroughly soaked and brimming with achievement-joy, Rosie continued down into town, legs gradually adapting to walking once more, the heat slowly dissipating out of her tired muscles. There was just time to cycle back to the marina to shower and change before returning for her 4pm meeting with Albert.

7: Galene's Mission

7/4

Albert

'So, you are writing about the drug-trafficking market, eh?'

Albert Astaveras was fortyish, moderately overweight, self-assured with a ready grin and attractive brown eyes. The meeting place, a bar-restaurant in Casemates, had been Albert's suggestion. Arriving before him, Rosie had been dismayed to see outside tables packed and noisy with people eating and drinking, children running around, and a dozen waiters in constant motion.

However, inside was more suitable: a long dark room with high-backed wooden seating booths along one side that allowed discretion and privacy. They sat in one of the booths now. Inside was quiet: the only sound, the gentle swishing of three overhead fans, battling the heat from outside.

As Bill had warned, Albert was indeed the overly tactile type of man that some women might find uncomfortable. But Rosie quickly taught him to

The Travel Agent

behave himself with subtle gestures and mildly admonishing glances.

'Well, no, not exactly,' she now replied, 'I'm writing a thriller set on the Rock that has a backstory of drug gangs, but it's not primarily about that. I'm keen not to go anywhere near what may or may not be going on here. My book's pure fiction, but I want to be fair to the enforcement agencies here.'

He frowned. 'Fair? How do you mean?'

Rosie smiled disarmingly and went into her well-rehearsed routine. 'Well, suppose I just ploughed into a story that concerned, say, a bust by the Borders & Customs Agency, without knowing anything about what you do or how you work. I might end up with a parody of incompetence that could naturally put a lot of backs up, quite rightly so. I want my book to sell *here*, as well as in the UK. The more I know about local procedures and facilities, the better I can avoid the story being criticised as poorly researched.' She gave a sartorial smirk. 'In short, Albert, I don't want to create colonial cartoon characters, I want to write you guys as the efficient border force on top of their game.'

Albert pulled a crooked grin. 'Good luck with that.'

Rosie snorted. 'I'm sure you don't mean that.'

He took a long swig of his beer, downing half of it, then wiped his lips on the back of his hand. 'Okay, my dear, so fire away – what do you want to know?'

They talked for an hour, but despite the several drinks she bought him, she learned little that was useful; little she had not already learned from her intensive briefings at Sparta.

According to Albert, the Borders Agency regularly spot-checked locally-based vessels transiting in and

7: Galene's Mission

out of the Territory but rarely boarded them without due cause. They co-ordinated with the Gibraltar Defence Police on which vessels warranted special attention, focussing on arrivals from the non-European Atlantic.

Responding to her question on terrorism and illegal immigrants, Albert told her that that was the Royal Gibraltar Police Marine Section's responsibility. They owned several modern, high-speed RHIB's. Unlike the UK-funded Defence Police who had only a couple of old range boats for Naval Base security.

During the conversation, Rosie was distracted when a man walked in, ordered a drink at the bar, then, glancing around, chose a bar stool opposite their booth. There was nothing particularly noteworthy in this. The man looked like a hundred other locals taking an after-work drink. Indeed, several others like him had drifted in during the past twenty minutes. But something in the way he surveyed the room - while seeming to avoid looking in their direction, a subtlety few would have noticed - had instantly tweaked the agent's curiosity.

'The problem with this place,' Albert was saying, 'too many cooks. The GDF, the RGP, the GDP, the BCA, the Navy, the Army, all with their own agendas, their own axes to grind.' He chortled as something came to mind, 'You could write a book about that, but it would need to be a comedy.'

Rosie dragged her attention back to the conversation, grinned belatedly at his joke, and said, 'The list of acronyms would give readers a headache. Is there nobody to co-ordinate?'

The Travel Agent

'Supposed to be the JMCC,' he said with evident scepticism, 'but they've only been in business a year or so, and it's hard to change a system that's been entrenched for a hundred years. Talking of which, you might want to have a chat with South Ops. They're all a bit, you know, geeks with heads up their arses, but they mean well and can tell you a lot about illegals and terrorists.'

The man at the bar was still there when Rosie thanked Albert for his time, leaving the disappointed customs officer to finish the fourth pint she had bought him.

Later that evening, Rosie met up again with Bill & Kate at the Marina Bar and told them how her session with Albert had gone. But Kate had come up with another idea.

7: Galene's Mission

7/5

Tash

The Sunrise Bar was close enough to Eastern Beach to attract a few sun-reddened holidaymakers cooling off before heading to their hotels for dinner. This allowed Rosie - in her shorts and flip-flops, evenly tanned from her sea passage - to blend in unobtrusively. According to Bill and Kate, it was also close enough to Devils Tower Camp to be a regular haunt for off-duty soldiers.

'Meet a nice army lad to show you what's what,' Kate had suggested, drawing a worried frown from her partner.

'Aye, they'll show 'er what's what alright,' grunted Bill.

'Better than trying it on with a fucking customs officer,' Kate argued, 'at least she can be sure he won't be in bed with the druggies.'

'They're squaddies, Kate,' Bill countered, giving Rosie a significant look. 'So ya right, it won't be the druggies they'll want to bed. Pretty lass like Rosie,

The Travel Agent

here? Them randy buggers'll be all over her like a bunch of rock apes in a banana shop.'

'So, we'll be nearby to make sure she's okay. That alright with you, Rosie?'

'Oh, you noticed I'm still here then?'

Walking in now, and feeling like a whore touting for business, Rosie clocked the pair sitting at a table on the patio and making a fair fist of ignoring her. Touched by their concern, Rosie chose an empty table as far as possible from her friends. She ordered a sangria from a passing waitress.

Too early for any military regulars, Rosie took out her Kindle, pushed up her sunglasses and settled down to play the lone tourist reading and resting after a hard day on the beach. She took pains, however, not to appear too engrossed to be unapproachable.

Bill and Kate were shortly joined at their table by a woman, someone they clearly knew. The pair seemed to be enjoying their impromptu evening out on its own merits. Rosie returned to her reading smiling inwardly, feeling less beholden to her self-appointed minders.

'We've got a plan B for you.'

Rosie looked up to see Bill standing there.

'I hope so,' she said, smiling to hide her irritation. 'Because you just blew my cover.'

Bill chuckled, 'You sound more like an undercover cop than a writer. This friend of ours works for the government. When Kate told her you were researching a book—'

'You told her about me?'

'Why not, pet? How else are you going to do research? Anyway, it turns out she can help. You interested or not?'

7: Galene's Mission

Rosie picked up her bag and her drink with a sigh and followed Bill over to their table.

'Tash works in the Ops Room up inside The Rock,' Bill explained after introductions.

'Joint Maritime Control Centre,' corrected Tash, a slim, attractive forty-something, neat mousy hair and wearing beach casuals.

'Bill says you might be able to help with some research,' Rosie said, pulling up a chair.

'Depends what you need,' said Tash. 'Some of our work is sensitive.'

Rosie nodded. 'Anything you feel you can discuss would be helpful. It's a work of fiction so I can always invent stuff to fill the gaps.'

As the conversation got underway, Bill and Kate made an unfussy departure and left them to it.

Tash turned out better than Rosie could have hoped. In what was colloquially known as The Hole, a Watch Supervisor offered to give Rosie a tour of the place tomorrow when she was next on duty.

'You'll need to dress for the office, though,' warned Tash, 'it's mostly military up there, and they expect visitors to conform to dress-codes. Plus, the aircon's a bit fierce because of all the electronics, so bring…' she looked up as a man approached their table and smiled broadly.

'Lev! How wonderful. Come and join us.'

And no wonder the woman was so delighted. The man was mid-fifties and handsome by any standards, with thick black hair, slightly wavy with a grey touch at the sides, beautiful dark brown eyes and a naturally-dark complexion; a winning smile showing a perfect set of white teeth.

The Travel Agent

'Natasha, darling, I hoped I might find you here,' he bent and kissed her chastely on both cheeks before turning a beaming grin on Rosie.

'And who is this delightful lady?'

'Rosie, I want you to meet my dear friend, Leviticus Danilenco. Lev, this is Rosie Winterbourne.'

'Hello, Rosie Winterbourne,' purred the charming Adonis. 'A pleasure to meet you.' He bowed and placed a feather kiss on her offered hand, sending an electric shiver down Rosie's spine.

'Likewise,' she smiled, meaning it.

Leviticus looked about five-feet-nine - Rosie's height - but carried himself like a taller man. Hitching up his elegant cream chinos, he took one of the vacated seats, his smoke-coloured sports shirt tightening briefly across a finely-muscled torso.

'Rosie's a writer,' Tash explained. 'I'm helping her with some research.'

'You have a wonderful name,' Rosie told him, cutting off any further musings in that direction.

'Thank you. I have a Greek mother and a Ukrainian father – they thought I should share both heritages. And Rosie, I am guessing, if you'll forgive me, is a shortening of Rosemary?'

Rosie grimaced playfully. 'Thanks to my Irish Granny. Only my Dad uses that name now.'

Rosie stayed chatting with the pair for another half hour. Although they took great pains to make her feel included, it did not take long to realise they were a serious item. When Leviticus called over a waiter to order more drinks, Rosie took the opportunity to ask for Tash's contact details and politely extricate herself.

7: Galene's Mission

She was halfway across the carpark to where she'd locked up her bike when quiet footfalls padded up behind her. She whipped around, tensed for violent action, but then relaxed and blew out a sigh.

'Sorry if I startled you,' said Leviticus, smiling his beautiful smile, 'I just wanted to give you this.'

She looked at the card he handed her, no business details, just his name and phone number. He came straight to the point.

'It would give me great pleasure were you to agree to have dinner with me, Rosie. I would like to know you better,' he waved a disparaging arm towards the bar. 'Without these frivolous distractions?'

Hiding her amusement, she gave him a withering look. 'Does Tash know you followed me out?'

The Ukrainian's smile was undiminished, and now she came to think of it, strangely beguiling.

He said, 'Natasha and I have, let us say, a flexible relationship,' clearly unabashed at being called out. 'You will call me tomorrow, yes?'

'I will call you tomorrow, no. I`m busy tomorrow night.'

'Oh, that is a pity.' He looked only mildly crestfallen, then brightened, 'Some other time, then, perhaps?'

She smiled then, despite her disapproval of the man`s brazen duplicity. 'I'll think about it,' she said. 'Now, if you'll excuse me, I have to go, so goodnight.'

And think about it, she did, all the way back across the airfield and Frontier to the marina. And by the time she was locking up her bike she`d decided that the secret paramour's role, however tempting, was not her style. Besides, there was much work to do.

The Travel Agent

7: Galene's Mission

7/6

The Hole

The taxi laboured its way up the Rock; a series of switchbacks then up a steep straight climb bearing numerous signs warning:

MINISTRY OF DEFENCE PROPERTY
AUTHORISED PERSONNEL ONLY

Before setting out this morning, Rosie had logged on to Marine Traffic to check up on Michael. Ever since her friend had told her about his final foray to Libya to extract Greta, she had felt a growing niggle. It was nothing Rosie could lay a finger on, but worrying, nonetheless. She found *Surf Warrior's* last position just off the Tunisian island of Djerba, seemingly heading for the marina there. There was an Italian naval vessel - *Comandante Borsini* – five miles to the north of Michael's boat and heading northeast. That was probably what had forced him to feint his destination as Djerba. She would check again later.

The Travel Agent

A final hairpin at the top brought them up at a barrier with a concrete security billet, a pair of apes gazing down disinterestedly from its roof. Beyond the checkpoint, the narrow road continued to wind upwards until lost among rocks and shrubs.

Rosie paid the driver and climbed out, gasping in the sudden heat after the car's aircon. She had chosen her grey worsted skirt, cotton blouse and low-heeled shoes, and already she felt the blouse clinging wetly to her back. As the car backed away to turn around, a soldier emerged from the billet.

'Hello. Can I help you?'

'Good afternoon,' Rosie said, smiling brightly as she handed him her passport, 'I'm here to see Natasha Marchant.'

He studied her carefully for a few seconds before opening the passport, then again as he compared her to her photo.

'Right you are, Miss,' he said, handing it back. 'Come inside and take a seat. I'll get someone to come and drive you up.'

Ten minutes later, a Landrover came snaking down the hill and turned around at the barrier.

'Hi,' said Rosie, climbing in.

'Miss Winterbourne, is it?'

'That's right.'

The driver did not speak again until the road levelled out and led into a brightly-lit tunnel.

'Been to The Hole before, Miss?'

'Huh, I didn't know the place existed till now,' she lied easily. 'Or that you could even drive in these tunnels.'

7: Galene's Mission

The vehicle had not slowed at all as it entered the narrow tunnel. The rough-hewn rock wall flashing by on either side felt disconcertingly close. Of course, Rosie knew about the JMCC from her mission briefing and had a fair idea of what to expect. Gaining access to it was part of her strategy; the serendipitous meeting with Tash had merely brought the plan forward. The Landrover entered a vast cavern - where several cars were parked - and pulled up outside a formidable steel door declaring in big white letters that this was

WESTMINSTER ADIT

Rosie shivered as she climbed out of the vehicle: the tunnel had the chilly, musty ambience of a natural cave. As she approached the armoured portal, a personnel door swung inward.

Tash looked quite different in uniform - long blue trousers and Border Force epaulettes on her crisp, white shirt. Seeing her smiling welcome in the entrance, Rosie felt an uneasy stab of disloyalty. Unreasonable, since she hardly knew the woman, she had anyway rejected the advances of the officer's inconstant lover.

At least, for now, whispered a mocking voice inside her head.

A uniformed guard in the entrance lobby ran a hand-scanner over Rosie and handed her a visitor's pass before Tash led her into the control centre.

A large digital map display dominated one wall of the room. Several smaller monitors mounted on the other walls showed live camera views of the Strait and Gib's territorial waters. A lighted display above the

The Travel Agent

map stated that the current Security Condition was Yellow. A row of consoles stood quietly humming in a semi-circle, behind which sat half a dozen headset-ed operators, their quiet communications chatter permeating the room.

'This is our principal focus,' Tash explained, running a laser-pointer along the Moroccan coast on the giant display. 'A potential launchpad for drugs and terrorists.'

'Looks like you've got it covered,' Rosie observed, looking about her, more impressed than she had anticipated. She turned her attention to the overhead display. It showed hundreds of ship symbols transiting from the Mediterranean and Atlantic, squeezed into the narrow Strait like sand in an hourglass. Their positions were updated microscopically every few seconds. The sand grains flowed both ways, a graphic illustration that, without the Transit Separation Scheme, maritime mayhem would undoubtedly ensue.

'What are the flashing diamonds?' Rosie wondered.

'Unidents - radar contacts of vessels without active AIS. Most of those will carry on into Spanish waters and get intercepted by the Guardia Civil.'

'And if they're heading for Gib, what then?'

'If they come into GTW we call them on Channel Sixteen to identify themselves, then there are several ways it can go. Worst case, they don't respond. Then we ask the RGP marine section to investigate - if the RPG don't like what they see they'll board and search the vessel. Ninety-nine times out of a hundred, it's a yacht or fishing boat with a faulty radio.'

'What about the boats that identify themselves? How do you know they're clean?'

7: Galene's Mission

Tash nodded. 'There are regulars, of course: sailing-school yachts that make frequent trips to Ceuta or Smir, local fishermen, motorboat day-trippers - they're all subject to random stop and search, but mostly they come and go unhindered. Visiting yachts from ports outside Europe is another matter, especially from South America.'

'Cocaine, right?'

'Uh-huh, Charlie - that's the big issue right now. If they've been to South or Central America, they can expect a thorough search when they get here, sniffer dogs, the lot.'

'What about dodgy contacts crossing the Strait. I'm thinking refugees, piracy, that kind of thing.'

Tash turned and gave her a puzzled look. 'I thought you were writing about the drugs trade?'

Rosie shrugged, unruffled. 'I might as well get the full picture while I'm here, eh?'

Tash grinned knowingly. 'Typical author, always an eye on the next story, eh?'

Rosie grinned back – it was a winner when they helped you fabricate.

'Fair enough,' continued Tash. 'So, in the case of suspected refugee activity, or if there is a risk of danger to shipping, I can activate Operation Sea Guardian. This gives the Navy permission to go out there with its NATO hat on and police the situation.

'As for hashish and weed, unfortunately, there's not much we can do until, and unless, they enter our waters. Quite often, we know who they are, and we liaise closely with our Spanish colleagues. But the usual suspects generally head for Tarifa in the west or up the Costa del Sol where the Guardia Civil are hard-

The Travel Agent

pushed to catch them landing it. Interestingly, most cannabis products come into Gib via the land bridge or jet skis racing across the front of the runway. Duty-free tobacco goes the other way.'

Tell me about it, Rosie thought. She remembered vividly when she and Doc had almost been mashed by a motorcycle laden with smuggled cigarettes, the Guardia Civil hot on his tail. That incident had triggered the psychotic seizure that had led to Rosie's discharge from the navy.

Rosie had lots more questions about crossings from Morocco, but now something else had caught her attention on the big screen.

'What's that out there to the east - IRP?' Rosie asked, quite sure there had been nothing in that location on the area sea charts when she had examined them a few days ago.

'Ah, the International Research Platform.'

'What do they do out there?'

Tash shrugged. 'Research, I suppose.'

'Mm, so who owns it?'

Tash shook her head. 'We have no idea. It's twenty miles offshore, well outside our jurisdiction. IMO officers inspected it after it arrived a few months ago. All above board, apparently, but commercially sensitive. All I can tell you: there's a Notice to Mariners to keep a mile clear due to underwater operations.'

Underwater operations! Rosie thought. Twenty miles from Gib? Interesting. Perhaps she was grasping at straws, but she would check it out.

7: Galene's Mission

'What about at night?' Rosie asked. 'A small rubber boat might not show up on the radar, could even come in on the east side and land stuff, say, in Sandy Bay.'

Tash shook her head and led her to one of the TV screens on the wall. This one showed a birds-eye view of a bay dotted with sunbathers and swimmers and surrounding coves and rocky shoreline.

'Is that live?'

'Uh-huh. Sandy Bay, as it so happens,' Tash moved a rollerball to zoom in on a couple lying prostrate on the sand, close enough to see facial features.

'A voyeurs dream,' the officer said with a chuckle. 'Be careful what you get up to on the beach. We don't even have to watch it – the auto-tracking system tells the operators over there when anything's moving. They can switch their own monitors to look at any one of these displays.'

'Mm, I'm impressed. I guess at night you've got infra-red imaging?'

'Of course,' the officer flicked a switch, causing the monitor to flare briefly before settling down to a ghostly green image of the same view. The sun-worshippers were now reduced to bright green stick figures. Rosie nodded glumly - the range of possible entry points was fast closing.

Arriving back onboard, Rosie unlocked the security container she had installed under the starboard banquet, replacing a redundant water tank. It was also a virtual Faraday Cage to keep her portable electronics safe from lightning strikes. On her Atlantic voyages, Rosie used to put it all in the oven when thunderstorms threatened. Now, as Rosie, she needed more room for

The Travel Agent

the box of toys they had issued her with for the mission.

Firing up her laptop, she searched for information on the IRP. She found nothing except the Notice to Mariners Tash had mentioned. The TOR search engine also drew a blank. She logged on to the Firegate Mailbox.

> From: Galene
> To: Housekeeper
> JMCC coastal security looks tight - no apparent gaps. Meeting with leader of volunteer SOUTH-OPS group tomorrow. One loose end, probably nothing, but worth checking: International Research Platform position: approx. 36 12N 4 48W. Owner/financier and purpose unknown. Lack of online data make claim to be 'International' seem suspect. Grateful any info you have.
> G.

Next, she logged in to Marine Traffic to check *Surf Warrior*'s progress. She was surprised to find the catamaran's position hadn´t been updated since this morning and was no longer live. Perhaps Michael had taken time out to visit the ancient Tunisian town with Astrid. It seemed unlikely but was all she could think of. Unless they were already back at sea, transponder off, and heading for home. If so, she calculated that they should reappear tomorrow near Lampedusa and pass through the Strait in a week. She grinned at the thought of calling Michael's phone while watching his

7: Galene's Mission

passage from the top of the Rock through her binoculars.

The Travel Agent

7: Galene's Mission

7/7

Captured

Michael was feeling bloated with constipation from a starchy meal last night; ironically, he had avoided the salad and raw vegetables because of the risk of the squits.

An Italian patrol ship had come up alongside the catamaran yesterday, asked the usual barrage of questions, then withdrawn to the east. But several times during the day, the warship's profile had reappeared hull-down on the horizon, watching - with probably the best of intentions - for the sailboat's safe passage through these troubled waters. This had constrained Michael to stand on for Djerba, his reported destination. He and Astrid had gone ashore to sample the Tunisian souk's delights and had decided to eat dinner there.

Now, having left the island's marina at noon with AIS in silent mode, he hoped to escape unseen to make the rendezvous at midnight tonight. The easterly breeze was inconvenient for sailing, so he had decided

The Travel Agent

to motor the hundred miles to Zuwara. An added advantage of bare poles was to make the cat less visible to both eyeball and radar. He scanned the seas nervously from *Surf Warrior*'s flybridge, frequently checking the chartplotter for contacts. The delay had forced Astrid to risk a text to Greta, rearranging the rendezvous.

By late afternoon, the sky had become overcast; the wind veered south and dropped to almost nothing, bringing in a stifling, sultry heat from the desert. As seven p.m. approached, the sun flashed brilliantly but briefly, then sank, projecting lurid fire onto the lumbering clouds. Half an hour later, with the sunset flames fading astern, the evening gloom turned rapidly to complete darkness. Beyond the dimmed instruments on the flybridge, only the sporadic flare of phosphorescence from the twin bow waves cut through the totality of the night.

With only twenty miles to go, the thrumming of the two powerful engines seemed suddenly loud, adding to the palpable tension of their covert approach to a potentially hostile shore. Michael eased back the throttle controls until the log showed a steady four knots.

'Relax, Captain,' cooed Astrid, coming up beside him, eyes gleaming in the light from the compass, 'this is the last time. And a perfect night for it. How is your tummy now? Did the pill work?'

Michael shook his head sadly. 'Hard as concrete.'

At a mile to the waypoint, Michael killed the engines, letting the boat's momentum carry them into the shallows with the sounding at three metres. The catamaran's draught was a mere eighty centimetres, so

7: Galene's Mission

they would be able to get closer in than usual, making for a shorter ride from shore.

Astrid took out her phone and speed-dialled Greta. The ring tone sounded for a few seconds, then cut off. The nurse shrugged her ample shoulders and tried again, and again the call went unanswered. Then her phone pinged as a text came in.

> We are ready – send a signal

Shaking her head, Astrid lifted the big torch and flashed it once to shoreward.

'Why didn't she answer like always?' Michael said, 'you don't suppose–'

'They're here,' interrupted Astrid, stepping down onto the sundeck. The soft splutter of an outboard drifted across the calm water, coming closer, and out of the darkness morphed a slighter darker shape. Astrid climbed out onto the starboard hull, preparing to take their line.

'As-salam alaykom, Boulos,' she called - her usual greeting to the driver - as the boat glided in. Astrid shielded her eyes as - instead of the customary return greeting - a powerful light pierced the night.

'Put that fucking light out!' shouted Michael from the flybridge, then saw in the glare, the dull gleam of a rifle barrel.

'Get back inside, Astrid, quick, move!' he called shrilly.

Michael dashed forward to start the engines as heavy footfalls sounded from astern, coming up the starboard transom steps. Before he could reach the ignition key, a bearded face peered at him through the spray shield.

The Travel Agent

A rifle butt arced over the plexiglass and cracked jarringly against Michaels skull, sending him staggering back. Stunned almost unconscious, the skipper was caught in the arms of another man coming up the bridge ladder. Concussed and barely registering what was happening, Michael was catapulted down the ladder into a sprawling heap on the sundeck.

By now, a dozen or so men had swarmed the cat. Astrid, protesting loudly, was forced onto the sundeck at rifle-point, her wrists bound with cable-ties. A stinking rag, stuffed into her mouth, reduced her protestations to frustrated grunts. She was then thrown down to join the dazed Michael. He too by now found himself bound at the wrists, though he was incapable of resistance; drifting in and out of consciousness until finally, he dropped into a well of oblivion.

The pain came first, dull but insistent, lurking in the darkness behind closed eyes. Other sensations jostled for attention; cold concrete against a cheek, pins and needles in a trapped limb, children's voices squabbling beyond unseen confines, a putrid stink from something terrible. The puzzling sensations were like disconnected elements of an action-painting that made no sense until the whole was complete. Recollection came last, creeping back in dreadful segments. Michael opened his crusted eyelids, and the finished picture was revealed in all its dismal portent.

Sitting up was a groaning, stiff-jointed effort and brought throbbing pain to his head and a sea of nausea. Easing his back against a crumbling plaster wall, the young skipper squinted around his dreary cell while pummelling life back into his benumbed arm.

7: Galene's Mission

A small unglazed window high on the opposite wall admitted daylight into a tiny room devoid of furniture. Slivers of light came from ventilation slats in a wooden door - no handle on the inside, though it looked flimsy enough to kick down. A shadow indicated someone moving outside. A sentry, perhaps.

Michael could now identify the sweet, metallic odour that had accompanied his awakening. It was a smell he remembered from his time in Rwanda. One particular time. When his team had crossed into DRC to assist a Hutu village after a visit by Rwandan troops. It was the smell of spilled blood and death.

Michael picked the dried blood from his eyelashes then tentatively explored the wound on his brow, winced as he felt the dried-up gash; forelock hair glued to a ridge of scabbed skin. How long had he been lying here? Someone had taken his watch and his phone.

Questions hounded him.

Where was he? Somewhere in Libya, undoubtedly, but by the coast or in the desert? Where was Astrid? Had they hurt her, was she even alive? And what of Greta? What had gone wrong? Where was she now? How would he explain to the catamaran's owner what had become of his half-a-million-pound boat? What *had* become of *Surf Warrior*, anyway? Should he, Michael, even care?

A male voice outside, Arabic, chastising. The children's squeals and shouts drifted further away. The shadow beyond the door moved again, the click of a lighter, cigarette smoke wafting through the slats.

Standing up, Michael swooned against the wall, dizzy and sick with fear. Then his bowel was on the move. When the moment had passed, he took two

The Travel Agent

steps across the room and slapped his hand against the door, rattling bolts on the outside.

'Hey, can I talk to somebody?'

He backed up as bolts scraped and the door swung inwards.

'So, English, you wake up, eh?'

The man wore a black turban: shiny black eyes, a sparseness of curly black facial hair - hardly a beard. The guy was young: early twenties, Michael guessed; skinny in black fatigues and military boots, a Kalashnikov swinging from his shoulder.

'Why am I here? And where is my crew?'

'No questions, you stay here until your time.'

'My– my time?'

A wild smirk, a black-nailed finger drawn across a spotted neck scarf. 'When we take your head.'

Michael staggered on fear-weakened knees. Swallowing bile, he croaked, 'Why, what have I done?'

'You are infidel. You try steal wife of my commander.'

'Your com– Who are you people?'

An evil sneer. 'Who you think, eh?'

Michael stared at him in petrified silence.

The militiaman nodded slowly, then reached for something on the ground. 'Here,' he said, kicking a plastic bucket into the cell. 'For you piss.'

With a final nasty grin, the guard pulled shut the door. The bolts slid home with the sound of a blade through gristle.

Michael groaned as his gut turned and rumbled ominously. Fear was achieving what Astrid's laxative pill had failed to do. With a feverish fumbling of his

7: Galene's Mission

shorts, he squatted over the bucket, evacuating his quivering bowel in an unstoppable splatter.

EPISODE EIGHT

Surveillance & Capture

8: Surveillance & Capture

8/1

Roberto

After ordering his breakfast, Roberto asked: 'So, what's the book about?'

'Are you paying for breakfast?'

'No, you are.'

'Then I get to ask the questions, right?' Rosie lifted the teapot, grinning. 'More tea?'

Her breakfast companion feigned an injured look. His name was Rob Marsa, a nerdy, sixty-something Gibraltarian: the man in charge of South Ops. Keen to promote the voluntary group and its work, he had agreed to meet Rosie for an al fresco 'full-English' in Ocean Village, the hedonistic heart of the territory's moneyed district.

'Maybe if I knew what you are writing about I could, you know–'

'Yeah, I know. I really appreciate you agreeing to help, but I prefer to curate my own research.'

Rob's brow creased in puzzlement while Rosie scouted her surroundings, something she did routinely.

8: Surveillance & Capture

She had already clocked several security cameras; Ocean Village positively bristled with them. As for hostile eyes and ears, there was one man she could not entirely dismiss. He sat three tables away, tapping away busily on his phone – he had arrived just after Rob and was on his second coffee. Rosie had nothing concrete on the man, merely a degree of uncertainty in his deportment. However, she had had several false alarms, and indeed, just at that moment, the man stood up and went to pay his bill.

'Okay,' said Rob, miffed at Rosie's harsh putdown. 'So, what you want to know?'

Rosie smiled an apology, 'Sorry, that was rude of me. Do you think we could start with a quick overview of South Ops?'

'Sure. Well, we're a voluntary group, as you know. Most of us worked for the government at one time. Some are ex-cops, some like me were in Gibraltar Defence Force. In the late eighties, we got together after Spain joined the EEC and British forces were being scaled down.

'Up till then, the place was a proper fortress. The Army had a full battalion here, plus a Royal Marine Commando. The RAF sent four flights a day to keep stores topped up. There were four phantoms, two buccaneers, and a couple of helicopters stationed permanently at North Front. The dockyard was just a mass of grey: destroyers and carriers, auxiliary ships, and submarines stopping off regular like, ships coming for refit: there was always one or two frigates in dry dock.

'Hey, here's a story. In the sixties and seventies, the Spanish had dis old corvette: *Smoky Joe*, we called it.

The Travel Agent

Every day *Smoky Joe* would come over from Algeciras and cross into UK waters, taunting us, you know? And out would go the Navy's patrol boat to shoo him away. It was like a tradition: every morning they'd sit off by North Mole, wait for our boys to turn up, then scoot back to Algeciras for their *almuerzo* and *siesta*. It went on for years, even after Franco died.

'After '85 the UK Government, in its wisdom, decided Gib was safe because Spain was now a European ally. Yeah, right? But when British started pulling back, dey left us open to illegal's from across the Strait. The government didn't think that was a big deal, but we knew it would be … in the future. Turns out, what with ISIS and da refugee crisis, we were right, and they were wrong. And it's getting more dangerous every day.

'Er, should you be making notes or something?'

Rosie grinned. 'I've got a good memory. So, how many of you are there in North Ops, and what do you do, exactly?'

'Only fifteen of us left now. We take turns to be out overnight in pairs. We drive along the east side, stopping to check out the places we know where people could sneak ashore.'

'Ever caught anyone?'

'Only a matter of time,' Rob grinned ruefully. 'I could take you on a tour if I knew what you wanted. My car's only in da carpark here.'

'Okay,' Rosie relented, lowering her voice. 'I'm researching a novel about the drug trade, pure fiction - no names, no actual events. I just want to make sure I get the right angle on security. How the stuff could get

8: Surveillance & Capture

in. It needs to be believable, even for people who live here.'

Rob shrugged. 'Most people wouldn't care, I think. A great story's a great story.'

'All the same, I like to get my facts right. Let us start with: what is South Ops for?'

Carefully, Rob lined up the knife and fork on his emptied plate, dabbed his mouth delicately with a napkin. Finally, he said, 'We're not about stopping the druggies, no point, really, with the er—situation here. We're just wanna protect our home from terrorists and illegal's.'

Rosie nodded. 'From Morocco, I presume?'

He shook his head. 'Today they come from everywhere, all over Africa, Mid-east, even from Asia. People on the move looking for a better life. We're a small island, already overcrowded; we have no room for dem. Bad enough wid tourists.'

'JMCC seem to have it well covered. Probably why you've caught nobody, don't you think?'

Rob gave a derisive snort, 'You been up there, yeah? Sure, they got all the technology, they got the staff. But this Rock, you know, little hidey holes, cracks and crevices, especially on the east side. I can show you where people could land; there's a hundred places and dose people up da the Hole, they're too– you know?'

'Complacent?'

'Yeah, complacent. Dey think they see anyone coming near in their little spy cameras. What about swimmers? I say.'

Rosie was quite sure a swimmer at night would light up an infra-red camera but did not argue the point.

The Travel Agent

'They think all illegals coming from Morocco go to Spain,' Rob continued, 'get picked up by GC. Up to now, it's true, but now we got Libya. They took out Gaddafi and got Al Qaeda, Muslim Brotherhood, all dat shit. Now ISIS; the new caliphate in the west. Tunisia and Algeria have weak governments, easy for exploit. They get closer every day. You see dis morning's news?'

Rosie let her mind drift back to one of her briefings at Sparta.

'Sirte,' Gadfly, pointing out the troubled metropolis on the map, 'Gaddafi's home city, and until recently, the hub of Daesh's new Libyan caliphate.'

A head-and-shoulders shot of a black-clad jihadist appears on the screen, an inset on the map: luxuriant black beard with shaved moustache, a single glaring eye, the other absent, the socket inexpertly sutured. Behind him, the now-familiar black flag of the caliphate.

'This is Rasheed al Basara, claims to lead the new Libyan caliphate after defeats in Iraq and Syria. But he was pushed out of the city in May by Misrata-based militias after six-months fighting. Al Basara survived with four-hundred fighters and moved south, capturing the desert town of Bani Waleed and its nearby oil fields. NATO estimates al Basara's forces now number in thousands.'

'Sorry,' Rosie said, returning to the now. 'Miles away. What news?'

Rob shook his head sadly, 'No, I don't expect you saw it. All we get on BBC these days is Brexit, Brexit, fucking Brexit. But guess what! There's a big wide world right here on our doorstep. The story's all over

8: Surveillance & Capture

CNN and Al Jazeera. The jihadists took Sabratha last week, and they'll soon be at the Tunisian border if they're not stopped.'

Rosie's heart almost stopped. Engrossed in solving the riddle of insurgent fighters she had focussed on little else since arriving here. Sabratha was only thirty miles east of Zuwara, Michael's destination.

'What's up? You look like you've seen a—'

'Rob, I'm so sorry, I have to go.'

The poor man looked bewildered. 'But—'

'I'd still like to take up your offer of a tour – can I call you?'

'Okay, no prob—'

'Can I leave you to pay the bill?' She pushed a twenty across the table. 'That should cover it. I'm really sorry, I have to go - no time to explain - I'll call you later, promise.'

Arriving back on board after a furious cycle-ride across the airfield and frontier, Rosie rapped the table with impatient fingers while her computer booted up.

But Marine Traffic drew a blank on *Surf Warrior* - last known position yesterday morning, in the Tunisian marina on Djerba. Checking the CNN website to verify Rob's news, she found the article and read it carefully. There was no mention of Zuwara, but it was only a small town and may not merit naming. The one ray of hope lay in the report of rebels consolidating their hold on Sabratha, which could mean they were in no hurry to drive further west.

As for Michael, he could be safely on his way with his AIS on silent - no real reason to suppose otherwise, just a bad feeling. She considered calling, but at sea, the skipper would be unlikely to be in signal range.

Next, she opened the Firegate encrypted mailbox and read the reply waiting there:

> From: Housekeeper
> To Galene
> Sea platform appears to be seabed research laboratory owned and financed by private business consortium. Legitimate private enterprise - NFA.
> Occurs to me South Ops ideally placed to run infiltration operation. Implausible, maybe, but running BG checks on members (in anticipation of your request).
> H.

She keyed back a hurried reply.

> From: Galene
> To: Housekeeper
> IMO South Ops just a bunch of conspiracy theorists who don't trust government. But will keep contact and open mind. Touring Rock with leader PM today to discover poss. entry points.
> G.

Rosie closed the lid of her laptop, took out her phone, and after a moment's lip-chewing, tapped in Michael's speed-dial.

8: Surveillance & Capture

8/2

Prisoner

Michael woke to the scrape of the bolts on his cell door. He sat up, head pounding, a squadron of monstrous black flies circulating; the stink from his shit-bucket was overpowering.

The door swung open, bringing a flood of blinding light. Michael cringed into the wall at his back, gut wrenched with fear, as a cloaked figure filled the doorway: a spectral shadow backlit by the desert sun. In his terror, he imagined the figure holding a crescent scythe. Is this it then, a gruesome and anonymous end to his twenty-six years?

'Ugh! You people! This is inhuman. Bring water, hurry.' A familiar Swedish accent.

Michael wanted to call her name to make sure he was not hallucinating, but his mouth was glued shut with dehydration. Instead, he just simpered as she knelt beside him. Her nurse's tabard had been exchanged for an all-covering blue abaya; her blonde hair hidden under a loosely-worn hijab.

8: Surveillance & Capture

'Sorry I couldn't come sooner, my Captain, but they made me treat their fighters first. They have no medicos here so, for now, I am useful to them, eh?'

Michael tried to return her smile but desisted as his lips cracked. Astrid dragged up a dusty leather suitcase and clicked it open, revealing an array of medical supplies.

'Thank our Russian friends for this,' she said. 'Now, let me look at your head. Oh! that will need some sutures.'

A black-clad militiaman entered and set down two bottles of water, then stood gawping down at Michael.

'Out, out,' shooed the nurse in matronly tones, 'and take that stinky bucket with you.'

She helped Michael drink, careful to see he took small sips, and then let him cradle the tepid bottle while she got to work washing his wound.

With his tongue suitably lubricated, he said, 'Russian friends?'

'Ya. I was very surprised to see the Russians here. I think they are playing a dirty game – that is what they do. We Swedes know Russians better than most.'

'Where are we, Astrid?'

'I am not sure - a city with many ruined houses. There has been fighting. We came here in the back of a lorry, for maybe an hour. I think we came east, on the coast road, but it is hard to know in the dark.'

'What happened, do you know? And where is Greta, is she okay?'

'Greta is back with her husband,' she said mournfully. 'We were betrayed, Michael, by one of our women. These bastards,' she jerked a thumb at the open doorway where the guard stood, 'killed poor

The Travel Agent

Boulos, the boat driver, and his brother. They cut off their heads right there in front of me.'

Michael shivered, icy fingers up his spine. 'Did you speak to Greta?'

'Only whispers in the back of the truck. We could not talk much. The poor child is frightened. She thinks they will kill her soon, maybe when the Russians have gone.'

'Who exactly are these Russians?'

'Two men, civilians maybe, but you can never be sure with Russians. I saw them talking with Rasheed - that is Greta's husband, he is the leader here.'

'Why would Russians be talking to ISIS? They're bombing the shit out of them in Syria.'

Astrid paused her work and met his eyes. His forehead felt cold where she had applied an iodine solution strong enough to make his eyes water.

'This is not Syria, here is oil, the best quality, and the caliphate control it. When it comes to business and resources, the Russians are pragmatic people.'

'Jesus! What a world.'

Astrid gave him a wry grin, 'It is a world I have lived in for twenty years, Michael. Nothing surprises me anymore. Remember our time in Rwanda?'

'Huh, do you think I could forget?'

'No, of course not. Your poor Sara−'

'They told me they were going to kill me,' Michael's voice quavered, 'do you think they mean it?'

'Both of us, probably, when I am finished repairing their broken fighters. But again, maybe not while the Russians are here, eh?' She squeezed his shoulder. 'We just stay strong and hope for a miracle, my

8: Surveillance & Capture

Captain. Now, hold still while I sew your brains back in. Lucky you're not President Trump, eh?'

'Huh?'

'Because then I would be sewing up your anus ... Michael, keep still!'

The Travel Agent

8/3

Alert

The Housekeeper's intercom buzzed.
'Moth on line three, Ma'am.'
Moth! The autistic geek at Camp Sparta. What the hell did he want?

'Right. Put him through … Good morning Moth, what can I do for you?'

The technician's words came in a nonsensical rush, *'He's in Libya. Do you−'*

'Moth, stop!' snapped The Housekeeper, 'Slow down, get your breath, and tell me what the hell you're talking about.'

'Michael McCaffey, he's in Libya.'

'Right. So, tell me, who is Michael McCaffey?'

'The man Galene asked me to put a watch on.'

'What, her yachtsman friend?'

'The alert was set to trigger if the subject's phone connected to any cell in Libya.'

Of course, the cyber-sleuth knew nothing of McCaffey's background. Given his technically-

8: Surveillance & Capture

obsessive and withdrawn personality, he would not anyway be interested. Galene had mentioned McCaffey to her during her mission briefing: something about a baby-adoption scheme. If his mercy operation was still ongoing, and his boat was close enough to shore, then what significance could be drawn from this? Probably none.

'Is this the first time this alert's been triggered?'

'Otherwise, I wouldn't be calling you,' Moth sounded offended.

'Yes, of course. You were right to. Have you got a better location than just Libya?'

'I'll need to hack into Al Madar's server in Trip−'

'Alright, just get me a location and if possible, a call transcript. And Moth, keep this to yourself – I don't want Galene distracted by this.'

She ended the call, and after a long moment's thought, buzzed her secretary back.

'Where are Gauntlet and Hammer?'

'Manchester, Ma'am, stakeout in Piccadilly.'

'Still? Wha… Oh, never mind. When Gauntlet next checks in ask him to give me a call – not urgent. And page Gadfly - put her straight through when she calls.'

8/4

Fingers Cave

Rosie peered dubiously into the entrance: steps cut into the limestone leading steeply down into darkness. She turned back to her guide.

'Fingers Cave, really?'

Rob had turned off the road that ran the length of the Rock's eastern littoral and drove inland along an unmade track that ended under one of the massif's pendulous overhangs. Parking up, he had led Rosie here through a jumble of fallen rocks and slid aside a rusty corrugated sheet to expose the tunnel.

'Army sappers excavated it during the Great Seige,' Rob explained. 'They named the cave after some composer.'

Rosie threw him a sideways grin, 'The renowned Felix "Fingers" Mendelsohn, probably.'

Noticing Rob's uncertain frown, Rosie quickly deflected, 'So, it's a well-known cave, then?'

'A rockfall blocked it years ago, and it got forgotten. It was only when construction workers took away the

8: Surveillance & Capture

rocks to build sea defences that it got rediscovered. But no, it's not well known - most people don't even know it's here.'

Rob shone a powerful torch down into the hole. 'Stay close behind me. It gets a bit slippery further down.'

A distant murmur of the sea accompanied their cautious descent down the long tunnel; a cool updraft carried the stink of dried-out seaweed. The noise level gradually increased: tiny fluctuations of pressure on the ears accompanied the slurping, and sucking sounds echoing up the shaft. Finally, the steps levelled. They entered a spacious cavern, onto a ledge with a swirling maelstrom a few feet below. They could go no further.

'Whoa!' shouted Rosie, her voice-echo buffeted on the tidal racket. 'Who knew?'

It was a sea cave, alive with movement. Daylight spilling in through a crescent gash in the rock shifted with the rise and fall of the incoming swell, casting ghostly rippling shapes on the curve of the rough limestone roof. A fine mist of spray hung in the air.

'I thought I'd save the best till last,' Rob shouted back, a sheen of spray on his grinning face.

The cave's entrance looked treacherous; any swimmer attempting entry from seaward risked being dashed on its jagged rim. Rosie stepped to the edge and peered down into the turbulence.

'How deep is it?'

'Quite deep.' Rob shouted. 'On a calm day, with a westerly wind, you can see the bottom. About twenty feet, I'd guess.'

Rosie checked her watch and did a quick calculation; it was about an hour after high water. She nodded toward the entrance. 'So, on a calm day, at low tide, could you get a boat through there, do you think?'

Rob shook his head. 'Not enough headroom - a surfboard, maybe.' He grinned and made a downward swooping motion with his hand. 'Or a submarine.' Noticing her frown, he added, 'No matter though, eh? In your book, you can make the hole as big as you want.'

Rosie nodded. 'True.'

Fifteen minutes later, they emerged from the tunnel into sweltering sunshine. Leaving Rob to replace the makeshift cover, Rosie studied the surrounding area. She estimated they were maybe a hundred metres from the road, with another fifty metres to the cliff edge. The overhanging precipice would provide cover from any camera above. However, Rosie still thought it unlikely that an approach from seaward could be made unseen. And as for that treacherous cave-entrance…

'That's it,' said Rob coming up behind her. 'The perfect smuggler's grotto for your story, yes?'

'Fingers Cave,' she nodded, putting on a smile. 'I like it.'

'Was that his nickname, then – Fingers?'

'Er … great pianist, I guess. It's getting late, Rob, let's get back.'

Rob dropped her off at Ocean Village where she had left her bike. He turned down her offer to buy him a drink for his trouble; said he never touched the booze but would settle for a signed copy of the book.

As Rob drove off, Rosie frowned after him. She was no closer to solving the riddle and was beginning to think she was on a hiding to nothing. Perhaps she was looking in the wrong place?

8: Surveillance & Capture

Strolling along the marina boardwalk, Rosie paused to look up and down the line of pleasure-boats. What if the answer lay closer to home? Perhaps among these numerous small vessels that each day plied the busy Straits? To find out, she needed to be here amongst them and start monitoring their movements.

8/5

Dog-walk

Rob Marsa parked in the carport under his residential block overlooking Rosia Bay. He hurried up the three flights to his apartment. The Rock tour with the writer had taken longer than he had anticipated, and his little dog, Bluey, would be desperate to go out.

Rob never got out much since his wife died of cancer four years ago. He was sixty-four now and had given up all hope of ever meeting anyone again, had resigned himself to a lonely and solitary existence. These days, the only highpoints in life were the night drives with watchmate, Danny, along the eastern coves and caves. Looking for the illegal's he knew deep down would never materialise. Rosie had it right: the new people up in The Hole with all that fancy gear had security well covered.

For Rob, the night-patrols were just a pointless exercise: for someone to talk to other than little Bluey, who never spoke back, and his nosy neighbour in the

8: Surveillance & Capture

flat above, who just irritated him. But Danny was thirty and single with an eye for the ladies, and just lately his lurid tales had only served to increase Rob's sense of isolation and loneliness.

His recent chat with two of the local druggies was a symptom of that loneliness. The younger Rob, the GDF Officer Rob, would have shopped the guys without hesitation. But now temptation hovered over his conscience and threatened to submerge him into the dark side. It was not the money, but the sense of belonging that urged him to join the gangland underworld.

But today was a boost. Today Rob had decided to reject the offer. The day out with a girl, chatting like regular people, sharing funny remarks, teasing and joshing, had felt good. Under no illusions about his chances with such a smart and pretty young thing – what would she want with an old fart? - he nevertheless felt encouraged. Even if he did not see Rosie again, the new confidence she had given him got him thinking maybe he should start getting out more, meet more people. After all, you never know what might happen.

Reaching his door, Rob could see Bluey's little grey shape bouncing excitedly through the frosted glass. As he unlocked the door, a dreaded voice rang down from the landing above.

'A man was here asking for you, Roberto.' It was Mrs Jervis, his neighbour from the flat above, leaning over the railing.

'Did he say what he wanted?' asked Rob, impatient to get to Bluey before it was too late; the little mutt had no control when she was excited.

The Travel Agent

'No. Big man, baseball cap and sunglasses. Didn't like the look, personally.'

Rob grinned to himself. Mrs Jervis, a small elderly woman, living alone, disliked the look of anyone she did not know.

Rob opened his door, and Bluey flew out, tail wagging furiously as she circled the landing leaving small droplets in her wake. Rob reached around the door and grabbed her lead from its hook, then pulled the door closed.

'If he comes back,' Rob called to Mrs Jervis, 'we'll be out for an hour or so.'

Rob followed his desperate Jack Russel down the stairs. He reached the patio to find the little dog already squatting in the acacia, splashing out the contents of her tortured bladder and grinning. When she had finished, she came to him, happily allowing her leash to be clipped on before trotting on ahead. Bluey was eager to be on the clifftop walk with its glorious smells and skittering lizards.

As the happy pair made their way briskly down the hill towards Rosia Bay, a large man wearing a baseball cap and sunglasses stepped from behind the colonnade and followed at a discreet distance.

8: Surveillance & Capture

8/6

Disturbing News

After making herself a light salad supper on-board, Rosie settled down in the cockpit to eat while checking Marine Traffic once more. *Surf Warrior* was nowhere to be seen – the catamaran's history track at Djerba was no longer registered.

The agent was washing up when her phone buzzed. It was Rob Marsa's number.

'Hi, Rob. What's up?'

'Hey, Rosie. Something I forgot to tell you this afternoon, one of the sites we visited.'

'What, Fingers Cave,' she laughed. 'Don't tell me, it's haunted.'

'No, not the cave. It's the little–'

…

'Little what? … Rob, you still there?'

Rosie checked her phone – the call was still connected.

8: Surveillance & Capture

'Hello, Rob, can you hear me? I think you lost your signal. If you can hear me call me back when you can. Cheers. Later.'

She ended the call and sat down, thinking. Little what? Little bay, little cove? They had visited loads of sites this afternoon – it could be anything. Oh well, he'll call back if it's essential. She put Rob Marsa out of her mind and stepped below to write her update for The Housekeeper.

Early the following morning, Saturday, Rosie paid her bill at the Spanish marina and motored *Pasha* to Marina Bay. Here she took the opportunity to top-up with duty-free diesel before slotting into a mooring between two school-boats. Mooring in Gib was much more expensive than La Linea, but Firegate were generous about expenses. Only one downside: the nights in Marina Bay, with its profusion of bars and restaurants, could get noisy, even more so at weekends. But, the agent supposed, she could always join in the partying. Earplugs were a last resort, of course.

Having booked in, Rosie now sat drinking coffee at a quayside café. With her mind on Michael and Astrid, she paid scant attention to the news's silent images on the overhead TV screen. And Rosie thought too of the little one-eyed jihadi bride going home to be deradicalized and reunited with her family.

Surf Warrior still had not shown up on Marine Traffic, which she should have done by now. There could be any number of explanations, she reasoned, but could not ignore the nagging doubt. Had she not

The Travel Agent

been so lost in her anxiety, she would have noticed the man before his shadow fell over her table.

'Mind if I join you?' a voice she instantly recognised, and a little shiver ran through her as he slid smoothly into the seat opposite.

'Looks like I don't have a choice, what are you doing here?'

Leviticus gave her an injured look that did nothing to diminish the amused twinkle in those chestnut eyes.

'You didn't call me,' he said. 'For dinner?'

As if she needed reminding.

'No, I've been busy. I said I'd think about it.'

'And are you still?'

'What busy, or thinking about it?'

He shrugged but said nothing, just a quizzical smile that made her tingle again. God, he was good-looking and did he know it.

Before she could stop herself, she blurted out, 'I'm free tonight.'

His smile broadened, and she noticed, not for the first time, how perfect and how white were his teeth.

'There is a beautiful restaurant not far from here.

'Are we talking Gaucho's?'

'Oh, you know it. No good?'

'I hear the food's amazing.'

'Good. Shall we say, seven?'

'O-kay.'

He frowned at her slight hesitation. 'You don't seem sure, Rosie. If you…'

She reached over and patted his hand, giving him her best reassuring smile, 'It's a good choice, Leviticus, I'd love to try Gaucho's and seven-o-clock is fine. I'm looking forward to it.'

8: Surveillance & Capture

A surge of excitement ran through her, despite hating herself for giving in so easily.

Rosie did not register what he said next, because suddenly her attention was drawn to the TV screen behind him: a visage she instantly recognised. 'Drowning in Rosia Bay' said the caption underneath Rob Marsa's grinning face.

'Huh! I'm sorry, Leviticus, I have to go.'

She picked up her bag and rose to leave, the Ukrainian's face a picture of bewilderment. On impulse, she leaned over and kissed his cheek. 'I'll meet you outside Gaucho's at seven, promise,' she assured him before dashing off to get her bike.

Reaching the police substation in Casemates Square, Rosie locked up her bike, then hesitated, debating with herself the wisdom of reporting her connection with the drowned man. The Housekeeper would be furious at the unwanted exposure. If it had been an accidental drowning, Galen reasoned, it would not be such a big deal. On the other hand, if foul-play were suspected the local plod would most likely track her down – her breakfast with Rob yesterday morning was bound to have been captured on CCTV. Wouldn't it be best to allay any suspicions by coming forward first? What about that call from Rob yesterday evening? Was that significant? No, she must not mention that – it might blow her cover. She took a deep breath and walked briskly into the police station.

8/7

Interrogation

For Michael, sleep is the only respite from utter wretchedness: fitful sleep, alternating with spasms of nausea and stomach cramps, not helped by the stinking, suspiciously-stained mattress they have provided him with. Sleep punctuated by sudden starts and sickening anxiety. This time it is men's voices outside that drag him back to consciousness.

Astrid had been allowed back in to see him yesterday; to clean and re-dress his head wound. Once again the nurse had cajoled the guard to empty Michaels shit bucket and fetch him fresh water to wash.

Astrid has not appeared today. Apart from the daily delivery of what passes for food - a sticky, foul-smelling brown mess – he has seen nobody. Once more, the stink of his faeces from this morning's ablutions is attracting a swarm of blowflies.

Recalling accounts of victims held in captivity - sometimes for years - by these people, he has begun a

8: Surveillance & Capture

makeshift calendar: two marks there now, scraped on the wall with a spoon. Perhaps, like in Shawshank Redemption, he can scratch out an escape hole in the wall. He imagines his secreted spoon worn down to a stump.

The voices, which sound like Arabic, cease. The two bolts are slipped, and the rickety door swings open. Michael looks up eagerly, but it is not Astrid. It is one of the militiamen.

'Get up, English, you have a visitor.'

The guard stands aside, and another man enters carrying a folding chair. Michael sits up and winces, a painful rash has developed in his crotch.

'Stand up,' orders the man with the chair.

Staggering to his feet, Michael holds up a hand against the light to get a better look at him. No jihadi fighter, this: tall, clean-shaven, dressed in smart desert-khaki. Hope stirs faintly amid the misery.

The man smiles, then opens the chair and bids Michael sit. Dull, stupefied, Michael sits.

'Now, tell me why you came here to Libya,' the man demands in faultless English with a faint accent. There are Russians here, Michael remembers Astrid telling him.

'Where's Astrid?'

'Why did you come to Libya?'

Astrid said they had been betrayed. They already had Greta back. How much had she told them?

'We didn't come to Libya. We were just anchoring offshore overnight.'

'To kidnap the wife of a hero of the caliphate.'

'That's not how it…'

'How do you know this woman, Greta?'

The Travel Agent

'We did…'

'Who sent you here?'

'Nob…'

'Who do you work for?'

'I don't …'

He does not see it coming; a numbing shock: Michael sprawls onto concrete, vaguely registering the chair falling on him. Blinding pain thunders into his brain. Vision all but gone, he is hoisted to his feet. His arms are pulled behind him, a click as cold metal closes around his wrists. Swooning, he is seated once more, his handcuffed wrists hooked excruciatingly behind the chair back. As vision returns, a smartphone appears under his nose.

'Who is this woman?'

Michael draws his head back to focus his blurry eyes on the screen. As the image slowly clears, incomprehension ties his tongue.

'Who is she?' insists the Russian in a reasonable tone.

Michael looks again, unable to believe what he sees. That ridiculous buzz-cut – she is in conversation with some scruffy-looking older man at a table, clearly unaware of being photographed. Moored boats in the background, a marina somewhere. *Gibraltar!* That's right, she is in Gib. Michael shakes his head slowly to clear the fuzziness of his thoughts. He remembers why she has gone there – to investigate the cocaine trade in Gib. What could that have to do with these people?

'Where did you get this?' Michael slurs. Too late, he realises he has just wasted the chance of denial.

'Okay, once more. Who is the girl?'

8: Surveillance & Capture

Michael looks up at his questioner and attempts a disdainful grin. 'Go fuck yourself!'

As he is again knocked to the ground, a searing pain shoots up his arm - jarred by the handcuffs.

'Fuck! I think my wrist is…'

Once again, head ringing, he is picked up and re-seated.

'You can answer my questions, or we can do it the hard way.'

Michael wonders how much harder it can get. Though dazed and hurting, he is determined not to get Rosie involved in this nightmare.

'Up yours,' he grates. 'You broke my fucking wrist.'

'We know you are connected with this woman. She called your phone. Who are you working for?'

Oh, shit! Did she speak to them, he wonders, or did it go to voicemail? If so, what message could she have left?

Michael groans. 'Look, she's my friend, okay? We don't work together. She just sails her dad's boat, that's all – you have to believe me. So what, if she sometimes calls me? We're friends - where's the problem?'

The Russian's face comes down level with his. 'I ask myself this: should I believe your story? We will see.'

The Russian straightens and beckons to a third man, also in khaki. But all Michael is focussed on is the hypodermic syringe descending as the other two men hold him firmly in the chair. The needle sinks deep into his upper arm. Another thought occurs to him even as his vision begins to shrink: Russians are in Gib, and they are after Rosie. Then, a closing dark– falling, falling.

The Travel Agent

A century passes.

…

'What is your name?'

A floating face on a sea of fog.

'Feel… sick.'

'It will soon pass. What is your name?'

'My wrist hurts.'

'What is your name?'

'Michael McCaffey.'

'Who do you work for, Michael McCaffey?'

'Nobody.'

'Then why are you here?'

'Last trip.'

'Last trip - you have been here before?'

'Babies. Astrid saves them. We rescue the kids.'

…

'Michael, who is the woman in the picture?'

'Russians. Astrid says you're Russian.' Michael giggles insanely. 'Ba-aad people.'

'Who is the woman, Michael?'

'Rosie… Smuggling.'

'Rosie? Her name is Rosie?'

'Yes,… Rosie.'

'What is Rosie smuggling, Michael?'

The floating face moves from side to side… no, he realises it is his own head, shaking. 'Government.'

'The British Government? Rosie works for the British Government?'

'Mm. Under-cover work. Please … don't hurt Rosie.'

8: Surveillance & Capture

8/8

Osprey

High on a bastion wall eating her lunch, Rosie gazed out over the shining strait separating two continents. Between her and the distance-misted mountains of Morocco sailed numerous ships, their stately progress discernible only by the silvery tracings of their wakes, like vapour-trails, melting into the pristine blueness of a tranquil sea. The agent looked down and wrinkled her nose at her dull cheese sandwich and sighed wistfully; such a panorama deserved oysters and champagne.

Leaving the police substation this morning, Rosie had returned on-board to pack her bag with the things she would need for her solitary vigil. Sometime during the morning, a cruise ship had appeared on North Mole, spilling its human cargo into the town.

Keen to avoid the milling crowds, Rosie had cycled instead along the Queensway Road, stopping to buy lunch at the supermarket, then on to Ragged Staff. She had locked her bicycle to a lamppost under the eyes of

8: Surveillance & Capture

dockyard security guards before walking up through the Botanical Gardens to Europa Road. From here the agent had followed the same route taken for her run on Tuesday: up to Levant Battery and the Med Steps. Still sunburned from Tuesday's run, today she thought it prudent to cover up: long sleeves and jeans, and a wide-brim sunhat.

Rock Gun Battery provided a commanding view of the eastern shoreline and Mediterranean approaches. Her initial motives had been vague, little more than an impulsive urge - to reconnoitre from above the possible gaps in security, to watch the comings and goings of shipping. And simply just to enjoy this godlike overlook.

But mainly, she realised, to be alone. To think.

It saddened her that she had met Rob only yesterday, and now he was dead. Although she would waste little time mourning a man she barely knew, she wondered if he had left anybody behind, a wife, children, perhaps? She had not thought to ask the officer who had taken down her details, and now wished she had.

He had apparently taken a fall from the quayside at Rosia Bay during the late evening. Police assumed he had hit his head on the rocks before tumbling into the water. It was hard to believe a sober man would be so careless; Rob had told her he never touched alcohol. There had been nobody about at the time to rescue the poor man. Otherwise, he might have survived. Apparently, the barking of his little dog had alerted a couple of walkers. There was to be a post-mortem to confirm the cause of death; the Coroner's hearing was set for Tuesday morning.

The Travel Agent

On her way up the Rock, Rosie had encountered crowds at all the usual tourist haunts. They poured out of their luxury coaches to marvel at the views and pose warily for selfies with the apes. But few sightseers ventured to this lofty redoubt. And that meant the apes were also absent. Happily, this left the agent to eat her lunch unmolested.

Finishing her sandwich, Rosie made a ball of her food-packaging and stuffed it into her rucksack, then hopped off the wall to brush the crumbs from her jeans. Suddenly something crashed into bushes behind her. The agent whipped around, tensed, primed to meet an attack, already planning her moves, her options.

There was only one way into the bastion: the rocky footpath Rosie had climbed to get here. Metre-high bushes crowded either side of the track. A tree branch hanging in a patch of acacia and bindweed was shaking as if it had just been struck. Rosie held her breath as the shrubbery around the bough shivered, a rustle of something moving.

Or someone.

The distance from her to the opening was a good five metres – an assailant with a firearm would be a problem. She glanced around her for cover – nothing close enough. But all was quiet and unmoving now in the shrubs.

Crouching, prone and ready, Rosie recalled her sense of being followed, of being watched: the suited man on the next table while talking to Rob at breakfast yesterday. And again, with Albert on Tuesday afternoon - the dodgy guy at the bar.

Paranoia? Perhaps. But the agent had been trained to observe, to be suspicious.

8: Surveillance & Capture

Pay attention to your instincts, Gadfly had cautioned, *it could save your life.*

Perhaps it had been just a small rockfall.

Suddenly, a kerfuffle broke loose in the bushes, and into view rose a shape: the head of a raptor. Rosie relaxed and straightened as, with a talon hooked onto the hanging bough, the bird struggled out of the shrubbery until most of its body was visible. The creature was enormous. Unable to emerge further, it began emitting a shrill *chip-chip-chip* while flapping and clawing to extricate itself.

Still hyped-up with adrenalin, Rosie walked over. The bird eyed her, ceased for a moment its frantic calls, and stilled its struggles. One spread wing pointed awkwardly skyward, the other was snagged with skewed feathers in a tangle of bindweed. The animal's position was clearly not great. Only the one talon gripping the branch prevented it from falling back into the trap. The other one flexed and clawed uselessly for want of purchase among the flimsy weeds.

Rosie gave a gasp of surprise as she recognised the species: it was an osprey. Briefly, she flashed-back to the nesting pair at Camp Sparta.

'Hello,' Rosie cooed. 'I'm Rosie, and I'm here to help, so don't peck me, will you?'

As the agent reached carefully toward the trapped wing, a scolding eye glared at her. The raptor's bill dipped hesitantly towards her face, obliging her to exercise extreme caution.

Rosie had once, while fishing on *Pasha*, caught a booby on her trawl line. That seabird, she was able quickly to subdue and fold under her arm while disgorging the hook from its snapping beak. However,

The Travel Agent

the osprey was a much larger beasty - a lightning-fast and robust predator - and presented a far more formidable challenge.

'Let's see if we can get you out of there,' Rosie purred. Gingerly she reached in and tugged free a tendril of weed, snatching her hand away as the opened beak lunged viciously. Reaching in again, this time from lower down, Rosie eased more of the bindweed away, gradually reducing its hold on the mussed-up wing. The distressed animal lunged again and this time almost caught her fingers as she pulled away.

'C'mon, be nice to your Auntie Rosie,' Rosie pleaded. 'I'm only trying to …'

Suddenly, the clinging tendrils of bindweed sprung apart, and the raptor was free, clawing itself onto the tree-branch and then flapping into the air with a high-pitched *tweeh-tweeh*. Rosie quickly ducked to avoid the talons that swept so close above her head she felt their draught.

Turning around, the agent was surprised to see the osprey had not flown far - it now sat on her wall preening its dislodged flight-feathers back into order. Rosie kept her distance, and she was suddenly reminded of Michael: his hawk nose and deeply inset eyes.

Finally, satisfied with its plumage, the bird spread its enormous wings and was lifted effortlessly on the Levantine breeze. It circled once, in what Rosie fancied was a show of gratitude, before continuing across the Strait with a prolonged and piercing *tweeeeh,* away at last to continue its winter migration.

8: Surveillance & Capture

When the bird was little more than a speck in the southern sky, Rosie sighed with an audible murmur, a kind of 'Oh well.' After a few more moments, she roused herself and got to work.

Taking out her binoculars, she focussed on the enigmatic research platform twenty miles away to the east. What was its *real* purpose?

The Housekeeper had ordered NFA, no further action, but that had only piqued Rosie's interest further. How could they be so sure that that oddly stationed platform was not part of the operation Rosie was tasked to uncover?

As the platform's image zoomed in, she noticed its shape seemed to have changed since the last time she had looked. She gave the lenses a rub with her shirt and looked again. Yes, something *was* different: the rig was no longer symmetrically square but somehow lopsided. The reason soon became apparent, however: the platform had a visitor: a ship. It was impossible to identify what type of vessel at this distance. Still, it was reasonable to assume an offshore platform needed support vessels for provisions, fuel, and personnel exchange.

But it still did not explain why the rig was there? According to geological survey reports, there was no possibility of oil or gas in that region. And even if there had been, the platform lacked one crucial detail: a drilling rig. IRP was just an unremarkable, flat, greyish disc stuck in the middle of nowhere. And that bothered the agent.

She took out her phone and logged in to Marine Traffic. As she had discovered earlier, the platform lacked an AIS signal, which was unusual for a large

The Travel Agent

marine structure. However, the ship had a number that began with 273, identifying itself as RFS *Ivan Peronovich*, a hydrographic survey vessel of the Russian Federation. Drilling down into the vessel's details, her last port of call was unspecified. But the vessel's destination was Gibraltar.

Before leaving her over-look, Rosie swept the sea with her binoculars in the forlorn hope of finding Michael's delivery boat. She located several white flecks of sails dotting the Strait and more out to the east that seemed to be heading westward. But none were catamarans.

As Rosie left the old gun emplacement, a white flash in the shrubbery caught her eye. Walking over, she saw what it was, stuck on a thorn and flicking gently in the breeze. Reaching in, Rosie plucked out the white feather and smoothed it with her fingers. Smiling sadly, she touched it to her lips. 'Be safe,' Rosie murmured, thinking not of the osprey but her best friend, somewhere between here and strife-torn Libya, off the grid since Thursday morning and out of contact. She slipped the feather carefully into an empty compartment of her purse.

Rosie took the shorter route down the Rock, past the Siege Tunnels and Moorish Castle, then walked quickly through town to retrieve her bike from Ragged Staff. She needed to get back to *Pasha* and her laptop – she needed to know about Michael.

Arriving back onboard *Pasha*, Rosie again searched Marine Traffic, this time on her laptop. She frowned as the map zoomed to the Tunisian island of Djerba; the catamaran's last position had not moved from the

8: Surveillance & Capture

marina at Houmt El Souk. That could mean of course that they had had trouble with the boat and were awaiting repairs. But then why had Michael not returned her call?

She tried Michael's number again, but only got a 'phone not available' response. Out of cell-phone range, perhaps, on their way with AIS in silent mode? Forgot to charge his phone? Possible, but unlike him. Or something more sinister? She huffed her frustration. She could not afford this distraction right now, but neither could she help the gnawing worry for her friend's safety.

Turning back to her mission, she panned back towards the Spanish coast. *Ivan Peronovich* was stationary, and therefore, she assumed, still alongside the transponder-less platform. She set up a Marine Traffic tracking notification to get an email when the survey ship moved.

Next, she phoned Albert, her contact in Customs.

'The Rusky survey boat? Yeah, she's a regular here, why, what's your interest?'

'Just an idea - a nice angle for my novel. I'd like to meet some of the crew. When are they due in next?'

'Early on Monday - hang on a mo… yeah, the pilot's booked out to meet her at Europa Point at seven. She'll go inside North Mole, her usual berth. But you should know, Rosie, those people don't socialise much, I've never seen any of them go ashore.'

'So why do they come here?'

'For the duty-free fuel and cheap provisions, I suppose. Somebody ashore organises the delivery, the van is usually waiting on the jetty when she docks.

The Travel Agent

They'll be at sea again by teatime, so you'll be pushed to get to see anybody. I wouldn't bother if I were you.'

8: Surveillance & Capture

8/9

Dinner-date

At five to seven that evening, dressed in her glad-rags with a touch of makeup, Rosie walked the short distance to Groucho's for her dinner date. Leviticus, looking debonaire in a white linen suit and silver-grey tie, stood waiting outside. He kissed her chastely on the cheek.

'So, what happened?' asked Leviticus after the waiter had seated the pair at their table.

'Sorry?' Rosie asked, her mind elsewhere.

'You rushed away in such a hurry this morning, nothing serious, I hope?'

'Oh. Yeah, the guy that drowned last night, in Rosia Bay? I knew him.'

Leviticus pursed his lips, eyes rounded with concern. 'Oh, I am sorry to hear that. No wonder you are so… preoccupied. Forgive me, we could have postponed tonight…'

8: Surveillance & Capture

She shook her head. 'No, it's fine. He wasn't a friend or anything, but I was with him yesterday morning and thought I'd better tell the police.'

'Ah, good. Then we can talk of more pleasant matters, no?'

She smiled. 'We can talk of more pleasant matters, yes.

'Then please answer me this,' he reached over and touched the lobe of her left ear, causing her an unbearable tingle of pleasure – God! Did he know how sensitive her ears were?

'There was an earring here, yes?'

Taking a firm hold of herself, Rosie replied, 'A diamond stud, yes. I lost it a while back.'

Her mother's gift had fallen out somewhere in the forest around Camp Sparta. A distraught Rosie had consoled herself with the notion that it might now adorn some magpie's nest.

'Why do you ask?'

'It would be a shame to let it heal up – something expensive there would enhance what is already beautiful.'

Keen to move the conversation on, she began, 'How was your…' then shook away the question and asked another. 'Do you know, Leviticus? I haven't a clue what you do. Tell me about yourself.'

'First of all, call me Lev. Leviticus is such a mouthful.'

'I like it, though,' she said.'It's so unusual and has a fine, classical ring. But if you prefer Lev, then Lev it is. Go on, what brings a Greek Ukrainian to this pile of crumbling rock?'

The Travel Agent

He grinned, 'A pile of rock that Plato called "The Pillars of Hercules".'

Rosie laughed and said, 'I never quite got that allusion. I was up there today, on Breakneck Bastion. It strikes me Plato must have meant that Gibraltar was only one pillar, the other being the mountains of Morocco across the Strait. It's still an absurd metaphor, though, don't you think?'

'I agree entirely. Now let us choose from the menu so we can order when our drinks arrive.'

Rosie picked up her menu, frowning at the long list of main course options, and gave a sigh of indecision.

'What do you recommend?'

'Well, if you like shellfish, their Cabo Verde lobster is a house speciality, cooked in Canino olive oil with orange and fennel confit. And to start, I can recommend the Cornish oysters, they are flown in fresh each morning from England.'

Rosie smiled relievedly and put down her menu.

'Sounds wonderful. I'll go for that.'

'Splendid! Then that is also what I will have. Now, I have a confession to make, and you may call me a philistine because although one should drink only white wine with fish, I have a… what? What is funny?'

'It's perfectly fine to drink red,' Rosie assured him, stifling her laughter, 'I do it all the time. How about a nice Rioja?'

When the waiter had left with their order, Lev raised his glass to her. 'I cannot tell you how delighted I am to be here with you, Rosie. Thank you for coming.'

Rosie felt herself blushing.

Get a grip, Girl! He's a player.

8: Surveillance & Capture

'No, thank you for inviting me.' She chinked her gin and tonic to his vodka tonic, and they drank.

'So, you were going to tell me what you do here.'

He grinned ruefully. 'I'm sorry to say, it is the god Mammon at whose altar I serve. My firm wishes to invest in this magnificently wealthy pile of crumbling rock.'

She shook her head. 'Nothing wrong with that, the place is built on money, it's the only reason we don't hand it back to Spain. So, what exactly is it you do?'

'I work for a Ukrainian property developer, and I am here looking for land to build a resort hotel. There is nothing available now, but as you know, the extensive land reclamation work will bring new possibilities. I want to be here when it comes onto the market.'

Trained to spot tells, Rosie tried to shake off a feeling that something was not quite right with his story and decided to explore further.

'And wh…'

Lev held up his hands as if in surrender but laughing genially. 'Please, enough about me and work matters. I wish to learn what brings such a beautiful young woman into my life.'

She blushed again – this was ridiculous. And the 'into my life' bit was worrying. Just what was he expecting from her?

'Look, Lev…'

'You have a boat, I understand?'

She nodded enthusiastically, happy to move on. '*Pasha*. She's an old lady now, a sailboat.'

'And you have had this *Pasha* how long?'

'She's always been in my family. Mum bought her the year before I was born. My father taught me to sail

The Travel Agent

when I was a kid. Now, unofficially, she's mine, because Dad doesn't sail anymore.'

The conversation continued throughout the meal, interspersed with occasional comments about the excellence of the food. Rosie fed him selected titbits of her life while taking care to avoid straying into dangerous territory. Her attempts to open him up on his own life story came to not very much. The agent realised that for all her probing, she had discovered only that Lev had at some period studied English Classics at Baliol College, Oxford. This, at least, explained his evident competence in the language.

By coffee, the uneasiness Rosie had felt earlier seemed to have melted away. This she put down to the twin effects of the second bottle of Rioja and the handsome Ukrainian's old-world charm. So comfortable was she in his company that, as they left the restaurant, she was almost tempted to accept his invitation to go home with him.

'I'm sorry, Lev, maybe another time.'

The agent gave him no further explanation, and he, like a true gentleman, did not ask for one. She did, however, submit willingly to a long kiss goodnight under the arches of Casemates Bastion.

Halfway back to the marina, Rosie stopped in her tracks when conscience and sensibilities prevailed, and it struck her like a punch in the gut. Apart from remorse for her betrayal of Tash, she realised she was behaving like a besotted teenager. And despite her silly infatuation with the handsome Ukrainian, the analytical part of her brain reminded the agent there was something off about him.

8: Surveillance & Capture

The Travel Agent

8/10

Execution

Michael is still groggy from the drugs when they come for him the next morning. Men are shouting outside in Arabic. The door crashes open, and two men rush in shouting in Arabic. Barely aware of what is happening, Michael is dragged out into sunshine so bright he closes his eyes. Stumbling blindly between jostling hands and rifle-butts, the young skipper tries to block out what is happening and distance himself from a terrifying truth. Staggering as he is shoved from behind, he opens his eyes and squints at a black flag draped across in front of him.

Jerked to a stop, they turn him so that his back is to the flag. In front, a town square, a row of grey adobe buildings, broken walls: their rubble remains strewn everywhere. Excited gabble. Music starts, faintly at first, as Michael's wrists are bound behind him with what feels like a cable-tie. He is forced to his knees. He closes his eyes again, afraid to see what is coming. The music is turned up, a crooning, almost sleepy male

8: Surveillance & Capture

voice, a chant, something about Allah, in time to faint drumming in the background. It might have been pleasing in other circumstances.

Michael's hair is grabbed roughly, painfully, from behind, his head pulled back. The gentle singing becomes layered, many voices joining in, the drumming more insistent.

The young captive opens his eyes. The grip on his hair tightens as he shakes away tears. In front of him stands a tall man with a black and white scarf around his head and neck. He glares at Michael with one fanatical eye - the other is missing; its purple socket crudely stitched.

'Ah'm Rasheed al Basara, and in 't name of Allah, ah charge thee with attempted kidnapping, waging war on 't caliphate, and crimes against Islam.'

Somewhere beyond Michael's terror lies the notion that the man's Yorkshire accent is absurdly out of place.

'Please, *please*, I haven't done anything. Oh, fuck, please don't… don't…'

But Rasheed's single eye shows only naked contempt: there will be no mercy here: 'Shut the fook up, infidel - the fookin' sentence is death. *Allah 'Akbar.*'

The music's volume increases, growing more strident, accompanied now by ominous sound effects: the metallic ring of a sword being drawn, sporadic gunfire, marching boots. Rasheed stands aside, revealing a tripod, a smartphone mounted on top.

Michael's head is jerked backwards onto cold, damp leather. His internal organs seem to be sinking, drawing all the strength out of his core. He feels

The Travel Agent

spreading warm in his crotch – Michael is pissing himself and can do nothing to stop it. His desperate crying is drowned in the fundamentalist anthem now raised to deafening levels. A glint of metal: a butcher's knife turning before his eyes; they want him to see the instrument of his death, a last cruel gesture to maximise his terror.

But then, something strange. An inexplicable calm descends, and Michael's horror becomes externalised. It is a dreamlike tableau where he is the observer, not the victim. In this tranquil state, the young man pictures his ageing parents: his Irish father's well-intentioned brutality, his mother, whose love and sensibility held the family together in the worst of times, and Julia, his beloved sister, also a victim of this distorted parody of Islam. And his lost love, Sara, herself executed by mindless prejudice. Above all, Michael's disembodied other self worries for Rosie, his beautiful friend and sometime lover. His hopes for something more in that relationship are now as dead as the headless cadaver he envisions for his own fate.

Bitterness rises dark and unstoppable like the banshee. As steel touches Michael's throat, he takes a final breath and shouts out, 'Fester in your own shit, you murderous cunts. Ali-fucking-akbar!'

Then it is over.

Michael is shoved forward, toppling into the sand. The diabolical anthem has stopped.

Someone stoops and snips his wrists free, rolls him onto his back, grins into his face. 'That was for YouTube, English. Next time, maybe for real. *Inshallah,* eh?'

8: Surveillance & Capture

The man steps away, and another takes his place, pointing a rifle. But Michael is past caring. For something else has caught the tear-filled eyes of the traumatised yachtsman. He is looking beyond the black-turbaned head to a dark cruciform silhouette hanging in the heavens. At first, he believes it is a message from the Almighty. But as his vision clears, he sees it is not The Holy Cross. It is a large bird of prey, head extended eagerly as if intent on some vital but far off destination. It is an oddly moving image, that solitary migrating raptor, and it bolsters Michael's heart with new hope. Faintly, as the bird passes out of sight behind the rifleman, Michael hears a shrill, mournful cry: *tweeeeh*, which for some unfathomable reason, conjures an image of Rosie.

Astrid comes to Michael's cell later that day.

'I hear you are a film star, now,' she says, kneeling beside him, not smiling.

He glowers at her, and she grimaces. 'I know, not very funny. I cannot imagine how that felt for you.'

'Don't ask.'

She studies his face and frowns. 'They beat you also?'

Gingerly he touches the swelling on his cheekbone. 'That was one of the Russians yesterday, asking me questions – then they injected me with something.'

Astrid nods. 'Sodium thiopental, probably. I think that would be better than letting Rasheed's men interrogate you.'

'They wanted to know about Rosie. I can't remember what I said. I hope I haven't dropped her in the shit.'

'Rosie? Your friend on our last trip?'

The Travel Agent

'Mm, they had a picture someone took in Gib. She's an undercover investigator there, chasing drug smugglers. At least, that what she told me, but now I'm starting to wonder.'

Astrid nods and begins cleaning his head wound while she speaks. 'You may be right. I was treating one of the fighters yesterday, Imran, a nasty case of gangrene. The opiates I gave him loosened his tongue, and of course, he was grateful to me for saving his leg. So, I asked questions, and he gave me some answers.'

'And?'

'Many of the Jihadi fighters here came to Syria from Europe–'

'Yeah, I know. Rasheed's a Yorkshireman.'

'They came to Libya when they started losing territory in Syria. They have much support in Libya, and many more have joined them, from other North African countries. They have taken over Sabratha and Bali Waleed, and control most of the oil fields.'

'Sabratha! That's…'

'Yes, only thirty kilometres from Zuwara, where Greta was hiding.'

'And only ten miles from the rendezvous waypoint,' says Michael bitterly. 'Someone should have warned us.'

'Greta tried, but it all happened so quickly. Rasheed had her phone, that is why he texted instead of answering my call.'

'I knew something was wrong with that,' Michael says, 'I should have…'

'Shh, my Captain, let us not blame ourselves. I too thought something was not right, but I was so happy to be taking Greta home… So, we are where we are, no?'

8: Surveillance & Capture

But Michael is distracted by a sudden realisation. Of course! Rasheed also has his, Michael's phone. If Rosie has tried to call him… but how would a bunch of rag-tag militiamen be able to trace an international call? The Russians!

'So, why are the Russians here, did the guy say?'

'It is about the oil, of course, but not the way I thought. They want Rasheed's people to set alight the wells, just as Sadam Hussain did in Kuwait.'

'Jesus! Why?'

Astrid shrugs, 'The usual reason, I suppose, so nobody else can have it. There is a world glut, maybe Putin worries about his profits.'

'And what's in it for Rasheed, do you suppose?'

'Ah, well this, I know. The Russians are secretly repatriating some of the foreign fighters. At least those from Europe. Imran told me they plan a big terrorist campaign. They have already sent some to England. I am afraid for your people, perhaps mine also, because there are Swedes here.'

'And the Russians are doing this, are you sure?'

Astrid gives a humourless chuckle. 'Imran couldn't stop himself telling me about it. A ship comes to anchor off Sabratha every month to pick them up. Imran himself is from France, and he wants to get well enough to go home. And he is totally committed to killing the infidel and believes he will go to Paradise if he dies for the caliphate. I find it quite disturbing.'

Michael does not speak, just shakes his head in befuddlement.

'First Trump, then Brexit,' Astrid says, 'and now the prospect of mass terror in Europe. Putin must be laughing his head off.'

The Travel Agent

Michael sighs, nods at the medical kit, 'Got anything in there for nappy-rash?'

'Ooh! You poor boy. Take off your shorts, let me see.'

Michael does not move – he just stares at her.

The nurse smiles sadly. 'What, you have something I have not seen before? Come, stand up.'

Reluctantly, with glowing ears, Michael complies.

8: Surveillance & Capture

8/11

Suspicions

On the morning following her dinner date with Leviticus, Rosie logged into Firegate and sent an update. In it, she reported her renewed doubts about the IRP in the light of the Russian connection. Rosie argued that it wouldn't, after all, be such a leap of the imagination to find the Kremlin up to its neck in sponsoring terrorism. She told The Housekeeper of her intentions to monitor the vessel's entry into Gibraltar and watch for anything suspicious during Monday, especially with the delivery van Albert had mentioned.

With the message on its way, Rosie checked the usual news outlets for Libya's latest fighting. While trawling the BBC pages, an item flashed by in the side panel that she would have missed, had the subject not been uppermost in her mind. Scrolling back up the page, she found the item again and stared at the headline.

8: Surveillance & Capture

'Marie Celeste' Mystery in Mediterranean. Search underway for missing crew

Heart in mouth, she opened the article.

Reuters: Saturday, Oct 7
Fears were growing tonight for the fate of two missing sailors after a sailing catamaran was found adrift off the island of Gozo. The fifty-foot (UK-registered) vessel was discovered this afternoon by an Italian frigate and handed over to Maltese authorities. The two missing crew, who have not been named, are believed to be British. Search & rescue operations resume tomorrow, say Maltese coastguard.

'No way!' she breathed. The voice of denial crept in: how many Brit-registered cats sailed the Med? Thousands, surely? But Rosie pushed those arguments aside. She had always had a bad feeling about this.

She now took out her Med Pilot and studied the currents around the area where the cat was found, and what she discovered seemed to confirm her fears. She searched for more information online, frantically banging the keys, but could find no further details.

Rosie slept poorly that night and got up at first light exhausted and feeling helpless. There was no further news about the missing catamaran, so she took a shower and tried to park her fears. After all, she

The Travel Agent

needed a clear head, feeling her mission was reaching some sort of conclusion.

After breakfast, needing some distracting activity, Rosie cycled around to see where Roberto had come to grief. It was too early for Camp Bay's usual Sunday crowds of sun worshippers. Apart from two men cleaning the swimming pools and café owners preparing to open up shop, she had the place to herself.

Locking her bike to the railings, Rosie wandered over to Rosia Bay's old harbour and was surprised to find her way barred by blue and white tape. Three uniformed policemen walked the sea wall inside the cordon, eyes downcast as if searching for something. She spotted another uniform on the landward side, this one with pips, talking to a man in a suit. Curious, Rosie ducked under the tape and approached the two men.

As Rosie neared the pair, they turned towards her. The uniformed senior officer rolled his eyes and said, 'I'll leave you to it then, Greg, see you later.' With a final withering glance at Rosie, he turned on his heel and walked off while his colleague moved to cut off her approach.

'You shouldn't be in here, madam, please—'

'Is this where Rob Marsa was found?' Rosie demanded.

The man adopted a belligerent expression. 'Look, if you're from the press you'll…'

'I'm not a journalist. I knew Rob. Why the crime scene stuff, I thought it was an accident?'

'And you are?'

8: Surveillance & Capture

'Rosie Winterbourne. I came forward yesterday at your Casemates office and gave my details to the desk sergeant. Was he murdered, then?'

'When did you last see Mr Marsa?' he said, clearly interested now.

'Friday, when he dropped me off at Ocean Village.'

'In that case, you might be the last person to have seen him alive, so I need you to come to New Mole House in an hour or so to make a statement. I'll be back there by then. Just ask for me.'

She looked at the card he handed her. Detective Inspector Greg Singleton, Royal Gibraltar Police.

'And I'll need your details, Miss: are you a Gibraltar resident?'

'No, I'm on a boat, *Pasha*, in Marina Bay.'

'Thank you, Miss Winterbourne. Now I need you to move back behind the cordon. I'll see you in an hour.'

'Fair enough. So, are you going to tell me what happened?'

'I'm afraid that's confidential. There'll be a police press conference later today.'

The Travel Agent

8/12

Gift

After leaving Police Headquarters, Rosie returned on-board to update The Housekeeper on events. Cycling back past Rosia to Europa point, she entered the road tunnel leading to the Rock's east side.

In her statement to police - which had been given under caution - she had left out mentioning that Rob had shown her Fingers Cave. She had a feeling about the sea cave and did not want to draw attention to her interest in it.

Neither had it escaped her that the circumstances of Rob's death could mean she was also in danger. And that spurred her to sprint through the narrow road tunnel very quickly indeed. Coming out into daylight once more, Rosie noted with satisfaction the sea's calm on this side due to being sheltered from the westerly breeze. It was also coming up to low water, which was why she chose this moment to take another look at the peculiar sea cave. Reaching the concealed entrance, Rosie parked her bike in among the rocks. She pulled

8: Surveillance & Capture

away the metal sheet covering the hole and then, taking *Pasha*'s heavy-duty boat-lamp from her pack, lit her way gingerly down the steps.

The cavern today looked quite different. Gone were the dramatic light effects of breakers roiling through a mostly submerged entrance; transformed now into a low arch looking out on a serene, shining sea, the waters inside undisturbed and crystal-clear. Although there was only a half-metre of headroom at the surface, she saw that the entrance extended far beneath and was wide enough to drive a truck through, albeit a submerged truck.

Charmed by the ambience of the quiet cavern, she sat down on the ledge and swung her legs over the lip. In that peaceful solitude, Rosie's thoughts drifted back to Michael and the abandoned catamaran. The boat's name was still withheld. Of course, it was apparent why: the missing pair's relatives would need to be tracked down and told before names could be released. Deep down, though, she could not help fearing the worst. She had thought of calling Michael's sister to see if she had had news, but what would she say? 'Hi, Julia, have you heard from Michael lately?' If they had not yet contacted Julia that would surely ring alarm bells.

Staring absently into the limpid water, Rosie caught silvery glint on the floor of the cavern. After a moment, she saw it again, flickering in the deflected sunlight at the entrance. Turning her lamp to full brightness, the agent directed its powerful beam vertically down between her trainers. And now she saw it clearly: a sliver of bright metal lodged between two limestone shards.

The Travel Agent

It could be something and nothing, she thought, but she had to make sure if possible. Springing to her feet, she surveyed the rock shelf. Where she stood, it would be too high to climb out again, but further round to her left the ledge sloped down closer to the water, to less than a metre. Doable. But there it was only a few centimetres wide, which might still give her a problem climbing out.

Coming to a decision, Rosie removed her shoes and socks and stripped naked. Then, without a second thought, she dived neatly into the pool, letting the momentum carry her to a couple of metres before pulling herself on downwards and turning back towards the wall. The water depth was more significant than it had looked from the ledge, and Rosie soon felt her ears popping, and her chest compressing. She fought to resist the reflex to breathe. However, her now neutral buoyancy allowed her to sink effortlessly to the bottom. After frantic moments of searching among the yellow rocks, she located the object. Snatching it up, she pulled triumphantly for the surface, feeling the joy of expanding lungs and returning buoyancy. Surfacing into blissful air, she breathed deeply to reoxygenate her starved body, then, treading water, examined her find. It took a moment to understand the significance of what she had recovered, and then her eyes widened in astonishment. After a moment she swam to the ledge and tossed her find safely onto the shelf then swam to where she had estimated she could reach. Hooking both hands over this lower edge, she worked her way back around the ledge. When there was sufficient lateral clearance, The agent heaved herself bodily from the water, finally

8: Surveillance & Capture

rolling safely and thankfully onto the ledge. The effort had been more than she had bargained for, and for some minutes she lay on her back breathing deeply, before getting dressed.

Rosie picked up the weapon for a closer examination. From the fittings on the carbon-coated handle, its purpose was clear. In her work with the Royal Marines and later at Sparta, Rosie had come across many types of bayonet. But she had never seen one quite like this: a beautifully crafted weapon. The thirty-centimetre-long blade was a classic bowie-style, razor-sharp with a partially serrated top edge. She held the knife up and pictured its function; a well-balanced instrument perfectly designed to deliver rapid and silent evisceration. Gardener would love it.

Returning to the marina, Rosie was ambushed on the pontoon by a security guard. 'Excuse me. *Pasha*?'

'That's my boat, yes,' she confirmed, casting an anxious eye to her mooring. 'What's the problem?'

'No problem, Miss Winterbourne, can you come to the office? There's a delivery for you.'

Emerging from the marina office, astonished and somewhat embarrassed, Rosie carried the ostentatious bouquet gingerly back to the boat, avoiding the eyes of admiring passers-by and fellow yachties. Manoeuvring the flowers carefully down the companionway hatch and laying them on the saloon table, she noticed an envelope attached. She slid out a card:

> *Rosie*
> Thank you for a
> wonderful evening
> (Let us do it again soon?)

The Travel Agent

> I hope you like the gift,
> a token of my affection,
> and trust you will wear it
> always.
> Your fond admirer
> Lev. xx

Intrigued, Rosie pulled out from the envelope a tiny silk bag and inside found an ear-stud. It looked expensive, and she had no doubt the gemstone, a dark, lentil-sized ruby mounted in a gold circlet, was the real thing.

It had been almost two months since anything had penetrated her left earlobe, and it took some manoeuvring to get the pin through. 'You were spot on, Lev,' Rosie told herself in the mirror. 'That ear does deserve a stud.'

After all, she was hardly likely to get into close combat situations. When she got home, she would replace it with her treasured diamond stud from Mum.'

8: Surveillance & Capture

8/13

Leviticus

From his luxury apartment overlooking Marina Bay, the Ukrainian watched the British agent collecting the flowers he'd sent her. Once again, he was struck by the way she walked along the pontoon. Such grace! Such economy of movement, the way she swung those perfectly formed hips. An almost feline stroll, yet somehow poised and alert. She put Leviticus in mind of some exotic, long-limbed creature.

He had been astonished by his physical response to their first face to face encounter: that night he had met Natasha in the Sunrise Bar. His attraction to the girl had been instant and almost overwhelming. Even now, as he watched her step lightly onto the boat with his gift, he felt his arousal stirring. Such a pity, but he could not afford to let his desire get in the way of what must be done.

Smiling grimly, the Ukrainian returned to the coffee table and opened his laptop. But his mind was still on the girl. He had seen her before that first meeting, of

8: Surveillance & Capture

course. He had known the agent was coming days before her yacht sailed into La Linea. On the morning after her arrival, he had hidden behind a wall by the Jewish Cemetery. She ran with incredible agility, this girl. She had the body of an athlete. He had studied her face through the binoculars: that elfin allure flushed with exertion, like a fresh peony beaded with morning dew.

Dinner last night had been his first and last opportunity to seduce this extraordinary woman. She had undoubtedly signalled her availability. But after that lingering kiss under the arches, she had demurred politely and skittered back to her boat.

Leviticus sighed wistfully.

When his machine had booted up, the Ukrainian clicked the tracker icon, opening a Gibraltar map. He zoomed in to the marina and waited for the device to connect via a satellite link. After a few seconds, a flashing cross appeared in the yacht moorings. He zoomed in some more and grunted his satisfaction that the symbol was correctly aligned on the girl's yacht. Now it was all down to her – he only hoped he had judged her inexperience rightly. And more importantly, that he had not raised her suspicions.

He took out his phone and speed-dialled a contact.

'Yes, Mister Danilenco?'

'Another delivery is scheduled for dawn tomorrow, Bernard. There are four of them. You are to bring the minivan to the Cable Car parking lot at midnight – I'll meet you both there.'

'Okay, Mister Danilenco, we'll be there.'

'Good. I will see you at midnight, and please do not be late.'

The Travel Agent

'Er, Mr Danilenco, we didn't get paid yet for the last ...'

'You and Enrico will have your payments in the morning, Bernard, with a rather big bonus for a job well done.'

'Oh, thank you. I'm sorry I had to ask, Mister Damilenco, but Enrico...'

'This will be the last one, Bernard, then we are done. Until tonight.'

Leviticus ended the call.

Tonight, was to be the Ukrainian's last night on the Rock, and he felt obliged to spend the evening with that goat Natasha one final time. He was finding it increasingly challenging to respond to her wooden and unimaginative performance in his bed. But Leviticus was a fair-minded man, and the woman deserved a final servicing for her assistance in the mission. The insurgencies would not have worked. The watch officer had not disabled the Levent Battery camera for that crucial hour on each occasion.

By this time tomorrow, the Ukrainian's last-minute change of orders would see him back aboard the ship and sailing for Tripoli. Putin, in his infinite capacity for chicanery, had once more switched allegiances. And because of this, the dawn would require of the Ukrainian the thing he most detested; Leviticus anticipated the coming violence with distaste and a heavy heart. For he was a man with murder on his mind.

EPISODE NINE

The Discovery

The Travel Agent

9: The Discovery

9/1

Backup

Sunday evening at Firegate's secret North London headquarters: the Housekeeper convened a meeting of the cadre she had curated as a contingency but had not expected to use. These were her field agents: Gauntlet and Hammer, and Covert Ops Training Officer, codename Gadfly.

'Back in August,' The Housekeeper began, 'based on certain information gained by one of our surveillance teams, I arranged for an agent to train and infiltrate into Gibraltar. Her mission: to investigate Daesh's travel arrangements.'

'Ooh!' muttered Gauntlet, 'not fake news then?'

Hammer's expression was implacable. Gadfly pulled a frown but declined to comment.

The Housekeeper ignored Gauntlet's taunt, and after a pause, said, 'Technically, it's a contravention of the rules. But because it was possible to insert this agent under cover of everyday pursuits, I felt it too good an opportunity to miss. I saw it as a chance to discover

The Travel Agent

what, if anything, is going on over there. And with minimal risk.'

Gadfly gave a little cough, 'Not sure about minimal risk, Ma'am, I'm guessing this is Galene we're talking about?'

The Housekeeper nodded, 'And you're right to question her lack of experience. But that risk, I felt at the time, for reasons I'll come to, was mitigated by the posting – this is a British territory we're talking about.'

Hammer sat up a little straighter, 'Felt at the time, Ma'am?'

The Housekeeper flashed him a frosty smile. 'Subsequent events have caused me to revise that assessment, though I hasten to add, that is no reflection on the agent's competence. Galene seems to be handling an unforeseen situation with a degree of skill and discretion, which is a credit to you guys at Sparta.' She directed this last at Gadfly. 'Anyway, let us cut to the…'

'Er, with respect, Ma'am, this was our investigation,' interrupted Gauntlet. 'How come we weren't in the loop?'

'Fair point, but as you'll see, I had my reasons.' She held up a hand to curtail further dissent. 'We are where we are, now listen up. Galene may be onto something, and she might be getting in over her head. She's going to need support, both here and in the field. So, let me bring you up to date with events so far. Firstly, I should point out that Galene has prior contacts in Gibraltar and they know her under her real name: Rosie Winterbourne.'

9: The Discovery

'You sent *her*?' said Gauntlet with a mixture of accusation and disbelief. 'She's only been with us a dogwatch for Christ's sake!'

Hammer said nothing but his eyes had widened noticeably.

'I did. You both said Winterbourne has unique qualities, and you were right. Gadfly?'

Gadfly nodded and pushed back her chair to address the room. 'Winterbourne came to us at Sparta on the twentieth of August and underwent a one-month course in fieldcraft, electronic surveillance, Krav Maga/Silat, and small-arms training–'

'A month!' objected Gauntlet, 'with no previous military? And she's thirty-two – that's too fucking old to start, if you ask me, excusing my French, Ma'am.'

'She worked with the marines in the Caribbean,' countered Gadfly, 'got cited for courage under fire while arresting smugglers.'

'It might be worth noting,' The Housekeeper added, 'that before her illness got her discharged, the Navy had earmarked her for training with the Special Boat Service.'

Gauntlet raised his eyebrows. 'I never knew that.'

From the agent's expression, the Housekeeper could see she'd scored the killer argument: she had recruited Gauntlet from that same unit. She grinned, 'No reason you should – and neither did Winterbourne.'

'We subjected Galene to a brutal physical regime,' continued Gadfly, 'far exceeding what your average recruit could expect; Jesus, what we put that woman through! But by the end of week two, she was nailing it. Gardener told me he was amazed by her combat performance in her final week. "Awestruck!" were his very words. I've never heard him say that about anyone, let alone a novice. And as for Moth... well, she had this way of getting past his misanthropic attitude.' She gave a short chuckle. 'I think she put a hex on the poor man.'

'Thank you, Gadfly,' said The Housekeeper, 'now let us catch up with events so far. Galene arrived in theatre on the second of October, last Monday, with her boat. Since then she's acquired several leads but seems to have fixated on a Russian-owned research platform stationed some twenty miles east of Gib.

'My initial response was to steer her away from this because, considering Russia's actions in Syria, it seemed unlikely that they could be involved with Daesh. Despite my brief of No Further Action, Galene continued her surveillance of the platform and yesterday observed a ship alongside. Following further enquiries, she discovered this was a Russian survey vessel. That in itself would not have been significant were it not for the vessel's next destination.'

'Let me guess - Gibraltar!' said Gauntlet.

The Housekeeper nodded. 'Apparently, the ship is a regular visitor, coming in once a month. She stays for about ten hours. Here's what is interesting: a delivery van invariably meets the ship as she docks, ostensibly to embark supplies. Galene thinks this could be how our returnees are making it back onto British soil.'

'I don't see it,' said Gauntlet, shaking his head. 'Where's the Libyan connection?'

'So far we've been unable to trace the vessel's last port of call. We're working on it. But given our zero-profile policy, it's risky to make direct enquiries. Galene may have better luck on that score.'

9: The Discovery

'What about passports,' said Hammer. 'To get a flight back to the UK, they'd need passports. They couldn't use their own: Border Force would get alerted and pick them up them on arrival.'

The Housekeeper smiled, somewhat disparagingly, 'And you don't think the Russians could manage fake documents? Team, I have a confession to make. When you first raised the possibility of Gibraltar being the entry point, I was more than sceptical. And not just because it looked like a typical Facebook spoof, but for the specific argument that Hammer just gave us: Gibraltar Customs scan passports just like anywhere else. When I sent Galene to Gib, I did so primarily to consolidate her training. To give her field experience in a relatively benign theatre and cover an angle that I assumed was unlikely to come to much. In the light of subsequent events, it seems I misjudged the situation.'

'If that's what's happening,' said Gauntlet, 'then this thing is bigger than we thought.'

But Gadfly and Hammer had detected the ominous inflexion in The Housekeeper's final words. It was Gadfly who spoke up. 'What aren't you telling us, Ma'am?'

The Housekeeper gave a resigned sigh – they might as well know.

'One of Galene's contacts was a man called Roberto Marsa, leader of a local voluntary group called South Ops. They're a kind of Neighbourhood Watch but watching specifically for illegal migrants. On Friday Mister Marsa took Galene on a guided tour of potential landing spots. Sometime that night, the poor man was found floating face-down in the sea.'

The Travel Agent

Grim faces as the implications hit them. The Housekeeper had their full attention.

'Cause of death?' asked Hammer.

'Not certain at present, but according to Galene, the local bobbies don't think it was an accident. The Coroner's Inquest on Tuesday will tell us more. Something else to consider: Galene may have been the last person to see the guy alive, so we can't discount the possibility she's on the bobbies' list of suspects.'

'And maybe on someone's target list,' added Gauntlet.

A tense silence ensued.

'There's another complication,' The Housekeeper said. 'Galene's last assignment at Mercury One was a yachtsman called Michael McCaffey? It appears he and a Swedish nurse have been snatching endangered infants out of Libya and sailing them here for adoption.'

Gauntlet whistled. 'That took balls.'

'Mm, quite. Well, we think McCaffey's in Libya.'

'Holy shit!' breathed Gadfly. ' And the nurse?'

'Probably her too. Yesterday the Italian Navy found a catamaran abandoned and drifting towards Malta. This afternoon the Foreign Office was informed by the Maltese that this a British-registered vessel called *Surf Warrior*. The boat left Greece a week earlier with McCaffey and Bannermann on board.'

'My God!' said Gadfly. 'Does Galene know?'

'Not yet. It gets released to the media tomorrow after the families have been informed.'

Neither did Galene know about the video The Housekeeper had received this morning from GCHQ that showed McCaffey undergoing what seemed to be

9: The Discovery

a mock execution. Thankfully, due to a new filter algorithm, the footage hadn't made it onto YouTube. The Housekeeper deemed it especially necessary to keep this development from the cadre if they were going to contact Galene, which seemed increasingly likely.

'I need your input here, Gadfly: how far will the news impact Galene's performance?'

The psychologist chewed her lower lip. After a few moments, she said, 'Galene and McCaffey are close. Nevertheless, I think she will try to shelve her emotions until she's completed her mission. But it's bound to affect her focus, and probably her judgement.'

'That makes her unreliable,' muttered Gauntlet, 'a potential liability.'

Gadfly nodded, 'I'm afraid I agree with Gauntlet, Ma'am, at the very least, this is going to impair her effectiveness.'

The Housekeeper said, 'I think we're all on the same page. It looks like time to put someone else in.'

'We can't pull her out now,' said Hammer. 'Not while she's on the police suspect list for this killing.'

'Agreed. So come on, Team, let's get our heads around a plan.'

The Travel Agent

9: The Discovery

9/2

The Hacker

It took Rosie about ten minutes on google to identify the bayonet. It was for an M-9 assault rifle used primarily by US Special Forces. Such a weapon could have been bought online, of course, but was it a coincidence that USSF was known to operate where Daesh had their bases? So, a captured weapon discarded by a returning jihadi?
If Rosie's inference was correct, this raised several questions. How did they get into that cave – JMCC's cameras would have picked up any seaward approach. If they had got through from seaward, what role did the mysterious IRP play? Rob Marsa had joked about a submarine, but that was ridiculous, surely? The cavern was not nearly big enough. Or was it?

The agent sat up straight. An idea had been lurking in a remote recess of her mind. Was it too outrageous to consider seriously? But what if…? In a flush of excitement, she dug Tash's card out of her purse and tapped the number into her phone, not sure whether

The Travel Agent

she would be home or on duty. She hesitated, spent a minute or so planning her ruse, then hit call.

'Hello?'

'Hi, Tash. It's Rosie Winterbourne – you were kind enough to show me around the Hole the other day?'

'Oh, yes. Rosie. How's the book coming along?'

'Still working on the research. Is this a good time? Only I have a quick question for you.'

'No problem. I'm off today. How can I help?'

'Just an idea for a plotline. Could a submarine approach here without being detected?'

'Wow, Rosie, that's some plotline! Are you writing a sci-fi?'

Rosie laughed, 'No, just looking at other angles for my fictional drug smugglers.'

'Well, let's see. A nuclear sub certainly wouldn't get near, those things chuck out so much heat they leave an IR trail on the surface like Oxford Street on Christmas Eve. We see them all the time transiting the Strait. Submerged diesel-electrics could get close, in theory. Still, they'd need to stick to the swept channel - otherwise, it would be damned dangerous.'

'Yeah. I was thinking more of those submersible thingummies that scientist use?'

It was Tash's turn to laugh. *'I know where you're going with this. That research platform you asked about, the IRP. I could see that got you fired up as soon as you spotted it on the map.'*

Rosie cringed but said nothing.

'Okay, supposing a consortium of smugglers owned a thing like that, operating a minisub from it to get their drugs into Gib. Yeah, it might work, on a moonless night. Those things are battery-driven and

9: The Discovery

have hardly any footprint. But here's the thing, and I'm surprised it hasn't occurred to you. An operation like that would cost millions, billions, maybe. Gib is is a tiny island, Rosie, the drugs market just isn't big enough.'

'Of course, you're right. Gosh, what was I thinking? Well, back to the drawing board, I guess. But thanks, Tash, I appreciate your help, and sorry to interrupt your day off.'

'Not a problem, Rosie. Happy to help. Call me anytime.'

'Er, just one thing before you go. I feel really stupid about that idea now, so could you please not mention it to anyone? It could damage any reputation I might gain in the future.'

A chuckle. *'Rosie, my lips are sealed. Good luck with the writing.*

I'm looking forward to my signed copy.'

Rosie ended the call with a grimace. In her haste for an answer, she had deliberately made herself a fool in the eyes of an important contact. The agent realised she could expect little more help from that quarter. The gregarious watch officer would be unable to resist telling the joke.

Why am I acting like an impulsive knothead?

She knew the answer, of course.

Michael.

She rechecked the news sites, but there was no further mention of the catamaran. The story seemed to have shut down. Then, a lightbulb moment. Logging onto TOR, the Dark Web, she accessed Moth's personal VPN messaging app and typed:

The Travel Agent

> Moth?

After a full minute came a reply.

> hello galene

> You remember the phone number you were monitoring my friend on?

> michael mccaffey, yes.

> Can you trace a call I made to that number on Thursday morning?

This time the delay was much longer. Eventually came the reply:

> off-limits hk orders

Rosie gave a start. Why on earth…?

> Can you at least give me the location of his phone when I called it?

> NO

Rosie sighed. There would be no bending that inflexible will – obduracy was in his soul.

> Thanks, Moth. Have a nice day.

> Okay, you too.

Moth was oblivious to irony or sarcasm.

9: The Discovery

Ten minutes later, Rosie's phone pinged. A text message! Disappointingly, it was only from ROCKCELL, the provider of her local SIM card. They were probably trying to sell her something. She opened it anyway, just to delete the message, but then stared at the screen, a pair of digits and nothing else:

32796852 12387391

But Rosie thought she knew what the numbers signified. Moth, you are a star.

But damn, how did he do that? He had to have hacked the ROCKCELL network through their Firewalls.

She logged onto Google Maps and transferred the co-ordinates. The map panned to the location and began to refresh at the speed of a charging snail. Rosie watched, with growing dismay, her worst fears assembling in blocks of digital cartography.

The Travel Agent

9: The Discovery

9/3

Preparations

After a late lunch, Rosie selected three items from her 'toy' box. Packing them carefully into her rucksack, she cycled over to North Mole to reconnoitre the area where RFS *Ivan Peronovich* was due to berth the following morning.

There were three ship-basins inside the North Mole, the first was jam-packed with fishing vessels of various types and sizes. The stink of rotting fish here burned in her nostrils, and she quickly cycled on. In the second, on the eastern side, a small merchantman was being attended by a crane unloading cargo. A tank-cleaning vessel lay opposite, leaving several vacant berths ahead.

A Tui cruise ship domineered the outer mole beyond the Passenger Terminal. She would be sailing once her day-trippers reembarked, and that would allow Rosie unobserved access to the terminal roof after dark. If she needed it.

The Travel Agent

The third basin stood empty. Rosie assumed this was where the Russian would berth, on the opposite side to the Terminal. The quay here supported a huddle of small workshops and, at the very end, three fuel storage tanks. Marked parking bays lined the unbuilt area, most of them unoccupied. The workday was over, so it was quiet, and few workers remained around the complex.

Locking her bike outside the Missions to Seamen Club, Rosie went walkabout for closer scrutiny of the docks. She noted six security cameras that could give her trouble: four under the eaves of the Terminal roof, one on the nearest storage tank, another on one of the outbuildings.

The survey vessel was due in at seven, almost ninety minutes before sunrise; if Albert's information were accurate, the delivery vehicle would arrive and unload in darkness. She noted the positions of floodlights and estimated their spread. She would have a better idea when she came back later tonight.

Returning to the Missions Club, Rosie studied the building's rear. A burglar alarm was fitted to the wall next to the top floor window - she was pleased to see no camera there. Male voices and the clacking of pool-balls drifted down from the open window. Rosie walked around to the front and entered the club.

'We close at five-o-clock,' lisped the man she encountered inside mopping the floor.

'Well, it's only half four,' she said evenly.

He paused his work and looked up, hand on hip in studied camp fashion, eying her dowdy pedal-pushers and trainers with disdain.

9: The Discovery

'This is a private club for seamen. What ship are you on?'

Rosie gave him her sweetest smile, 'Only sea-men? Are sea-*women* not allowed?'

He straightened, visibly taken aback.

'Just thought I'd pop in for a look around,' she explained, 'and maybe a drink?'

'You'll need to sign in,' he relented, indicating a visitor's book open on a small table. 'And sign out again when you leave.' He resumed his mechanical mopping. Rosie signed in as Davida Jones, and her ship as M/v Hardship, Grey Funnel Line, Gibraltar.

The room upstairs was cosily austere, a small bar on one side with two bar stools, both occupied. The pool table took up a disproportional amount of space but left room for two circular tables with chairs. A narrow passageway led to the open window at the back, a sign indicating that was the way to the toilets.

The two men playing pool looked up when she entered, mildly surprised – Rosie assumed they did not see too many women here. She gave them a friendly smile and made for the bar, where one of the men shuffled his stool aside to make room for her.

The barman, a wiry man in a grubby grey tee shirt, gave her an enquiring look without speaking.

'Hi,' she said brightly, studying the small selection of beer taps. 'I'll have half a Stella if that's okay.'

He nodded. 'More than okay,' he said, reaching under the bar for a glass, 'it's the only one that's on.'

Sniggers from the two men.

Rosie carried her beer to one of the two empty tables, took out her phone and feigned scrolling through her emails. The pool game resumed, and the men at the bar

The Travel Agent

continued their banter with the barman. They all ignored Rosie, which suited her fine. After a few minutes, she stood and headed for the passageway leading to the toilets, gentlemen to the left, ladies to the right, the open window straight ahead. She entered the ladies and removed one of her toys from her bag and switched it on. When it connected, the agent flushed the loo and washed her hands, wiping them on her jeans because there was no towel.

Emerging from the toilets, Rosie moved to the window, made sure nobody was about outside and checked the men could not see her from the bar-room. Leaning out of the window, she fixed the magnetic wide-angle webcam to the top of the metal alarm case. The camera was the size of a matchbox and would not be visible from the ground. Satisfied it covered the angle she wanted, she returned to the bar. Seeing the current pool game was almost over, Rosie offered to play the winner.

It soon became apparent that the five-o-clock closing rule was not enforced while people were drinking. Rosie won her game and played the other guy, winning again amid much friendly ribbing from both men. She said goodbye to her two new friends at six-thirty, hoping never to see them again.

The agent had two more webcams to position in the area, but that would have to wait till after dark. Meanwhile, she cycled out of the docks and to the supermarket for an anonymous dinner in the cafeteria.

It was almost ten when Rosie got back to the boat, having installed all three of her webcams. With an early start in the morning, she wasted no time getting

9: The Discovery

on with what she had still to do. First, the agent connected her laptop to the SIM cards installed in the three cameras via the ROCKCELL network. She then activated each camera in turn and checked the live feed, pleased to see that the wide-angle lenses gave an acceptable margin of error. She then connected an external hard drive to store the MPEG files and set recording to start at five a.m. Satisfied that all her preparations were complete, she leaned back and grinned. Who said you couldn't be in two places at once?

Before turning in, the agent laid out some suitable clothing for her morning vigil; a dark, heavy shirt, lightweight black salopette, and suede leather seaboots. She planned to be back on-board before sunrise so was unworried about getting overheated.

Setting her alarm for four, she climbed into her bunk. But thoughts of Michael kept her awake far into the night. She would need to learn the truth of his situation, or it would drive her to distraction. An audacious plan was beginning to assemble in her mind. But first, she must concentrate purely on the job in front of her.

The Travel Agent

9: The Discovery

9/4

Morning Vigil

Moonset came two hours and fifty minutes before sunrise. It was 0530. Out to the east, a black sea slumbered under a sullen overcast, contrasting with the limestone massif's unsleeping realm that guarded the Mediterranean. Rosie had been surprised to see how well-lit it was on this side of the Rock. Upturned floodlights and powerful sodium lamps combined to deny any semblance of night-time. Only in the Rock's numerous tunnels and caves can real darkness be found.

Reaching her chosen spot an hour ago, Rosie had hidden her bike and placed her fourth webcam pointing at the tunnel entrance. She then made herself comfortable on a flat rock overlooking the approach road. Rosie was now more confident than ever that she had made the right choice. The survey ship had left the platform some hours earlier than needed and was only making three knots. This gave credence to Rosie's

The Travel Agent

theory that the vessel was shepherding a submerged vehicle.

The cameras at North Mole were her backstop in case she was wrong. After all, moving ISIS veterans from a legitimately berthed vessel into a van, in darkness, was, without doubt, the more straightforward choice for the Russians. On the other hand, it was the most apparent ploy to anybody investigating them and the most manageable foil strategy. Entering the territory via a hidden sea cave was a wonderfully inspired choice. Who would believe such a tactic? Not the observers up in the Hole, who, according to Tash, had the cocaine trade as their primary focus. The Border Force officer had seemed oblivious to the danger of insurgency. In this respect, Rob and his geeky band of brothers may be right.

Rosie could now see the survey ship's nav lights out to the east, four miles to run; another hour or so. She turned back to watch the approach road - rolling onto her stomach - and wondered how the reception crew would arrive, she wanted a good look at Rob's killers. Despite the early hour, she had heard one or two cars passing on the main road below …

Rosie froze, in a sudden a chill of precognition. Before she could move, a voice behind her growled, 'Waiting for someone?'

In the microsecond it took to understand her grave misjudgement, a heavy knee on her back knocked the wind out of her. Whooping for breath, the agent felt cold metal pressed against her ear.

'Keep still, bitch. Move, and you die.'

9: The Discovery

9/5

Duplicity

There were two of them, big men clothed in dark coveralls; Rosie was still gasping for air as they hoisted her to her feet and dragged her down the slope, past the metal sheet covering the tunnel. The gravity of her oversight became apparent when they passed the tunnel entrance – the cover had been moved aside. They must have been down in the cavern when she arrived, with the steel cover pulled back in place to avoid discovery. She had overlooked that possibility.

The men marched her for ten yards back down the track and turned right between two enormous boulders. And there stood a black minivan. Rosie cursed herself for the inadequate recce.

The agent now forced herself to loosen up, surrendering her body to the skills and practised muscle-memory of her training. When one of the men relaxed his grip on her arm to open the vehicle's back doors, Rosie took her chance. The guy who'd eased his hold on her was first. A roundhouse kick to the groin

The Travel Agent

doubled him over. This freed her right arm to deal a devastating two-fingered *jab jari* up into the other's right eye. The practised blow exploded the eyeball and punched through the socket into the brain. She then twisted, as Gardener had taught her, to maximise the damage. It felt a lot different to watermelons. The man went rigid, and there was a sickening slurp as Rosie withdrew her fingers. He stood there a moment, dropped his pistol, then crumpled.

But before Rosie could claim the weapon, the other man straightened and snatched a punch at Rosie's head that caught her a glancing blow and left her reeling. Stunned and seeing double, she forced through a *pukulan tinju* to his throat that, correctly delivered, should have crushed his windpipe. However, the botched move did leave him clutching his throat and gasping for air, giving Rosie time to stagger away to gain recovery time. But the thug rallied quickly and came after her, bellowing like a bull. The agent's training had shown her how to exploit both her fear and her opponent's rage, and those vital seconds had been enough for her vision to clear.

Dodging under a flailing fist, Rosie slipped sideways past the man and unbalanced him with a kick to the back of his knee and an open-palmed blow to the neck. As he toppled, she followed through with a well-timed kick to the solar plexus, which folded him into a wheezing wreck on the ground. A *cap kaki* to the kidney would finish the guy, but Rosie hesitated.

Hurt 'em bad and get away! The Gardener maxim.

Calmly the agent assessed her opponent. It was clear the enormous brute was by no means finished. He looked up at Rosie and snarled and began to struggle

9: The Discovery

to his feet. In his condition, Rosie could quickly finish him. Equally, she could run for her bike and just cycle off – he would never catch her. But the flat shape of the dropped automatic beside the van decided it for her. She stepped away and tensed herself for further action as the brute charged.

'That's enough, Bernard,' came a voice from behind Rosie. 'You had better quit while you are behind.'

The creature stopped in his tracks, wild-eyed and snorting.

Rosie turned slowly to face the newcomer. A linen suit and a tie - and a laconic grin. He was pointing a handgun at her.

'Lev!' she gasped. 'What the--?'

'Rosie,' the Ukrainian purred, 'What a pleasant surprise. That was very impressive.'

Rosie pulled herself together. She had missed all the signs in her stupid attraction to the man. Now it was clear just how far the charming Adonis had duped her.

'Bernard, get that cadaver below into the cave,' Leviticus told the snorting giant. 'We'll take it with us.'

'Sorry about your thug,' said Rosie. 'I didn't have many options.'

The Ukrainian shrugged. 'Enrico was careless - he got what he deserved.'

'I knew there was something fishy about you. Does Tash know you work for the Russians?'

As Bernard set about his task, Leviticus turned back to her and shook his head sadly. 'Poor Natasha, she is too infatuated to suspect my duplicity. I have been using her, of course. And as for working for the Russians? Yes, Rosie, or should I call you Galene?'

The Travel Agent

Leviticus grinned at the agent's stunned face. 'Such an enigmatic name suits you admirably. Yes, I work for them because I *am* Russian, Ukrainian-Russian, to be precise.'

Rosie was in no doubt this man, who could so easily have been her lover, was about to kill her. She stepped aside to keep both men in sight and readied herself for any opportunity to reverse her fortune.

'Ah, do not make the mistake of underestimating me, Rosie. I have seen what you are capable of and will not give you the opportunity you seek. I detest violence. That is why I employ these meatheads.'

'Are you going to kill me?' Rosie asked, with just the slightest trace of a quiver in her voice. She thought she knew the answer, not least because of the suppressor attached to the Ukrainian's pistol barrel. But his reply surprised her.

'I would hate to have to do that. You are a fine woman - it would be such a waste.'

He glanced to seaward – the survey ship was nearing her closest point, dimmed running-lights less than a mile away, gliding south towards Europa Point.

Leviticus said: 'My time here has been a wonderful experience, Rosie, but unfortunately the adventure is concluded. It is time for me to go home.'

He circled widely around her to the minivan and picked up the dropped pistol.

'How did you know where I was?' Rosie asked.

'I saw the light from your phone when I came out of the cavern. I suppose you were tracking our ship out there. Tut-tut, careless.'

She had screwed up. Again!

9: The Discovery

9/6

Insurgents

Bernard had disappeared down the hole with his deceased companion, and the Ukrainian now urged Rosie to do likewise: 'Walk ahead of me. And please, if you wish to live, do not be a hero.'

Rosie complied. As she felt her way carefully down the treacherous steps, Leviticus followed at a cautious distance, holding high a pencil torch to light her way ahead. Curiosity held her back, for the time being, from preparing an escape plan. Indeed if he had planned to kill her, he would have done so by now. The wistful tone of his words about going home held her in intrigue. And why the flowers, and the expensive ear stud, if he had known who she was all along? Was Leviticus planning to do a bunk in the minisub and take her with him? The agent found the notion of abduction both disturbing and perversely thrilling.

Emerging into the cavern, Rosie was astonished to find it brightly lit with portable floodlights. She turned

The Travel Agent

to face her captor, 'I was right, then. It's a minisub, isn't it?'

Leviticus smiled broadly, 'It appears we were both right: I for not underestimating you. Natasha told me you were thinking along those lines with your wretched subterfuge of researching a novel. Clever girl. I almost feel sorry you will not impress your employers with the capture of your so-called Travel Agent.'

He motioned her to stand at the left-hand wall of the cavern.

'Now, be a good girl, and you will learn all, and perhaps survive to tell the tale. Not that there will be any evidence to support such an outrageous theory – you may be assured of that.'

Rosie frowned. The Ukrainian's strategy made no sense, and that needed investigation.

'But why would you leave me alive?' she asked. 'Not that I'm complaining,' she added hurriedly, 'but will you at least explain…'

But Leviticus had switched his attention to the cave's seaward entrance. She followed his gaze, and there, beneath the water, an amorphous white shape moved slowly into the arc of the floodlights. As the submerged vehicle approached, Rosie felt her sanguinity about her situation beginning to waver. Would ISIS terrorist be among the occupants? And if so, would such men tolerate her presence here, or would they decide to terminate her after the subs departure?

'Lev, who's on the minisub?'

For a long moment, he gazed at her, a look of puzzlement on his handsome face. 'You are frightened,

9: The Discovery

Rosie. I had not expected fear in such a gallant warrior. It is our passengers that worry you, yes?'

Rosie stared back in silence, ashamed of the telling emotion she had, up to now, kept concealed behind the shield of her training.

'Trust me, Rosie. You have nothing to fear, I promise.'

Mystified by his enigmatic reassurance, Rosie turned to watch the minisub as it glided toward the ledge. Bernard - the sad crumpled heap of his erstwhile colleague at his feet - watched in rapt fascination as a shiny white carapace rose out of the swirling pool. A circular hatch cracked with a hiss and was then swung fully open. A head emerged - a young man's grinning face.

But the grin morphed quickly to a frown as its owner took in the scene: Lev holding a strange woman at gunpoint, Bernard with a corpse at his feet. As the craft manoeuvred carefully alongside the wall, Rosie saw faces peering anxiously out of portholes below the waterline. Leviticus gabbled in Russian, and the crewman's eyes widened progressively at his new instructions. With a slow nod of assent, he climbed out onto the casing, dragging with him a folding passerelle. When the gangway was firmly in place, he used it to step ashore.

'Give them a hand, Bernard,' ordered Leviticus, as the first passenger's head appeared, casting fearfully around at the unlikely surroundings of the cavern. With Bernard guiding them over the gangway, the four jihadi killers stepped ashore to stand bareheaded and bewildered on the limestone ledge. They were all clean-shaven: sun-darkened faces with pale chins

The Travel Agent

where beards had been. They wore jeans and various coloured tee-shirts that appeared brand new. The men looked anything but the seasoned desert fighters they undoubtedly were.

When they were all ashore, the crewman stepped back onto the sub's casing and looked on, waiting with a look of apprehension.

The fighters looked about the cavern, at the slime-covered rock face and roof, disorientated and wary. One of them stared at Rosie, sitting with her back against the wall. The other three began to notice, with visible consternation, the tableau before them: the Ukrainian with a pistol pointed at Rosie, the dead Enrico at Bernard's feet.

'What the fuck?' muttered one.

'What happening, man?' asked another.

'Just relax, guys,' grunted Bernard to the men, trying to defuse the suddenly charged atmosphere.

The four exchanged worried glances as Leviticus turned their way. Long used to carrying weapons, the unarmed men began visibly to sense their vulnerability. Rosie had caught sight of Leviticus' face and started to get a bad feeling – this was not going to end well.

Bernard stepped over the body of his friend. 'This way,' he piped, walking towards the tunnel entrance and beckoning the fighters to follow. 'First to the safe house, and tomorrow you'll…'

'Er, just one moment, Bernard,' said the Ukrainian.

Bernard stepped back and looked at his boss with an expectant frown.

'What's up, Mr Danilenco?'

9: The Discovery

Despite all the distressing events so far, what came next shocked Rosie to her core.

'I am sorry, gentlemen,' said Leviticus regretfully to four men. 'There has been a change of plan.' He raised the silenced weapon in both hands. Without hesitation, he fired four shots in rapid succession: *flup, flup, flup, flup*—such an innocuous sound. Rosie watched in astonishment as the four would-be terrorists crumpled to the ground, each with a neat hole in his forehead.

'Wha…?' gasped Bernard, staring disbelievingly at his erstwhile charges, just before another soft *flup* relieved him forever of any further thoughts.

The Travel Agent

9: The Discovery

9/7

Submersible

'You cold, callous bastard!' breathed Rosie, wondering if the next bullet would be hers and for the moment too shocked and outraged to care.

'I do what is necessary,' said Leviticus. He gave a grim smile, 'At least they never saw it coming.'

'Phew! You're all heart.'

Impervious to the irony, the Ukrainian now issued a stream of orders to the minisub's crewman. The man, rendered pale by what he had just witnessed, called down the hatch and then stepped back onto the ledge. The pilot climbed out and followed him, and the two of them began the grisly task of heaving the six bodies across the gangway and down the hatch. Still in partial shock at what she had witnessed, Rosie slid down the cave wall and sat watching.

'Won't it be a bit cramped in there, you three and all those corpses?' Rosie wrinkled her nose. 'Not to mention, smelly?'

'It will not be for long…'

The Travel Agent

Again, Lev must have read the question uppermost in her mind because he gave a mirthless chuckle and added, 'You are wondering if I am going to take you with me. The thought had crossed my mind. You excite me, Rosie. It is a pity we never had a chance to make love - even looking at you now I am becoming aroused.'

Leviticus guffawed loudly at her pained expression, a sound that reverberated hideously around the cavern.

'But something tells me you would make a difficult sex-slave.'

She snorted. 'In your dreams, you… you snake-in-the-grass, you bloody *murderer*.'

He grinned, and after a moment, said, 'But I intend to release you, Rosie.'

She stared at him. 'Do you mean that?'

'Of course.'

…

'So, tell me, why did you kill Rob?'

'What, the South Ops, guy? Why on earth would I?'

'But…'

'Rosie, my hand is on my heart, that man was of no interest to me. We had nothing to do with his death. Please believe me. What I *can* tell you, however, is that he had recently become involved with the local drugs cartels. Perhaps your Police should be looking closer to home.'

'Oh?'

He nodded. 'That aside for the moment, there is something on another matter I wish to impart. Call it a gesture of friendship between agents.'

'*Friendship between…* Phew, you've got a fucking nerve.'

9: The Discovery

He lifted an eyebrow, 'Shall I go on?'

Rosie blew out, hesitated a moment, then sighed. 'Okay, I'm intrigued.'

'I believe you have a friend who is in trouble, a sailor?'

She gaped. 'How... how the hell ...?'

He smiled. 'He and the woman, the Swedish nurse, are being held in a place called El Habar, a few kilometres south of Sabratha. The last I heard they were both alive and well.'

'Thank you,' she said with feeling, 'that's good to know.'

They were silent for a long moment, watching the two crewmen lowering the last of the bodies down the hatch. Finally, she shook her head in bewilderment and then sighed.

'What has this all been about, Lev? Help me understand why Russia would want to run an operation like this.'

Leviticus sighed, his expression rueful. 'You and I, Rosie, we are merely foot-soldiers - the men of power give orders, and we obey. But in the end, it is all about the money. The Politicos give no measure to their hypocrisy. They happily deal with whoever controls the sinews of capitalism. And when those people are no longer of use, they cheerfully drop them and support their enemies instead.'

'Is that what's happening here, why you're leaving? Is it because your bosses have switched their allegiances?'

The Ukrainian chuckled. 'In my case, only one man pulls the strings of power. But yes, as I understand it, that is what seems to have happened. The people

The Travel Agent

holding your friends were my country's friends because they controlled the Libyan oil. And now they are the enemy because they control it no longer.'

'So, who does?'

Leviticus gave a mirthless smile.

'That, Rosie, is the billion-dollar question. Since Gadafi's death, the country has polarised as never before, and choosing the winning side is an international gamble. In her autocratic wisdom, Mother Russia believes the winner will be Khalifa Haftar and his so-called Libyan National Army. And so Putin has taken his side. The Americans and their allies are gambling on Sarraj's government in Tripoli. With UN support, I might add, which leaves our glorious dictator once more the world's pariah. But Libya is a mess, and nobody knows what will happen.'

He glanced at his watch and then at the sub where the crew sat on the casing waiting to leave, their ghastly work complete. They had even sluiced down the ledge where the bodies had lain. And they had taken away the portable lamps, their light replaced by a rising sun spreading a shimmering orange glow into the cave. The agent had barely noticed how much the time had passed since being discovered at her surveillance.

'And, Rosie, one more thing. General Haftar has begun an offensive against the caliphate, which may soon affect the fate of your friend. I am not sure there is much your people can do to help him, or whether they will even want to, but I thought you should know.'

'Thanks a bunch,' she said. 'Oh, that reminds me, I dumped the flowers, but thanks for the stud.' She

9: The Discovery

fingered the jewel in her earlobe and smiled, 'You were right, the ear needs it.'

'My pleasure, something to remember me by, and perhaps wonder what could have been. But now we must leave you.' He shot a glance at the tunnel steps. 'Please do me the grace not to enter the tunnel until we are clear of the cavern. It is imperative, you must promise.'

'No problem, good luck.'

He hesitated. 'I would offer you my hand in friendship, but I think that might be dangerous.'

'It might be,' she grinned, stood and walked towards him extending her hand. 'How lucky do you feel?'

Leviticus moved forward to shake but then, glancing down at her hand, hesitated. 'I think not,' he said, a wry smile.

Rosie looked down at her hand and winced at the dried gore from the man she had killed. 'Sorry,' she said and moved the offending hand behind her back.

'It has been a pleasure to know you, Rosie Winterbourne.'

With that, the Ukrainian turned and stepped onto the sub.

'How did you know?' she called out.

'About Firegate?' he turned and grinned at the startled look on her face. 'Very well, a consolation prize: you can tell The Housekeeper that it was a Russian agent who furnished the tip-offs. We played a double game, Rosie. Although we valued their help, we were not prepared to allow Daesh to follow through with their nasty campaign in Europe. Because they would eventually have turned on us as well.'

The Travel Agent

He turned, then hesitated a moment, seemed to come to a decision, and turned back to her. 'And here is another morsel: your South Ops murder mystery? The police should look for a man named Anthony Littlejohn. Do what you will with that information.'

Rosie stood watching as Leviticus followed the crew below. He turned in the hatchway, pointed at the tunnelled stairway and waggled a warning finger before ducking his handsome head down and pulling the hatch closed. Rosie watched with mixed feelings as the craft submerged in a storm of bubbles and glided out of the cavern. Then she turned to leave, not knowing quite what her next move should be, but feeling her mission all but accomplished.

The agent had taken but a single pace towards the stairway when the blast hit her.

9: The Discovery

9/8

Trapped

Thrown like a rag doll to sitting splay-legged against the cavern wall, Rosie stared incredulously at the grey dust cloud rolling out of the tunnel. The ominous rumble had now stopped, but she knew the way out above would be blocked. Leviticus must have somehow caused the explosion to collapse the tunnel, trapping her inside.

The agent drew her legs up under her chin and waited glumly for the dust to settle. She bore no hatred towards the Ukrainian for his duplicity. It was only natural that he would want to delay her for as long as possible to ensure his escape. He could more easily have just shot her and left her to rot down to bones, undiscovered for perhaps years, if ever.

She circled her arms about her knees and stared at the brown crust and dried grey matter on the digits of her right hand in the growing light. She smirked. It was little wonder the Russian had declined her handshake. Then, unaccountably, she began to shake.

The Travel Agent

Her eyes filled, and as she sat there weeping on a wave of visceral self-loathing, the memory of Gadfly's prescient warning came to her:

Trust me, Galene, it will get to you, your first killing, no matter how tough you think you are, and the dam will burst when you least expect it. When it does, let it flow. Then learn to live with yourself.

Sometime later, when her remorse had subsided, Rosie began considering her options. Firstly, how certain was it that the tunnel was blocked? There could be a way through. With a renewed sense of purpose, she rose and entered the tunnel. However, within a few metres, she could see nothing at all. Worse, pulverised limestone from the explosion layered the steps, causing her to lose her footing once or twice. It took her half-an-hour to reach the point where she could go no further, and sadly, there was not the faintest chink of daylight in the rockfall. The blockage, like the darkness, was total. Her return to the cavern – a helter-skelter ride down the dust and scree - took far less time than the ascent.

Rosie had resigned herself to swimming out of the sea cave. She had no idea what the cliff conditions would be like out there or whether there was any climbable route up within convenient swimming distance. But it was her only way out – the only way out Leviticus had allowed her, maximising his time to get out to his rendezvous with the survey ship.

Rosie slipped off her Dubarry seaboots and stood them reverently against the wall. They had been together a long time, her and those weathered boots; a birthday present from Dad back in the day. They had served her through two Atlantic crossings, and she was

9: The Discovery

saddened to be deserting them. Perhaps one day somebody would discover them and give them a new life.

The heavy denim shirt would have to go too. At least the tropical salopette would not hamper the swim too much. Otherwise, the agent would have faced the prospect of emerging naked onto the busy roadway. She snorted a laugh at the image of someone stopping to offer a ride.

Rosie stood at the lip of the ledge looking apprehensively at the jagged cavemouth, which now, at high water, slurped and sucked dangerously beneath a growing swell. Taking a deep breath, she dived into the limpid pool and struck out underwater. She swam cautiously deep beneath the entrance, fighting a powerful vortex as she passed through the narrows, before surfacing on the other side.

Treading water, Rosie got her first external view of the cavern, not that anyone who didn't know it was there would recognise it as such. It could have been mistaken for an eroded cavity briefly exposed in the troughs of the shallow swell.

Few significant features in the near-vertical cliff face offered aid a climber. But happily, a short distance off to the right lay a small deserted beach, with an access road leading up to a derelict fortification and a carpark. Fifteen minutes of vigorous swimming took her to the shallows. Lamenting her lost boots, the agent hopped and shimmied barefoot up the sharp-shingled beach, each step punctuated by painful oohs and aahs.

Cars passed her on the road, some drivers slowing to stare at her sopping salopette and bare feet. Thankfully, she had emerged not far from the tunnel's

The Travel Agent

access road. Reaching the site, Rosie paid tribute to Leviticus's demolition skills. The entrance was now just a shallow hole among the rocks, and the corrugated cover lay redundant a few yards away. There was little evidence remaining of what it had been. Rosie mourned her lost boots – unlikely they would evermore see the light of day.

The agent retrieved the webcam she had hidden amongst the overlooking rocks. Hopefully, the footage on her laptop would provide evidence of what had occurred here. Though she doubted any of it would be made public. Collecting her bag and bike, she set off cycling back to the marina.

Rosie had considered taking the minivan and stowing her bike in the back. But the site would be investigated at some point. Somebody must have heard the explosion. And no doubt the deceased Rob's South Ops buddies would eventually discover the tunnel's collapse and report it. Either way, the agent wanted to leave no evidence of her ever having been there. So the van had to stay to be discovered.

Rosie now looked forward to a long hot shower. After that, she would return to the Mission Club; their formidable 'Seaman's Breakfast' would provide the opportunity to retrieve her webcam. The other two cameras would probably have to wait until after dark. In the meantime, the agent had much work ahead, including a couple of favours to ask of Moth. And to book herself a flight to the UK.

EPISODE TEN

The Rogue Agent

The Travel Agent

10: The Rogue Agent

10/1

Gauntlet

Along with an assortment of servicemen and women joining their new units, Gauntlet filed quickly down the Galaxy transporter ramp and headed across the apron. Ignoring the waiting military bus, he hurried past the two parked Tornado fighter-jets, to RAF North Front's Reception Centre. Production of his Special Ops ID Card got him a priority wave through.

There goes my zero profile, he thought, as he crossed the Frontier approach road, making straight for Marina Bay. He would probably end up in a training job after this - he did not possess the psychopathic mindset to be a Cleaner. No, he did not mind Camp Sparta – he was becoming bored lately with his surveillance role, and Hammer's plodding ways were getting on his nerves. He did not relish the prospect of working with the taciturn Gardener either. But then there was Gadfly, the alluring and remarkably intelligent COTO. The brightened mood quickened his step. Yeah,

The Travel Agent

romance had been missing from his life since leaving the Squadron. He might just bend the rules and take a punt at the sexy West Indian.

'Yes, *Pasha* is on berth F25,' said the girl at the marina reception. 'But I'm afraid you've missed her. Miss Winterbourne notified us she would be away in the UK for a few days and asked for extra security watch on her boat.'

'When was this?' asked the agent, getting a bad feeling in his gut.

'First thing this morning, she was waiting here when I opened at seven.'

'When was her flight, do you know?'

'She didn't say, but the only morning flight at this time of year is the nine-fifteen EasyJet, though of course, she could have gone to Malaga. Had she been expecting you?'

'Clearly not,' he grimaced. 'But thanks for your help.'

Leaving the marina, Gauntlet took a taxi to the Rock Hotel. He had a reservation under Mark Henderson, the name on his false passport. He had calls to make.

At that moment, not far away in Mackintosh Square, Detective Inspector Greg Singleton was entering ROCKCELL's impressive second-floor executive suite.

'Yes, can I help you?' smiled the predictably stunning receptionist.

Greg flashed her his Warrant Card. 'DI Singleton, RGP. I'm here to see your Technical Director. I believe he's expecting me?'

10: The Rogue Agent

Ah, yes, it was me you spoke to. Please take a seat, sir, and I'll tell Mr Lynch you're here.'

The policeman's interviewee did not keep him waiting long.

'Detective Inspector? I'm Liam Lynch, welcome to ROCKCELL.'

The two men shook hands. Lynch was a smartly dressed, smallish man of middling years.

'Let's go to my office. Would you like a drink?'

'Thanks, water would be good.'

'I'll bring it right along,' purred the receptionist.

'Now, how can I help you, Inspector?' said Lynch when the two of them were seated in his office.

'It's about...' he stopped as the receptionist knocked and entered with his glass of water.

'It's about a text I received this morning,' he continued when the girl had left. 'From a number registered to ROCKCELL.'

Lynch shrugged. 'It's perfectly legitimate for a provider to offer add-on services, Inspector. You can always scroll down the page and unsubscribe. We always respect our...'

'It wasn't that kind of text, Mr Lynch.' He activated the screen on his phone and showed him the message.

> Marsa killing – suggest interview Anthony Littlejohn, look for drugs motive.

Lynch read the message, mouthing the words, alarm spreading on his face. He reached across the desk.

'May I see?'

Greg handed over his phone, and for the next few moments, Lynch tapped away at it with growing

The Travel Agent

consternation. Finally, he shook his head in bewilderment and handed back the phone. He then began tapping keys on his computer.

'Well?' said the detective.

'Please, Inspector, give me a moment.' He continued tapping away, his face was beetroot. Eventually, Lynch gave a resigned sigh and looked up.

'I've tracked the message – it came from us, but I don't understand how.'

'One of your employees, perhaps?'

Lynch shook his head despairingly. 'That would have been the easiest to resolve. Although it was indeed sent to you by us, it didn't originate here. It came from an external source via one or more proxy servers. Our firewall should have made that impossible.'

'So, you've been hacked?'

Lynch grimaced. 'It would seem so, Inspector.'

10: The Rogue Agent

10/2

Desolation

More than anything, the boredom was the worst. The days seemed endless: days of scratching graffiti on the cell walls, making up stupid songs and reciting the few poems he remembered from school, singing to himself, thinking about his sister, his parents. And Rosie, especially Rosie. And contemplating a God in whom he did not believe but wished he could. The days were stifling, and the nights were bitter. In the night came the flying cockroaches: clicking on the walls, scuttling across the floor. And the irritating whine of mosquitos, the breeze of wings on his face in the dark. He thought to have heard rats, though he had yet to see one.

Michael could take all that. But the boredom? The boredom was driving him to wonder if it was worth surviving at all. Life in captivity had gotten so dreary and empty that he looked forward to the guard's daily ritual of entering the cell to kick, taunt and humiliate him.

The Travel Agent

On the plus side, the caliphate zombies had upgraded Michael to business class. He had a luxury new bed: a pair of wooden pallets pushed together, topped by a marginally more hygienic mattress, and a coarse, motheaten blanket that was relatively free of vermin. They had even afforded him a rickety chair and folding table. His daily meal was invariably a spicy goat stew brought in a bakelite bowl – at least he hoped it was goat meat. At regular intervals, the guard tossed in a bottle of tepid water.

Each morning, two militias escorted Michael to a filthy bathroom swarming with flies to take a shit and a cold shower under their contemptuous stares. Gone were his stinking shorts and tee-shirt, replaced by a baggy orange jumpsuit reminiscent of those worn by Guantanamo Bay detainees. Ominous for his prospects; he was still traumatised by the memory of that terrifying mock execution.

Michael knew he had Astrid to thank for his modest comforts. There was, apparently, a constant influx of casualties, and being the only medico available gave the Swedish nurse a degree of influence with their captors.

But the young man could see the work was taking its toll on the nurse – it showed in her face where the strain-lines were deeply etched. In the first days he had resented, even hated, that she was helping them.

'We do what we have to do to stay alive, Michael,' she had chided. 'It is not the first time I have fixed up the bad guys.' She had grinned then, and whispering because her minder was outside the door, said, 'I am very sparing with their morphine.'

10: The Rogue Agent

As the benefits accrued, Michael had gradually learned to tolerate his friend's collaboration.

It was late afternoon on his fifth day of captivity. Astrid was supposed to remove his stitches today, but she had so far failed to make her usual appearance. The sounds of battle were more frequent today. Was it his imagination, or was that gunfire getting closer?

The Travel Agent

10: The Rogue Agent

10/3

Missing

'Damn the girl! Are you sure?' The Housekeeper's pinched face glaring out from Gauntlet's laptop display looked thoroughly pissed off.

The agent reduced the speaker volume and said evenly, 'I checked with EasyJet, Ma'am. She was booked on the 9.15 to Gatwick this morning; she'll be home by now if that's where she was heading. What exactly did she say in that last report?'

'Not a bloody lot,' snarled his boss, 'I quote, "Shutting down this end. Travel Agent was Russian, but their operations are now terminated. Full report to follow, but be assured, case closed. Galene."'

'Is that it?'

'Yes, the cocky little madam. Oh, and a PS, "Taking a few days off - personal matter." Don't ask me what that means.'

Probably exactly what it says, thought Gauntlet.

'What do you want me to do, Ma'am?'

The Travel Agent

'Stay where you are – she'll be back there before long, if only because her boat's still there. In the meantime, I'll task Gadfly and Hammer to try and track her down this end. *Case closed* indeed! Who the fuck does she think she is? I want to know exactly what Galene's been up to. After that, we'll decide on your next move.'

But Gauntlet was not thinking about Galene's mission. He remembered a woman he had met six weeks ago, a woman who had, according to his contact in SIS, hopped on a plane to Turkey to spend six weeks at sea just to help a friend. That friend's name was McCaffey.

'I know that look,' intoned The Housekeeper. 'Come on, Gauntlet, out with it.'

'They won't find her in the UK, Ma'am.'

She blinked in surprise. 'Oh? Go on?'

'I think, if she was on that flight, it was to get a connecting one, most likely to somewhere in North Africa.'

The woman's eyes widened. '*Jesus H. Christ!* You think… But how could she know? Nothing's been released yet.'

'Nothing specific, maybe. But the clues are all there: the abandoned boat, Daesh pushing west and no word from McCaffey. She must be worried shitless.'

'Mm, maybe. But think about it. A huge, lawless country with a hundred different militias fighting it out, and a young western woman travelling alone? How does she expect even to survive, let alone find her boyfriend? She doesn't know if the guy's even alive. A bit of a leap, don't you think?'

'Did I hear Gadfly say she speaks Arabic?'

10: The Rogue Agent

The Housekeeper stared at him in silence for a long moment, then gave an exasperated sigh and came to a decision.

'Right. I'll get a check running on any outbound flights the girl could have connected with, starting with Tripoli, Tunis and Cairo. Stay put, get some rest. I'll get back to you.'

The Travel Agent

10: The Rogue Agent

10/4

Off-grid

Following a breakfast of tomato tostadas and strong coffee, Rosie picks up her backpack. She makes her way to the starboard gangway. She joins a small group of foot-passengers waiting in the pre-dawn light to disembark. Finding space on a bench, she watches the harbour lights of the Spanish enclave of Melilla, and the brightly-lit channel markers winking their identities as the ship glides past them. High above, the great fortress stands in its own shadow: an amorphous beast looming above the harbour wall's darker line.

Undoubtedly, Housekeeper will not take her disappearance lightly and perhaps even suspect her some sort of defection. At least her subterfuge of a booked flight to Gatwick should send whoever they send to look for her in the wrong direction. Moth will, of course, have worked out her intentions. Still, unless interrogated directly, the introverted geek will not volunteer the information. Not least because he has broken the rules himself on her behalf.

The Travel Agent

There are fewer qualms over that tip-off to police about Littlejohn. Hopefully, they will find enough evidence to convict the bastard of Rob's murder.

The only real regret is having had to shop Natasha. The officer has clearly compromised herself for sex with the handsome, silver-tongued Ukrainian. In her exalted position, there can be no excuse for what she did. Treason is treason, and despite being way beyond Rosie's brief, her conscience could not have let it ride. But still ...

The overnight passage from Malaga has been smooth and uneventful. Despite the hoots and running feet of a handful of overactive children too excited to sleep, the night on the lounge couchette was comfortable and slumbersome.

She will need to improvise the next leg of her journey, for now, she is on her own – on a rogue mission.

Yes, Housekeeper will be furious.

She smiles to herself, though she will be lucky to keep her job after this.

If she even survives.

Nevertheless, her mood is upbeat. Despite the uncertainties ahead, she feels remarkably content with her decision. Yeah, it is reckless and scary, what she is doing: the thought of it sends a thrilling shiver through her inner core. But that other fear lurked in the darkest recesses. The fear that, when allowed to manifest, projects no such visceral charge. The fear that she will arrive in Libya too late to save Michael.

Thank you for reading *The Travel Agent*, the second in the Rosie Winterbourne Series. I hope you loved Rosie as much as I enjoyed, and continue to enjoy, writing her story.

But, whatever your experience, please remember to post your review on Amazon (and any book club sites to which you subscribe, such as Goodreads).

I hope you continue to follow Rosie's adventures.
Happy Reading

About Michael Rothery

I divide my time between writing at my home in Elgin, cycling around the Highlands, and cruising the Atlantic/Caribbean islands in my yacht, *Island Spirit*. In past lives, I served twenty-five years in the Royal Navy and then another twenty as Director of a computer software company in the Midlands.

My other books available from Amazon:-
To Run Before the Sea
Diddle Dee

IV

THE CONFLICTED BRIDE

Rosie Winterbourne Book 3

Hunted by former colleagues from the Firegate agency, Rosie Winterbourne continues her solo mission to find and rescue her friend. With the help of Moth and a tipoff from the enigmatic Leviticus, Rosie has discovered Michael's whereabouts: the new caliphate holds him captive in a battle-scarred Libyan town.

Rosie's most dangerous challenge yet unfolds in this explosive sequel.

The Conflicted Bride **is due for release on 16th April 2021**

Weatherdeck Books

Printed in Great Britain
by Amazon